Ron

by Debra Kayn

This is a work of fiction. Names, characters, places, and incidents are products of the author's imagination or are used fictitiously and are not to be construed as real. Any resemblance to actual events, locales, organizations, or persons, living or dead, is entirely coincidental.

Don't Say It
Ronacks Motorcycle Club
1st Digital release: Copyright© 2016 Debra Kayn

All rights reserved. No part of this book may be used or reproduced electronically or in print without written permission, except in the case of brief quotations embodied in reviews.

All rights reserved. This copy is intended for the purchaser of this e-book ONLY. No part of this e-book may be reproduced, scanned, or distributed in any printed or electronic form without prior written permission from Debra Kayn. Please do not participate in or encourage piracy of copyrighted materials in violation of the author's rights. Purchase only authorized editions.
www.debrakayn.com

Dedication

To those who can see past stereotypes, gossip, lies, and realize there are always two sides to everything. Two sides to a coin. Two sides to a door. Two sides to people. It's what you don't hear/read/see that will tell the true story.

Acknowledgements

Haugan, Montana —In real life, Haugan is an unincorporated community in Mineral County, Montana. It's sixteen miles from the Idaho border and not far from where I live in Idaho. Haugan is the home to only one business, which happens to be one of my favorite places to go, Lincoln's 50,000 Silver Dollar Bar. I've fictionalized the town to include a main street with enough businesses to keep a motorcycle club afloat.

Chapter One

Swiss's stomach vibrated. He opened his eyes and found himself on the couch. The lights still on in the living room.

He picked up his phone off his stomach as he rolled into a sitting position on the sofa and shut off the alarm he'd set earlier. He'd fallen asleep with the television on while watching the football game. That was four hours ago. The longest stretch of sleep he'd achieved in a long time.

It was time to leave. Pine Bar and Grill would close in twenty minutes, and he needed to meet Raelyn, the manager, to pick up the cash from what the bar brought in with business today.

As a member of Ronacks Motorcycle Club, it was his job to hold on to the money overnight and pass it off to his MC brother, Grady, in the morning for drop-off at the clubhouse. Battery, the president, wanted no incentive for someone to break into the bar and put Raelyn and her son, Dukie, at risk.

As a widow, Raelyn had enough worries as a single parent living above the bar. The club tried to keep any added stress from hitting her on top of her already busy schedule.

Swiss took a piss, splashed water from the faucet over his face, and grabbed his leather vest. His stomach growled, and he stopped to eat the half of a deli sandwich he'd left out on the counter earlier. He finished in three bites.

He shut off the television, locked the front door behind him, and stopped in front of the duplex.

Something was wrong. He listened, peered down the street, and whipped his gaze to a car next to the curb behind his Harley.

Following his thoughts, he gazed over at the other side of the duplex. A light was on inside.

"Fuck," he muttered, grounding his teeth together.

He must've slept harder than he'd thought. Usually, even when he got some shuteye, he continued to hear every noise, inside and out, from voices to car doors.

Damn, he was getting old.

While he'd slept, someone had moved into the other side of the duplex. Nobody had rented that side for over twenty-two years.

The roof leaked in the back bedroom, thanks to the holes he tapped into the 3-tab shingles to keep anyone from moving in, and over the years, the carpet had rotted from moisture in the winter and heat in the summer.

Hell, the out-of-state landlord never came by, and Swiss made sure never to mow the joined front patch of yard to keep the appearance up that the building was abandoned. There weren't even appliances on that side of the duplex.

Even if the renter believed a good cleaning would get the place livable, the first good rainfall would have them running away from their lease when they discovered the mess the weather created inside their living room. Besides the unhealthy conditions, he had enough reasons to make sure whoever moved in moved right back out.

His good mood ruined, he walked to his

motorcycle under the glow of the streetlight and glanced over at the early nineteen-eighties Honda. Maroon paint with a faded hood, the car had seen better days. He threw his leg over his bike, started the engine, and pulled a U-turn in the street.

Looking at the car as he rode away, he noticed the back tire was flat. He hit the throttle harder than he usually went around the block in the middle of the night. His new lowlife neighbor would probably let the car sit at the curb and junk the place up even more.

He pulled out onto the main street of Haugan. The small, rural Montana town only a bird's throw from Idaho and smack dab along Interstate 90. Most of the people milling around during the day were tourist traveling through the state. At night, the locals went to sleep as soon as the two bars in town closed.

Three blocks later with the bar insight, he slowed down. A handful of customers flowed out the front door happier than when they went in and leaning heavily on each other. Swiss turned left and pulled in behind the bar beside three other motorcycles tagged as belonging to Ronacks members.

Sander and Rod, his MC brothers, and to his surprise, his president, Battery, were inside the bar. Battery rarely showed up at the bar, even though the club owned the establishment. He preferred to stay away from the place that had changed the direction of his wife's life and almost got Bree killed back when her parents owned the joint.

Swiss strode through the back door and raised voices coming from the other room greeted him. He hurried through the kitchen and came out behind the counter of the bar to find Raelyn standing beside Battery. Sander and Rod blocked an angry woman from getting any closer to their president and their responsibility.

"I'm only asking if you've seen her." The woman, he guessed in her early twenties, raised her hands out to her sides. "Was she here or not?"

"I've already told you that I don't believe anyone fitting her description has been here and even if she had visited the bar, I cater to customers. Adult customers who have a right to come and go as they please without the stress of knowing they're patronage to my business will be questioned." Raelyn's shoulders drooped, and she looked up at Battery. "I believe we've done all we can to help the lady. It's time for her to leave."

"Go ahead and escort the lady outside and make sure she gets back on the road safely," said Battery in a tone that stopped the woman from arguing.

Rod and Sander bookended the woman and herded her toward the front door. Swiss waited until the members trespassed the woman from the bar and cleared his throat.

Raelyn swiveled around, her blondish ponytail swinging behind her, and sighed in relief. "Hi, Swiss."

"Hey, honey." Swiss then glanced at Battery. "Exciting night?"

"Some woman looking for her sister and thought getting in Raelyn's face would get her the answers she was looking for." Battery ran his hand down his full beard. "Where've you been?"

"Home sleeping." Swiss reached up and pulled his skullcap down to his brows. "I planned to go over to the clubhouse earlier, but grabbed some sandwiches at the deli and turned the game on. I crashed until it was time to come pick up the bag."

Raelyn placed her slim hand on Swiss's arm. "Speaking of which, let me get you the money."

Swiss watched Raelyn go to the end of the counter and open the cash register. There was something off with Raelyn tonight. She usually was in the mood to talk when the bar closed and would even sit down and share a beer with him to relax after a busy day before she had to go upstairs and relieve the babysitter. Tonight, she seemed distant, rushed, and serious.

"Is she okay?" Swiss lifted his chin in Raelyn's direction.

Battery lowered his voice, "Today's the anniversary of Duke's death."

"Jesus," he mumbled. "Can't believe it's been two years."

Raelyn and Duke had only found out they were going to be parents before Duke was shot and killed when the Russians came looking for Bree. Sorrow laid heavily on him. He'd been there the day Duke took the bullet and tried to stop the bleeding and get the lead out, but the high caliber shot had taken most of Duke's neck out. His MC brother was dead before anything could be done.

"Here you go," said Raelyn, stopping in front of Swiss.

He put the bag under his shirt in the back and

tucked the material under his belt, covering the bulk with his leather Ronacks vest. "How's Dukie?"

"Running everywhere." Raelyn smiled tiredly. "He's only eighteen months and has already discovered how to climb up on top of the dining room table. I've resorted to locking the chairs in my room and out of his way unless we have company. I'm afraid one of these days, he's going to jump off and crack his chin open. He's a real daredevil. As it is, Pepper does such an awesome job keeping one step ahead of him while I work. Jana and Bree watch him for me when Pepper has to go to her college classes on Tuesdays and Thursdays. I don't know what I'd do without the women in my life."

Swiss leaned in and kissed her cheek. "You're a good momma, Rae."

Raelyn's eyes misted. Swiss squeezed her hand. Duke would be proud of his woman. She'd stayed strong throughout everything and lived for their son. Managing the bar gave her income and security. Along with the club supporting her, Raelyn would be fine.

"Oh, I can't believe I forgot." Raelyn stepped away and put her hand on her head. "I didn't wrap a piece of pie for you to take home. Let me go—"

"That's okay. I'm still full from dinner," Swiss lied. "Why don't you go put your feet up. I'm going to hit the road."

He motioned at Battery. "Walk out with me?"

"Yeah. Give me a second." Battery turned to Raelyn.

Swiss left through the kitchen and walked out the back door. He lit a cigarette and waited by his

Harley for his president. The wait wasn't long, and Battery came outside before he could finish his smoke.

"What brought you to the bar tonight?" asked Swiss, knowing Battery wouldn't have come over because a woman came around looking for her sister. There were always two Ronacks members who stayed during working hours to make sure there were no problems.

"Bree wanted me to check in on Raelyn and give her a gift for Dukie. I got tied up earlier and couldn't get away." Battery pulled out a cigarette and sat his motorcycle. "We decided to hand over Duke's vest. Told Raelyn to keep it for the kid. You would've thought I brought Duke back to life when she held the leather, man."

Swiss flinched and shook his head. "She loved him."

"Yeah, wholeheartedly," mumbled Battery. "Makes me want to go home and crawl in bed, keep Bree a little closer."

Swiss nodded. He understood the sentiment but had no desire to feel that way about another person. The solitary life fit him fine.

He only worried about himself. Life was simpler that way.

"I'll see you tomorrow." Battery stepped over to his motorcycle.

"Ride with purpose, Prez," said Swiss, stating the club's pledge.

Battery mumbled, "Always, man."

The president of Ronacks started his motorcycle and rode away from the bar. Swiss looked at the back door, found it closed, and the outside light turned off. Raelyn had already shut down for the night to be alone with her memories.

He started the engine of his Harley and followed Battery out of town. At the last street, before the speed limit raised to forty-five miles per hour, Swiss turned right and headed toward the duplex, knowing it would be another long night since it was unlikely that he'd be able to go back to sleep.

He swung over to the curb, backed his bike into position, and pocketed his keys. Glancing over at the rusted piece of shit-mobile next to the curb, he walked around the vehicle and kneeled down beside the flat tire, running his hand over the surface in the dark. Near the bottom, he felt the tell-tale sign of a nail protruded from the rubber.

It'd take more than a simple inflate to get the car drivable. The owner would need a spare and a trip to Leery's Tire Supply for a patch.

He straightened, knowing it wasn't his problem, and walked around the back of the car and up on the sidewalk. A dark shadow appeared alongside the car, and he turned, his hand going to his vest pocket where he kept his pistol.

"Don't move," said a feminine voice.

Swiss held his hands away from his vest. "Easy, there."

"Who are you and what are you doing snooping around my car?" she asked.

In the dark with the streetlight behind her, all he could make out was a woman with dark hair, probably brown, about five-feet-five-inches, and average weight. Her voice tremored when she spoke.

Apparently, she was his new neighbor.

"My name's Swiss. I live behind you on the left side of the duplex." He waited for her to look over her shoulder, and when she continued to hold a pistol on him, he said, "Why don't you point that somewhere else and I can go inside and get out of your hair."

"You live on the other side of the duplex?"

"Yeah." He lowered his hands. "Let's put the gun away, sweet."

"You're in a gang?"

He chuckled. "This would be a nice conversation of getting to know you if I felt more secure about you handling a weapon."

She lowered the gun and aimed it at his feet. Though he'd prefer she put the pistol away before she accidently shot him, he let her have her protection and hoped if her finger squeezed the trigger, she'd hit the steel toe of his boot.

"Answer my question." She straightened her arms and yet followed Swiss's request to keep the barrel pointed lower. "Are you in a gang?"

"Motorcycle club." Swiss kept his gaze on her hands. "Ronacks Motorcycle Club."

"You said your name was Swiss," she said.

"That's what I'm called."

"You live here?" She tilted her head to the side.

He'd like to see her in the light. Going by her voice and the way she held her position, he liked where his mind took him. She had guts.

With a gun in her hand, he'd be foolish to believe her stupid or predictable. But, it was the middle of the night, and he wasn't planning on standing around with a pistol pointed at him answering her questions twice because she failed to understand him the first time.

"Already told you where I live and as much as I'd like to discuss this more with you until you believe me, I need to get inside." He stepped to his right, keeping her in view in case she made any sudden movements.

Aware of the package of cash against his back, he'd at first thought someone was trying to lift the money bag off him. Haugan was a small town, but travelers passed through, often desperate for money or thinking they could skip town and never be caught after taking advantage of one of the locals. He couldn't be too careful.

He reached for the door handle and his nighttime rebel said, "Swiss?"

The insecurity in her voice stopped him. He turned around. "Yeah?"

"You're right. It's the middle of the night, and it's dark." She remained on the sidewalk. "I apologize for pointing my gun at you. You startled me."

He moistened his lips and gazed around her. The whole town slept. The houses along the street remained dark, and they were the only two awake and outside.

"No harm done. You can't be too careful," said Swiss, taking in the silence.

While moving in or not, a female shouldn't be out at three o'clock in the morning by herself. Even the town of Haugan had its good and bad areas where a woman should pay attention to curfew. He preferred to stay in the south part of town where most of the petty crime happened because he found it easier in the chaos to mind his own business. But, there were meth-heads, heroin users, and men who would think nothing of taking advantage of a woman alone.

"Why don't you wrap up what you're doing and catch some sleep until the sun comes up. That way you're not startled anymore if you happen to run into someone when you're going out to your car." He opened the door, reached inside and flipped the outside light hanging above him on.

The light temporarily blinded her and gave him time to see who pulled a pistol on him.

He was right about her size. All woman with curves in the right places. Though, she was better looking than he'd imagined—beautiful. She had thick, long, black hair and wide eyes. He dropped his gaze to her ripped jeans that hugged her thighs. Thighs he could dig his fingers into and hold on. Her waist indented nicely above her wide hips. He raised his gaze higher and appreciated the full breasts contained in her tight shirt with a low front that gave him a nice rack to admire.

"Sorry for disturbing you," she said, sidestepping to break his ogling.

He jerked his gaze to her face and openly stared. Her full lips gave her a sad expression. A susceptibility that confused him. She'd pulled a gun on him and seemed perfectly capable of taking care of herself.

She turned her dark eyes away and walked toward the door, fifteen steps to his left, and slipped inside her part of the duplex. He shook his head at the turn of events and went inside. He had no use for a neighbor, especially not a female.

The duplex was his, though he rented from the landlord, too. He'd made sure that nobody in their right mind would want to live on the other side of the wall from him.

She better not come over and try to get him to fix every electrical socket that wouldn't work or bitch about the noise of the plumbing.

It was a duplex. Not a condominium in Missoula. Shit broke down all the time, and he lived in the better half for a reason.

Chapter Two

Gia sat down on the scungy, shag carpet that reeked as if rats had died in the bedroom of the duplex. She held the cell phone she'd bought somewhere in Idaho at a Walmart store, and used cash to put twenty dollars on the account knowing she'd never use all the money.

She only needed to make one call. Then, she'd destroy the phone.

She punched in the phone number she'd memorized by heart and put the cell to her ear. The time of day or night she called no longer mattered. She had an emergency on her hands.

The phone stopped ringing. "Hm?"

"Please, please, wake up. It's Gia," said Gia on a whispered hiss of urgency.

"I'm here. I'm awake," said Bianca, the female crisis worker who helped Gia escape Seattle and found her the duplex in Montana to stay in.

"I arrived late this evening and met the man next door a few minutes ago. He said his name was Swiss, not Greg Jones." Gia let her chin fall to her chest. "I came all the way to a different state and the shelter sent me to the wrong place."

"Swiss? Like the cheese?"

"That's what he said his name was when I finally caught him outside the duplex in the middle of the night." Gia pulled up her legs and leaned her elbows on her knees. "What am I supposed to do now?"

Bianca had gone over every detail with her on how to cover her tracks. Gia made sure she gave no verbal clues to her location.

"Don't panic, yet. Let me think."

Gia raised her head to the empty room. "Think fast. I'm freaking out and feel like screaming or crying, maybe both."

"Okay, listen to me. The rent is paid for six months." A heavy sigh came over the phone. "It'd take me awhile to get the money together for you to go anywhere else. I'd have to go in front of the board again because we normally don't send women out of the state. Our budget is low. There are women who get turned down when all they need is a hotel room for a few days until a family member can help them find somewhere safe to stay."

"I know, but you have no idea how scary it is here. The duplex is a dump. I'm not just slumming. It's a health hazard living in this place," whispered Gia. "And, Swiss is big. I'm not talking fat. He's huge. He wasn't even scared when I pointed the gun at him. If he's the wrong guy, I'm in more trouble staying here."

"You showed him the pistol?" Bianca groaned. "Gia, I gave you the weapon off the record and went against the rules of the shelter. You're only supposed to take it out of your bag if you feel your life is in danger."

"It could've been. I don't know the man or what he'd do to me." Gia pushed to her feet and paced the bare room. "I thought for sure when I arrived, the man you sent me to was here. There was a motorcycle parked out front and everything."

"Wait. Why didn't you say he had a motorcycle?" Bianca scoffed. "Did you find out if this guy named Swiss is part of a motorcycle club?"

"Yes, I asked him. He said Rowacts or Ronacks. I'm not sure what the guy said because I was shaking so bad I couldn't even hear, and it was dark out so I couldn't read the patches on his vest." Gia peeked out of the bedroom into the living room and lowered her voice. "You don't get it. This place is nothing like back home, and the men do not wear suits or look like yuppies."

"What's *he* look like?"

"I told you, big and scary. Rough and physical. He's got tattoos, and he probably beats people up in his spare time." She walked back into the room. "I don't know anything else about him. It was dark, and I could barely see."

Even the lack of light couldn't hide what she had seen.

Swiss had arms on him bigger than her thigh—that was saying a lot. Her legs weren't skinny. He'd shown no fear at having a gun pointed at him, and that bravery in the face of danger frightened her more than being alone with him. Who knew what he was capable of doing.

She'd barely got a good look at him before he turned on the light and she had to look away from his face. All she knew was he had short hair, almost a military cut, and a dark goatee. He had black tattoos over both shoulders and at first glance, she thought he wore a black T-shirt, but when she looked longer, she made out a flannel shirt with the arms cut out under his vest.

"Did he have a scar on his face? On his cheekbone?" asked Bianca.

Gia pressed her fingers against the bridge of her nose and tried to picture the man's face. He had a wide forehead, broad nose, and he squinted. She dropped her hand, excitement filling her.

"Yes," she said, echoing in the empty room. "I think so. I can't be positive, but he squinted, even when he wasn't talking or looking at me."

"It's him. It's Greg Jones."

"You're sure?" she said, stepping away from the dirty, curtain-less window. "This isn't something to guess about. I'm living in a disgusting room and worried about not having a current tetanus shot. You need to be positive."

"Gia." Bianca's stern voice got her attention. "If he has a scar that affects his eye nd it makes him look like he squints, it's him. He got shot. It's not the kind of scar a person would get from falling and smacking their head on the coffee table or from a bar fight."

"I'll need to see his face in the daylight. I'm not taking any chances." Gia swallowed, not looking forward to the sunrise.

"When you do get another look at him, call me back."

Gia groaned. "I can't. I'm going to get rid of this one. You'll have to wait until I can get another phone or find somewhere to make a call."

"I hate that you're in this situation, but you need to stay safe. Be extra careful."

Tears gathered in Gia's vision, and she swallowed the weakness. She had to remain strong. With no one else around to help her, she'd need to set everything up herself and make sure the man on the other side of the duplex was the right one without screwing up. "I will. I'm too afraid to do much."

"You're going to be all right."

Gia inhaled deeply. "I hope so."

"I'm serious. Repeat after me, you're going to be all right."

"You're going to be all right," Gia mumbled.

"Smartass." The voice on the other end of the phone softened. "One day at a time, Gia. Be aware of your surroundings and don't ever go anywhere alone. When you must go out, stay where there are crowds and don't be afraid of yelling for help. Don't talk to too many people or raise any attention to yourself in the meantime. You want to be forgettable."

"Okay. I don't even want to leave the duplex. Though it stinks in here and I'm surprised the building hasn't been bulldozed."

"Don't focus on the living conditions yet. A lot can be fixed by soap and water."

Gia rolled her eyes. Bianca had no idea what the place looked like.

"Be smart, Gia. Call me when you can, okay?"

"I will. Bye." She lowered the phone and disconnected the call.

Before she fell apart, she walked into the living room and dug through her bag until she found a screwdriver. Then, she laid the phone on the carpet and stabbed it over and over, until the screen broke, the back came off, the battery flipped out. When she'd broken the cellphone in enough pieces, she felt confident that *if* the phone had somehow been trackable, she'd successfully stopped anyone from finding her.

She put the pieces in a bag and set the garbage by the door. Tomorrow, she'd find a place to throw the broken phone away where nobody could find it.

Chapter Three

By six o'clock in the morning, Swiss could no longer stay inside the duplex after returning from the bar, running into his new neighbor, and unable to go back to sleep. He walked out the door swinging his keyring on the tip of his finger. His work day started at eight when Watson's Repo and Towing opened for business, and he planned to waste time grabbing a couple of cups of coffee at Brewers beforehand. Hell, maybe he'd grab breakfast, too.

He'd need food to keep him going while he put in his time running security at Watson's during working hours while the owner dealt with a lawsuit from two brothers who thought they'd do a little pushing around in the form of vandalism and threats. His job was to make sure the brothers never set foot on Watson's property.

Metal clanked by the car at the curb. He walked around his bike and found the woman from the middle of the night on her knees struggling with a tire iron. Beside her sat a wienie balloon spare that wouldn't take her a mile down the road without throwing off the front alignment on her car.

"Hey," he said.

She startled and fell back on her ass. "I'm sorry. Did I wake you?"

"No." He leaned over and peered under her car. "Where's the jack?"

"I don't have one." She pushed to her feet and held the iron at her side.

"How did you plan on changing the tire?" He rubbed the back of his head and checked out the curve of her hip.

She made a soft mewl sound as if she were thinking the question over. Attracted to the sound, he raised his gaze to her face.

"I thought if I could manage to get the nut-bolt things loose, I could use those concrete blocks in the flowerbed and maybe it would give me enough height under the car to wiggled the tire off." She half turned and pointed toward the duplex. "I'd put the blocks back when I was done, and straighten up the dirt. All I need is something strong enough to hold up the car, but so far, I can't budge these nuts loose."

At least she had the basic idea, though an impossible task with the lack of tools. He stepped away and walked back to his side of the duplex, went inside, and found a jack in the pile of tools in the corner of his living room, then returned to the car.

The woman jumped out of his way when he stepped in front of her. He held up the jack. "I'll do it."

"Oh, thank you," she said with an exhale. "I appreciate the help."

He squatted down, found the frame, and placed the jack on the ground. "Iron?"

She passed him the tool. He stuck the end on the lever. A dozen pumps and the flat tire lifted off the ground, giving him more height to prep for the new tire.

"Is that the only spare you have?" he asked.

"Yes."

He pulled out his cell, pulled up the contact number for the Ronacks Vice President, and put the phone to his ear.

"Yeah?" said Rod.

"Are you working at Leery's today?" He gazed at the woman's hands until she crossed her arms and kept them from his view. She wore no wedding ring.

"I start at eight."

"Do me a favor and roll aside a 70R13 for me." He peered at the condition of her other tires. "Better yet, if you have a used one with enough tread to make it safe, I'll take it.

"Will do. I've got a delivery at four thirty this afternoon and will be out with the truck. Do you want me to drop it at your place and save you a trip back to town?" asked Rod.

"Yeah, that'd be good. Thanks." He disconnected the call and directed his attention to the woman. "I'm not putting the spare tire you have on the car."

"Why not?"

"Unsafe."

She sighed. "Well, I can't help that. It's the only spare tire I have, and it came with the car. It's inflated and holding air."

"Still not going to put it on."

"But, you…I can't…" She blew out her breath, sending her hair away from her cheek. "I can't afford a new tire at the moment, and it sounds like you just asked someone to get me a new one."

"Never asked you to buy it." He picked up the jack, handed her the tire iron, and stepped away. "I'll put it on around five o'clock when I get back from work."

She stepped toward him. He turned and walked away, leaving her by her useless car.

"Wait," she called. "You really can't buy me a tire."

"Already done."

She tugged her shirt over her flat stomach. "Can you wait a couple of weeks until I can pay you back?"

"Never asked for money, —" He frowned. "What's your name?"

She worked her lips in worry and finally said, "Gia."

"Gia," he said and nodded. "Fits you."

Swiss turned and unlocked his door, set the jack down inside, and went back out. Gia stood in the same spot frowning at him. He walked to his motorcycle. It wasn't his problem if she hadn't liked him getting her a new tire. He wasn't going to be responsible for not stopping her from driving around on a spare that could abandon her at any time. Probably in the worst place.

He straddled the Harley. Out of his peripheral vision, he watched Gia step toward him. He slipped his key in and looked at her.

"Anything else?" he asked.

She glanced away and studied the road. "Is there a coffee shop within walking distance?"

"You don't have coffee?"

She shook her head.

He removed the key, hopped off the bike, and walked past her to his side of the duplex. He left the door open behind him. She could follow or not, that was up to her.

He could take the time to make enough coffee for two people easily enough. Usually, he stopped at the coffee shop in the morning, because it was one of the businesses Ronacks protected. He dumped a half a pot of water in the maker, filled the coffee filter, and pushed the power button.

Gia cleared her throat behind him. He glanced over his shoulder. She stood in the doorway watching him.

"You might as well come in and wait." He removed two mugs from the cupboard and turned around. "It won't take long."

Gia inched her way in, looking all around. For the first time, he picked up her shyness. What she'd given him during the middle of the night and that morning was fear. A fear he couldn't pinpoint the cause.

"Wow, your place is nice." She peered around the room.

He grunted. "Nobody has lived in your side for a long time."

"Right," she whispered, frowning.

"Where are you from?" he asked, not caring where she originated, only that he wanted her gone from living beside him.

Gia stepped up to the other side of the open-faced counter. "All over. I was an Army brat until I went to college at U of W. Then, I lived in the Seattle area and...I'm living in Montana now."

"Yeah?" He pulled the container of sugar toward him. "What are you going to do in Haugan? Not much around here requires an employee with a college degree."

"I don't know yet. I have some time until I have to make a decision." She glanced down at his arm. "You were in the service?"

He looked down at his squadron number tattooed on his upper arm. "A long time ago. Learned enough skills to survive and left the career side to better men than me."

She bobbed her head and glanced at the counter. "Coffee smells good."

"You probably don't have much in the way of groceries yet." He turned at the sound of the last gurgle and shut the maker off. "Only have sugar and milk."

"Sugar is perfect."

He handed her a filled mug and motioned with his chin toward the canister in front of her. "Help yourself."

Without any hesitation, she removed the lid, reached in for the spoon stuck in the sugar, and loaded three mounds into her coffee. Amused, he grinned at her eagerness and guiltless calories. He enjoyed a woman who could also enjoy eating good food or drinking flavored coffee.

She glanced up at him, set the spoon on the counter, and lifted her mug. Her eyes closed as the aroma of coffee hit her and her mouth opened. He forgot about his coffee. He forgot about getting to work. He forgot about his dislike of neighbors and keeping to himself.

Her lips puckered, and she blew the steam away from the hot coffee, gingerly putting her lips on the mug. His cock pulsed, hardening in his jeans. He stood enraptured at the way her lips sought the liquid, teasing and tempting.

Gia moaned at the first sip and opened her

eyes. "God, that's good."

"How long has it been since you've had coffee?" He widened his stance, easing the pressure in his crotch.

"A couple of days." She shrugged. "With the move, the flat tire, and everything, I haven't made it to a grocery store. Actually, I don't even know where one is in town."

He pulled out his phone, glanced at the time, and took a big drink of coffee, scalding the tip of his tongue. "I need to get going."

"Oh." She drank a bigger swallow, grimaced, and set her cup down on the counter without finishing the drink. "I've taken up too much of your time."

"Hey," he said, grabbing the pot and filling her cup to a hair of the brim. "Take the cup. When you're done, you can leave it in front of my door. I'll get it tonight after I put your new tire on."

"About that…" Her brow furrowed. "I'm serious. I can't let you purchase a tire for my car. I'll figure something out."

"No worries. It's already done." He walked around the counter. "I need to get to work."

She walked ahead of him. He ogled her ass and his fingers curled into his palms. She had hips with a nice flare he could hold on to and keep her close.

Gia stopped in front of the door. Swiss followed her gaze to the right. All that was there was his television, a couple of empty beer cans, a picture, and a helmet he rarely wore sitting on his console.

"Something wrong?" he asked.

She jolted and stepped through the door.

"Thanks again for the coffee…and the tire."

"No problem." He locked the door and strode to his bike.

Removing his skullcap out of his back pocket, he pulled the tight material over his head to his eyebrows, started the bike, and looked over to the front of the duplex.

Gia had already gone inside, shut up tight in her part of the building with the only coffee mug he owned that had no chips. He pulled away from the curb and headed to work. Once he got the damn tire on her piece of shit car, he'd have his quiet existence back.

Chapter Four

A white truck with Leery's Tire Supply written on the side door stopped in front of the duplex. Gia peeked out the window, holding the pistol in her hand. Her last mini bag of Doritos gone, she blamed the shakes that riddled her body on hunger. Unused to living on junk food from a convenience store for two days, she needed something solid to eat.

A man with long hair tied at the back of his neck wearing the same type of black leather vest Swiss wore both times Gia had seen him stepped to the back of his truck and lifted a tire out. Gia sagged forward and set the pistol down on the windowsill. It was the man Swiss had called that morning asking about a tire for her car.

The thunder of a motorcycle vibrated the window. Gia looked past the man and spotted Swiss. Her pulse thrummed with the rumble boosting her energy. There was no mistaking the big, black bike and the large man heading toward the duplex. Her excitement at seeing Swiss wasn't over how incredibly sexy he was or the way he promised to fix her car and refused to take no for an answer. Around him, she had a lot more protection than she had by herself.

She felt safer.

That's why she'd rented the duplex. That's why she'd come to Montana. He provided a protection he wasn't even aware of, and if she thought long and hard about what she was doing, she'd hate herself for the risk she added to his life.

She picked up the pistol and put the weapon in the waistband of her jeans, pulling the hem of her shirt down to cover the bulk. The urge to go out there and be with Swiss after spending a paranoid day shut up in the duplex without a television or radio to distract her from her troubles set her to pacing.

The fewer people who knew where she stayed and could recognize her if anyone asked, the better. Nervous energy, hunger, and fear kept her inside all day. She stopped at the door. The polite thing for her to do would be to oversee Swiss putting on the tire, then thank him, and also thank his friend.

Swiss knew nothing about her, and she only knew a little about Swiss's background from Bianca at the woman's shelter in Seattle.

Apparently, he'd served in the Army—which was a good enough recommendation in her mind. Since arriving, he had never asked anything in return for the tire, the coffee, or for her pulling a gun on him. If all men were like him, she wouldn't be in the mess she was currently in, and she'd probably be married.

She stared up at the ceiling. It figured that she'd meet a perfect man at the absolute worse time and be a complete mess. Who knew what he thought of her.

She hadn't planned on getting a leak in her tire as she rolled into town on the first night. At least she'd made it to the duplex before the air went completely out. She counted herself lucky to have made it to her destination. She could go without a car while in Haugan. Though knowing she had a workable vehicle now in case she needed to get away meant everything to her.

She needed to thank Swiss again and acknowledge what he had done for her without any reason or motivation. Patting the pistol and making sure her shirt covered the handle, she inhaled deeply and opened her door. Swiss had disappeared behind her car, and the other man stood at the rear of the vehicle and glanced her way.

"Thank you for the tire," she said to the man.

"No thanks required. I'm only delivering the tire." The man reached out his hand. "Name's Rod."

She shook his hand and looked down at Swiss working on putting the new tire on to keep from giving Rod her name. Swiss glanced up at her, dipped his chin, and went back to working. Her heart fluttered.

He looked huge, scary, and standoffish, but he'd shown her how willing he was to help her. Thanks to knowing who and what she was headed toward when she set her car toward Montana, she'd made the right decision. Deep down, she finally had the sense that she'd found a safe spot for a while.

Swiss lowered the jack, and then went over each nut again with the crowbar. "That should do you."

"Thank you so much," she said, holding out her hand, sounding like one of those birds at the pet store that mimics the same phrase over and over until you wished you had a spray bottle of water to shut it up.

Swiss gazed at her fingers and frowned. "Better not. I've got road dust on me."

"Oh." She lowered her hand, embarrassment

warming her cheeks.

She should offer him something in return for all the work and money he'd spent. Paying for the actual tire was out of the picture. She only had enough money to survive. A new tire, new shoes, and even splurging on groceries would mean she'd need to go back to her condominium in Washington sooner than she'd planned. Right back to where men looked for her and would kill her if they found her.

"You're probably tired after working all day and having to come home and change the tire." She glanced over at Rod who watched her carefully and then turned toward Swiss. "Thank you again."

"No problem," said Swiss.

She walked backward a few steps, turned, and hurried into her new home for the next six months. Alone inside the duplex, she stared at the bare walls and braced herself for nausea to hit her from the rancid smell in the room.

She'd left what she thought was a good job. A job that provided her a condominium with a swimming pool, tennis court, and a walking path through the woods. A gated community she claimed as home. Enough money to live comfortably, and like any single thirty-two-year-old, she never thought of saving any cash for emergencies.

She had owned a car. Her pride and joy. She groaned. The perfect car she had to trade for the older car outside to make the trip to Montana. The old man who she traded with looked at her as if she'd lost her mind, but willingly took the upgrade instead of cash. She only had money to buy enough food to keep from starving to death.

She shuddered. Starving to death would be her least concern. If she died in the disgusting duplex, the coroner would have a hard time telling the exact reason for her demise. Almost everything could kill her. Mold infestation. Biohazard fibers from the rotting shag carpet. High toxic levels of flaking lead paint.

In the end, her death wouldn't matter anyway. If she weren't in Montana, she'd be dead in Seattle, likely from a bullet.

An engine turned over outside. She stayed away from the front window and yet close enough to peer outside. Rod drove off, and Swiss carried the jack back to his side of the duplex. Curious about the man she'd heard little about and yet was sent to trust, she wanted to find out more about him.

Swiss wasn't at all what she'd expected to find on her arrival to Montana. He was younger looking than she'd imagined a forty-five-year-old man to look, but that could have something to do with his body. Men his age usually leaned toward the skinny side or the dad bod. Swiss definitely worked out, and probably not with weights but lifting grown men above his head and slamming them to the ground. Yeah, he could be a wrestler.

He also had an attitude. She gathered her hair at the back of her head and rotated her head side to side, stretching her neck. Swiss weren't smug or rude. Quite the opposite.

He came across quiet and strong, weighing each word that came out of his mouth. A mouth with full lips. She let her hair fall down her back and rubbed her arms. Men usually had thin lips. Swiss's lips always remained relaxed, never pressed together. She liked his goatee. Not enough whiskers to call it a beard, but more than a five o'clock shadow. He kept it trimmed around his mouth.

She sighed, and a shiver ran up her spine. Mouth. Lips. Body.

What was she doing?

Delusional from lack of sleep and stress, she verged on turning him into a saint or a knight in shining armor. He was a biker. She needed to remember that.

She spied Swiss's coffee cup on the empty counter that he'd let her borrow that morning. Afraid if she left his mug by his door, someone would steal it, she'd held on to it until he was home.

He was home now.

Walking across the room, she picked up the mug and before she could change her mind, she walked out the door, locking the handle behind her. She'd only stay long enough to return what she'd borrowed, breathe the fresh clean scent of his part of the duplex, and tell him thank you again, and then she'd leave him alone for the evening.

She walked with determined steps. Unless Swiss asked her to stay and visit longer. Her ass would appreciate an hour on his couch. Living without furniture was harder than she'd imagined.

Chapter Five

Swiss turned the shower off and grabbed the towel before stepping out. His knuckles stung and he fisted his hand, stretching the skin. Brogard, one of the two brothers suing Watson's Repo and Towing, had shown up before closing and forced Swiss to use his fist to show the man the way out. Lucky for Brogard, he only had to nurse a split lip tonight. One more appearance and he'd find himself locked up for a few nights in the county jail for breaking the restraining order.

He toweled off and walked naked into the bedroom.

A knock came at the front door. He grabbed a pair of clean Levi's off the dresser and slipped his legs into the jeans bare-assed, preferring nothing constricting on him. Running his hands through his hair, rubbing the wetness away, he walked into the other room to another knock.

"Give it a rest, Mel," he muttered, prepared to do nothing else but advise the prospect on how to install a new chain on his motorcycle. It was his week to spend time with the kid before the vote went to the Ronacks members on whether to patch him in.

He opened the door to someone who looked a hell of a lot better than Mel. His next door neighbor held his coffee cup in her hand.

"I wanted to give you back your mug." Gia thrust her arm toward his chest.

He took the cup. She remained outside his door in front of him. He waited to find out what else she wanted. She had a look about her he couldn't pin down. Half anxious, she leaned her weight from one foot to the other. Whatever else was bothering her, she kept well hidden behind a brave front.

"I also wanted to thank you again for the tire." She waved her hand over her shoulder in the direction of her car. "C-could you tell me the direction to the nearest store."

"It's Bitterroot General. It'll pop up on your GPS," he said.

She looked away, and he caught a frown before her hair covered his view. He hooked his hands under his armpits.

"I don't have a phone and my car…it's old, so I don't have a GPS, either." She turned back around toward him. "Is the store on Main Street?"

He nodded. "Two blocks on your left. You can't miss it."

Her shoulders sagged, and she smiled. "Thank you."

"Let's cut all the thanks you're throwing my way. They're not needed." He unfolded his arms and watched her gaze lower to his chest and her head tilt to the side.

He glanced down. She studied his tat that covered the front of him and went over both his shoulders. He tensed his muscles making his pecs jump, and Gia snapped her gaze up to his face.

"It's beautiful." She pointed at him. "Your tattoos, I mean."

He cocked his eyebrow.

The base of her neck constricted with her heavy swallow. "When did you get them?"

"A long time ago." He reached up to swipe away a drip of water off the back of his neck and remembered he held the mug and lowered his arm. "Was that all you wanted—?"

A roar of a motorcycle cut his question in half. He looked out to the street and shook his head.

"Damn, kid," he mumbled.

Mel rode up to the side of Gia's car, swerved toward the curb and cut the engine. Swiss stepped away from Gia, lifted his hand, and made a circle with his index finger.

Mel took off his helmet and said, "Huh?"

"Move the bike and back it in." Swiss widened his stance. "Always back to the curb."

"But nobody is—"

"I'm not going to ask again," said Swiss.

The kid needed to learn every rule, every reason, every order that came from a member of Ronacks must be followed, not questioned. If he failed and fucked up, he'd never get his patch.

As it was, Battery delayed Mel's vote an extra year because the kid hadn't been ready. One of the lucky ones, Mel got a second chance.

Mel glanced at Gia behind Swiss, plopped his helmet back on his head, and pulled a U-turn in the middle of the street and straddle walked the bike to the curb until the back tire touched the concrete.

Under no circumstances should a biker park the front tire against the curb and make it impossible for a fast exit. Taking an extra thirty seconds to roll your motorcycle backward in a dangerous situation or during an emergency could cost someone a life.

Mel swaggered toward him and held his

skinny arms out to his sides. "Parked it like you said, Swiss."

Swiss cleared his throat and motioned his chin toward Gia. Mel raised his brows and looked back at his motorcycle, then directed his attention toward Swiss in concentration.

The kid's lack of education when it came to women was going to cost him a patch. Swiss looked Mel in the eyes. "There's a woman present. Introduce yourself."

"Oh, yeah." Mel stepped forward and held out his hand. "Name's Mel, ma'am."

Swiss growled and turned to Gia. "He's young. He's stupid. But, he's harmless. At least right now."

"What'd I do?" Mel glanced between Swiss and Gia.

"Does she look old enough to be your momma?" Swiss shook his head. "Stop the ma'am shit unless a woman is old enough to see you naked without rolling her eyes or you plan to give up your dream of patching in with the MC and want to sign your life over to the military service."

Mel's face reddened. Swiss lifted his chin in Gia's direction. "Her name is Gia."

"Hi, Gia. I'm Mel." Mel held out his hand. "I guess, I said that already."

Gia accepted the offered shake. "Nice to meet you."

Swiss clamped his hand down on Mel's shoulder, turned him, and pointed him back in the direction of the motorcycle. "First thing you need to do is get the back wheel off."

"Without a jack?" asked Mel.

"You won't have a jack on the road. Use the tools under your seat, look around where you're parked, and figure it out. One of these days, you'll be on the road, alone, and stuck. You don't ever want to be stuck." Swiss stepped back. "I'm going to finish getting dressed and then I'll be out to talk you through the change."

Mel walked off, scratching his head through his shaggy hair. Swiss turned to go back into the duplex and stopped at the look Gia gave him. From the curious lift of her brows, she wanted to ask him something.

He stepped closer. "Go ahead and ask."

"Who…?" She shook her head. "Is he your son?"

"Mel?"

She nodded. He chuckled at her sincerity. The noise took him by surprise and made him exhale to contain his amusement. Hell, he hadn't laughed in a long time.

"No. The kid is a prospect for Ronacks Motorcycle Club. He spends a week with each member before coming up for vote. What he learns now will last him a lifetime if he remembers and I aim to make him recall every single thing," said Swiss, stepping toward his door.

She followed him. "A vote for what?"

He walked inside and left the door open. Somehow, he knew she'd follow, and he continued. "For becoming a full member."

"That's a lifelong commitment?" She stood inside his door.

He set the mug down on the counter and walked out of the room, grabbed a shirt, socks, vest, and his boots, and then returned to the living room.

"Yeah. Once you wear the patch, it's for life." He slipped on his shirt and put on his vest.

She rubbed her lips together in thought while staring at his chest. He moved over to the couch, hitched up the leg of his jeans, and put his sock on. The only part of Gia that moved were her eyes. She followed him with her gaze. He put on his boots and stood.

Gia looked up at him. "I'm sorry I asked if Mel was your son. It was rude of me."

"No problem," he muttered, grabbing his skullcap off the end of the couch and stepped toward the door.

"So…" She stepped in front of him. "Do you have children? A wife?"

He studied her. "Why are you asking?"

She shrugged. "I don't want to make any assumptions like I did with Mel."

Swiss ran his tongue over his teeth. "No wife. I have a daughter."

"Oh." Her brows lifted, and she looked around the room. "Does she live with you?"

"No." He pulled his skullcap down. "She's grown and lives somewhere else. If she's happy, that's all that matters."

"That's…big of you." She shook her head. "I mean, that you put her happiness first."

He talked to no one about his life, and she'd already got more out of him than he was comfortable with.

He stepped around her and headed out to help Mel with his motorcycle. Squatting down beside the hand-me-down Harley, he glanced over at the duplex and found Gia standing in the grassy area in between his place and hers — watching him but deep in thought. Her gaze void of connecting with his.

Not one to talk about his past in the Army, his first marriage, his daughter, or how at one time he believed love played a hand in life, he picked up the wrench and helped Mel disconnect the drum brake before they could get the rear tire off.

He'd liked his life well enough without a nosy neighbor hanging around.

His hands worked automatically, knowing the tension, the caliber, the mechanics of the brake cylinder by heart and kept his eyes on Gia, who hadn't moved. A single woman moving to Montana without a job lined up, living in a rundown duplex without a second thought of talking to a biker or pulling a pistol on him in the middle of the night failed to add up to him.

His gut told him something was wrong with the situation.

Chapter Six

Gia turned to her right after the motel and made a quick left onto the street before her turn to go back to the duplex. She tightened her fingers on the steering wheel. Fear made her grip slippery.

The blue colored car behind her had followed her for three blocks after she'd left the store parking lot.

She glanced from the road to her mirror in a rapid pattern. They couldn't have found her already. Not yet.

The car continued to follow her.

She'd done everything possible to make sure she left no trail. Her eyes burned. Afraid to blink, she kept watching behind her.

Two months ago, she never would've imagined her life would take such a drastic change.

She peered in her rear view mirror. The dust covering her back window from her trip made it nearly impossible to see anything but a dark moving car. Without using her blinker, she turned to go back to the main road. There was no way she'd lead them to the duplex if there were a slim chance they hadn't found out where she was staying.

The car turned, too.

"Shit," she whispered, leaning closer to the steering wheel, concentrating on keeping the vehicle on the right side of the street and not hitting the cars parked at the curb.

She gazed all around her looking for someone, anyone, who she could seek out for help if she needed to make a run for it. The men after her had already run her off the road back in Seattle. Forced to flee for her life, she'd drove through someone's yard and missed crashing into a big Fir tree by a foot. The commotion of her erratic driving made the men take off and leave the area. Maybe if she pulled out on Main Street and weaved through traffic, they'd take off in the other direction.

A break in traffic came, she pulled out onto the main road and headed toward the store. She needed to keep herself surrounded by people. The men—she couldn't even call them by name, because she had no idea who they were, only what they wanted—would have no choice but to leave her alone. That's why she'd left her condominium and Seattle. There were too many places they could get to her back home.

Ahead, in the other lane, a motorcycle rider rode toward her. Her body tightened with adrenaline and hope. The rumble of the engine roared past her feeding her with relief. She stared in the rearview mirror and squinted, studying the biker until she had a good look at the back of him.

It was Swiss.

She'd recognize his size and skullcap anywhere. She slowed down and made a U-turn in the middle of the road, getting a look at the driver in the navy colored car behind her and almost slammed on her brakes.

The middle-aged woman only glanced her way and continued driving.

Gia sagged in the driver's seat. A female? One who appeared harmless as if she was coming home from a PTA meeting or the library.

She looked in the side mirror. The car continued on in the opposite direction, growing smaller in her view. Caught in confusion, she jerked her gaze to the road in front of her and panic-slammed her foot on the brake.

Swiss had stopped his motorcycle in the middle of the street. The forward movement coupled with the tension in her shoulders left her breathless. She stared at the back of him and panted. What was he doing?

He took off, roaring ahead of her. She groaned seeing the stop sign that almost had her rear-ending Swiss with her car during her negligence. Caught up in her drama believing it was the men after her that had followed her from the grocery store, she'd almost killed Swiss. She needed to get a grip.

Double checking for traffic to her left and right, she pulled across the road safely and drove slowly to the duplex. She parked behind Swiss and instead of getting out of her car, she sat inside and tried to stop shaking. It would do no good to have Swiss witness her falling apart.

Her plan to act normal, hide out in Montana and have the security of knowing someone capable of protecting her lived next door came down to her holding it together and appearing normal.

Swiss swung his leg over his bike, looked her way, and lifted his chin before heading to his side of the duplex. She waited until he'd closed the door, and then got out on shaky legs and opened her trunk to carry her groceries inside.

The hair on the back of her neck tickled. She

glanced behind her, dropped the sack loaded with cans of vegetable soup, and groaned as she heard the telltale sign of tin rolling over the pavement in all different directions.

There was nobody behind her.

Her paranoia beating her at every turn, she needed to get inside and regroup more than she needed to eat.

Grabbing the other two plastic shopping bags, she used her elbow to close the trunk and hurried across the overgrown lawn to the door. Her anxiety heightened the closer her hand got to the lock until her keyring rattled against the slot. The urge to run inside and shut herself away from the outside world overwhelmed her, and she stumbled inside when the door came loose.

Throwing the lock, she sank down on the floor and hugged the grocery bags. She rocked back and forth, pushing herself out of her fear. As strength came back and her heart rate calmed, she stood and went into the kitchen. Only a small tremor remained in her body, leaving her exhausted.

Without any cookware to prepare food, she relied on prepackaged dinners and grab-and-eat snacks. The cans of soup and cheap, manual can opener she'd dropped under her car were to fill her stomach and comfort her during the long evenings when she let her mind go places she wanted to forget about.

Nevermind, that her main meal of the day would be cold soup. She was desperate.

She opened a bag of pretzels. If she ate ten sticks at a time, the bag would last her a long time.

A knock startled her. She gasped in surprise, swallowed wrong, and choked. Pressing her hand to her chest, she tried to muffle her cough and failed, sending a spray of pretzel pieces out of her mouth.

Using her forearm to cover her mouth, she hurried to the window and peeked out. Swiss stood on the other side of the door and with her relief that it wasn't a killer, she gave way to a harder and deeper cough to clear her throat and stop her esophagus from strangling her.

When she caught her breath, she inhaled deeply to test if the tickle stopped. Hopeful that her coughing fit was over, she opened the door a crack.

"Hey," said Gia, then coughed hard, tears filling her eyes. Her throat seized, and she needed a drink. "Sor…hang…"

She shut the door, bent at the waist, and coughed as hard as she could. Her throat protested every attempt to talk. She walked into the kitchen, put her head under the faucet, and drank from the stream of water. Wiping her mouth, she coughed one more time and cleared her throat.

"What happened?" said Swiss behind her.

She jolted and turned around. "Shit. I…what are…?"

She cleared her throat again and wiped underneath her eyes. He wasn't supposed to be in her side of the duplex. She'd shut the door to keep him out. She was sure of it.

"I swallowed a pretzel wrong." She pointed to the door and inhaled a hot breath. "We can talk outside. The fresh air will probably help sooth my throat."

He held up a bag containing her cans of soup. "You dropped them at the back of your car."

Oh, God. Her chest warmed, and she ducked her head to hide the pleasure. He'd picked up her mess for her. She'd have substance to put in her stomach. He saved her from going back outside.

"Thank you." She took the sack from him and put it on the counter. "I was going to pick everything up and then I got hungry."

"The pretzels," he said.

"Yes. The pretzels." She shook her head, covering her embarrassment. "Thank you, again."

"You need to stop with the thanks," he muttered.

"Oh…" She bit her lip. "It's the polite thing to do."

"No needed with me." Swiss stepped back, took one full sweep of her side of the duplex and frowned.

She walked around him to the door and held on to the handle. The excuses she'd planned in the chance that he'd glimpse inside her place fled. She couldn't come up with even one believable justification for having no furniture or even a fork. Or, leaving the place in the hideously slum-like condition she found the duplex when she'd arrived.

"What's going on, Gia?" Swiss's eyes softened. "You've been here four days and today was the first day you've bought groceries."

"Are you keeping track?"

His cheek twitched, deepening his scar and making him squint more. "Gia?"

"I had a flat tire," she said.

"Which was fixed two days ago."

She laughed his concern away. "You work during the day. How do you know this wasn't my second or third trip to the store?"

"I know what goes on where I live, and lady, you live on the other side of the wall from me."

"But, that's—"

"You have nothing in here. Not even a suitcase," he said.

She gave him a slow blink. "Everything is in my bedroom. Furniture will have to wait until I get a job. Maybe you don't understand that money doesn't materialize because we wish it and…"

Swiss walked away from her, deeper into the room, and stopped when he had a view of her bedroom. She gritted her teeth at his audacity to look at her living space.

"What are you doing?" she asked.

"You have a backpack and a black garbage bag on the floor in your room. Where's your bed?" Swiss walked toward her, and she pressed her back against the doorframe.

He seemed twice as big stalking her way.

"I'll get one," she said, hating the way her voice cracked. "Really, Swiss. I don't know where any of this is your concern."

"Because this part of the duplex isn't livable or can you not smell the mold or see the rot all around you?"

"Again, it's not your place to question how I live," she said.

He turned around and stepped into her kitchen, went through her bags, and finally looked at her. "Are you running from an ex?"

"No." She crossed her arms. "Of course not, and stop looking through my stuff."

"Who are you running from?"

"Stagnant life." She shrugged. "My last job wasn't a comfortable fit for me. The area I lived in no longer seemed exciting. I needed a change, and the timing was right for me to take another step toward my future. I'm hoping Montana will give me somewhere to call home, and I can find a job that brings me happiness. Are you telling me you've never picked up everything and taken off for somewhere better?"

"No."

His sharp, blunt answer brought her head back. "Maybe because I'm younger, you can't understand a single woman's wanderlust to try new things and meet new people."

Wanderlust? She had to shut up. Explaining herself for no reason when he had no need for the false information she fed him, served her no purpose.

Whatever stance he took in life, he'd never know how desperately she needed his presence to keep the men hunting her away.

"Yo, Swiss," yelled a voice outside.

She recognized Mel's voice and stuck up her chin. Swiss could leave now.

His eyes hardened, and a huff of air escaped his lips and fanned her cheek. She stepped back, only now aware of how close he'd come to her. The intense strain between them bowed tight, her skin itched.

Swiss glanced into her kitchen and said, "Come with me."

She pressed against the doorframe. "Where?"

"To get food." He walked past her, brushing his arm against hers.

She only took a second to make up her mind that wherever he would take her, she'd go, because it was better than being alone and even though the car following her ended up not being the people she feared, she still shook from the fright.

Chapter Seven

Mel handed Swiss the bag from Jolyn's Burger Barn and opened his mouth. Swiss shook his head, cutting off any talk. The only thing he needed to do at the moment was feed Gia and get her situated on his couch before she fell over from whatever bothered her.

She shook, and her voice had trembled the whole time he stood in her part of the duplex. The other times he'd been around her, she held her own. Something fucked up was going on, and the last thing he needed was to get involved with a woman running away from trouble.

He pointed at the sofa. "Sit."

Gia stepped over to the couch and sat on the edge. He grabbed a plate out of the cupboard, took one of his hamburgers and half his fries out of the sack and dumped everything on the plate. Most of all, he wanted Gia sitting down with a cushion under her ass, no smells interrupting her appetite, and a meal in her. Maybe then, she'd feed her nervous energy.

She had no furniture, not even a bed in the fucking place. How long had it been since she'd relaxed?

He returned to her and put the plate in front of her on the coffee table. "Eat."

"I can't eat your dinner," she said.

"There's enough for both of us. Get some food in you. I'm going to go outside and talk to Mel. When I get back, make sure at least half of that's gone." He walked out the door not giving her a chance to argue with him.

Outside, Mel pointed behind Swiss toward the duplex. "What's going on in there?"

"Nothing." Swiss lowered his voice. "Do you have your phone on you?"

"Yeah."

"Do me a favor and take down the info on the license plate of the Honda parked at the curb, along with the name Gia." Swiss lowered his voice. "Send it to Rod and ask him to pull the specs and get me everything he can on Gia."

"Is she in trouble?" whispered Mel.

"Are you going to do the run or not?" Swiss stepped backward toward the door. "Do this for me, and our night of working together is good."

Mel grinned. "Got you."

Swiss turned and went inside. Hopefully, Rod would run the plates with no problem, and he'd have answers before it got dark outside.

Gia sat on the couch where he'd left her. The plate now on her lap and only half the burger remained in her hand. He grabbed the sack with his food in it, skipped sitting on the bar stool, and leaned against the edge of the counter facing his guest.

She chewed rapidly gazing at him. He took a bite of his burger and let her have time to get used to him. To know what motivated a person, he must first observe.

Hell, he'd observed her from the moment he surprised her in the middle of the night and almost got his head blown off. In the looks department, she couldn't be ignored. He'd have a hard time finding any man who wouldn't enjoy sitting across the room from her watching her eat.

A solid woman. Not too skinny. No extra weight that wasn't appreciated. Hell, she walked out of his fantasy and into his side of the duplex, and he still wasn't sure why.

He wiped his mouth with the back of his hand. "How old are you?"

Her chin dipped with her swallow, and she said, "Thirty-two."

He nodded. That proved his theory wrong. She wasn't alone and out on her own for the first time, and her recent tire blowout wasn't the end of the world to have upset her enough she showed fear. Not at her age. At thirty-two years old, women had a good grasp of life and how to adjust to changes without falling apart.

Gia stood holding her empty plate. "Thank you for dinner. Can I pay you back tomorrow night by cooking for you?"

His chest warmed, surprising him. He'd seen what Gia could offer him for a meal, and yet she'd offered. Her manners more than what he was used to, he had a hard time thinking of how to answer her. One thing was for certain, he wasn't stepping back in her side of the duplex because the noxious fucking smell even ruined his appetite.

"I'll tell you what." He set the almost empty bag on the counter beside him. "I need to go to the clubhouse tomorrow after work. You can come with me. The members usually hang around, drink, eat, and whatever. We can eat there."

"That sounds fun." She approached him. "Will I need to bring anything?"

"Nope." He slid off the countertop and took the plate out of her hands. "I'll swing by here after work, take a shower, and then you can ride with me out to Prez's house."

Her eyes rounded. "On your motorcycle?"
"Problem?"
She shook her head. "I don't think so."
"Good."
"I should probably go and leave you alone to enjoy the rest of your evening." She inhaled deeply, raised her shoulders, and never made a move toward the door.

Her hesitation had him opening his mouth. "I'm not doing anything."

"Oh?" She dropped her encouraged gaze when he continued looking at her.

The hope in her voice called to him. If any other woman stood in front of him, waiting around, hoping to spend time with him, he'd know exactly what she wanted and how to entertain her. He'd take her right back to his bedroom and fuck her.

Gia was different. The vibes she gave off weren't centered around sex.

Usually, he hung around women who hung around the club. They were after companionship and to feel good, and expected nothing in return. Solitary women who enjoyed their independence. And, they enjoyed sex.

Gia needed more, or maybe she expected more from him. He had nothing to give her, except a place to sit and waste an hour or two. He inhaled through his nose suddenly and ripped off his skullcap. He had Rod on point to get him information on Gia.

Maybe it wasn't a bad idea to keep her close until he found out what she was doing in Haugan.

"Remote control for the television is on the coffee table." He stepped away.

She could quietly watch a show and get comfortable on his couch, and he'd find something else to do. He walked into his bedroom, scanned the area, and grabbed the weakened chain Mel had taken off his motorcycle the other day, and Swiss had promised to fix and returned to the living room.

He opened the toolbox at the end of the couch and removed a screwdriver.

Gia turned the volume down on the television. "Is it broken?"

He fingered the chain until he found the bent bar on the bad link and held it up. "I need to switch this link with a new one."

"Is it Mel's chain he took off the other night?" she asked.

He glanced at her and nodded. "Riders always care a spare. Mel will need this one for a backup once I fix it."

Gia scooted sideways, forgot about the show on television and watched him. He used the screwdriver to slip the bar out of the link, held the chain in position, and laid it out in front of him on the coffee table.

"Where did you learn to work on motorcycles?" she asked.

He formed an oval with the chain. "Here and there."

"The army?"

"No."

She leaned against the back of the couch. He rolled to his hip, stretched his leg, and reached into his front pocket of his jeans.

"It's only a little bar that needs to fit inside the link." He held the part he'd picked up on his lunch break "Then it'll be fixed."

Gia watched him carefully as if someday she'd need to repair a weak chain by herself.

He approved of her attention to detail, regardless of the situation. If he had more patience, he'd call Mel and tell him to get his ass back to the duplex and take lessons on paying attention from Gia.

"Where do you work?" she asked, breaking her two-minute silence.

"All over." He leaned closer to the coffee table, held the link blunt end down, and worked the chain into position.

"Well, that doesn't help much." She laughed softly.

He stopped what he was doing and looked at her. He'd never heard her laugh before, and the softness of her voice laced with humor covered him. Covered him as if someone had thrown a blanket over him and he'd closed his eyes.

"Do you need help?" he asked.

"Knowing where you work?" She shrugged. "Not really. I was only making conversation."

If she wanted to avoid answering any questions about herself, she was doing a good job. "What about you? Are you going to get a job?"

"A job?" She inhaled deeply and put her head back on his couch. "Yeah, of course. I'll need to go to work soon."

"I thought you had plans."

She moistened her lips. "I do. I just thought you might know of someplace with a job opening. You've lived in Haugan your whole life, not me. You probably hear people talking about who is hiring and who isn't."

He studied her closer, trying to follow the back and forth questions that skipped from him to her. Nowhere in their talk had he told her Haugan was his hometown. He'd confirmed he was in the Army when she'd questioned him before. There was no way she'd know more.

He stood, knocking his knee into the coffee table, and sent the chain sliding across the surface disrupting the perfect alignment. Pulling out his phone, he walked out of the duplex and called Rod.

"Yeah?" said Rod a second after Swiss hit connect.

"Stop the search." Swiss glanced back at the closed door.

Rod grunted. "Too late. I already ran the plates."

"Fuck," he muttered, hooking his hand behind his neck. Needing privacy so not to be overheard, he walked to the curb. "Is there any way to erase your tracks. I'm not sure what kind of shit will come down by our getting the information."

"Hang on." In the background, a door clicked shut. "Before you jump to conclusions, the car is registered under the name Harold D. Pepperstone. Ring a bell?"

He blew out his breath. "No."

"Registered address is seven-four-one-two

Oak Street, Tacoma, Washington."

"Tacoma? Where the hell is that?" He lowered his hand.

"About forty minutes south of Seattle."

Swiss walked over to his motorcycle. "Gia said she lived in Seattle before coming to Haugan."

"Another thing…" Rod paused. "Your girl isn't in the system. Gia. Giavonni, Gianni, Gial, none of the names I tried came up. Now, Mel said she was probably between twenty-five and thirty years old, so I ran every name starting with the letters G—I—A between twenty and thirty-five, in case Mel couldn't recognize a woman in a lit room. Nothing. Either Gia's not her name or she's clean with no record."

Swiss stared at Gia's car. "None of this makes any sense."

"Want to feel me out with what you do know?" asked Rod.

"Not yet." Swiss blew out his cheeks. "I'm bringing Gia to the club tomorrow night, in the meantime, I need one of the prospects keeping an eye on my place while I work until I have something more concrete. Something's off, and I haven't fucking figured it out yet."

"With Gia?"

"Either with her or she's running from someone. There're too many things that are grabbing my attention and it makes me uneasy. Give me a couple of days, and I might have more for you." Swiss walked back toward the duplex. "I'll talk to you later."

He disconnected the call and slipped the phone into his back pocket. It looked like he was going to get to know Gia better, which went against the way he lived his life. Though he was far from disappointed. Away from the odd sense that something else was going on, he'd become fascinated with her and why she felt so comfortable around him when others would go out of their way to avoid him.

Opening the door, he glanced at the couch and found Gia leaning against the arm of the sofa, her feet still on the floor. Her eyes were closed, and her mouth was slightly open in sleep. He shut the door quietly and stepped into the room.

What the hell was he going to do now? His chest tightened.

He couldn't wake her up and send her back to her side of the duplex knowing she'd be sleeping on the floor. She probably hadn't had a good night's rest since she started the move. He stepped over the coffee table, lifted her legs onto the couch and leaving her shoes on, so as not to wake her, he pulled the blanket from the back of the couch.

Gia continued to sleep, her hair sprawled over her curved arm under her head. He spread the blanket over her body, tucking it over her shoulders, and hesitated. It'd been twenty-two years since he tucked anyone into bed. His daughter had been four years old. The next weekend when he came home from working at the base, he entered an empty house.

His family gone.

That was the last time he'd seen his baby.

Standing up and moving away from Gia. He let her rest. There was no sense in making her go back to her side of the duplex when she had no bed. The couch would do. For tonight.

Chapter Eight

Gia paced the length of the six-foot-long kitchen area because it was the only part of the duplex—besides the bathroom—that had linoleum, and she'd used the oldest shirt she had to wipe the floor clean. Manual labor gave her something to do besides worry about going out with Swiss to his clubhouse.

Yesterday, she felt safe with him and looked forward to eating real food without having to get into her stash of supplies, essentially saving her money. A night away would distract her and anywhere outside of her part of the duplex was a good thing.

Now that it was time for Swiss to show up, she regretted her hasty acceptance to go with him.

Her doubts came after she'd woken up early this morning and had to pee, and then quickly realized she wasn't laying on the floor and had fallen asleep at Swiss's place. She'd hurried out of his place in embarrassment and into hers. The shock of letting her awareness for her safety slip, she'd stayed by the window on her side of the duplex, until Swiss rode off to work.

The rest of the day, she'd gone over every little detail of the night before and finally before five o'clock, she'd showered and slipped into the last of her clean clothes. She looked down at the baseball jersey top with no sleeves and a pair of old cutoffs with the pockets now longer than the fringe. Her outfit was either too casual and would be considered indecent, or make her overdressed.

She assumed a biker get-together would have other women around who wore a lot less.

She lifted her hand to rub her face and stopped. The added eyeliner to cover the worry around her eyes would come off if she one-finger rubbed.

What was she doing?

If she had any sense, she'd drive into town and ask someone to borrow their phone. She needed to call Bianca and check in. Though they had the understanding that her phone calls would be far and few between, any contact helped Gia feel not so alone.

Swiss, while he brought her security, also distracted her. She never dreamed she'd arrive and be sexually attracted to him. The thought had never entered her mind.

Her whole focus was getting somewhere safe and biding her time until it was possible for her to return to her former life. A career she enjoyed. People she knew. An area she was familiar with and called home.

She never wanted to become one of those women who clung to men because any attention they received bolstered their self-confidence, but that was exactly what was happening to her. She wasn't immune to Swiss's helpfulness and yes, his overbearing need to take care of her simply because he had a deep belief that he was the man, and she was the woman.

It was rather caveman-like, and she practically panted at his feet offering her hair and begging him to drag her over to his side of the duplex.

God, she hated the whole situation. When everything was over, she hoped to gain her self-respect back.

A motorcycle rumble filled her empty room. Gia walked to the window and peeked out. Her stomach fluttered, and she rubbed her hand across her ribs. She'd come here seeking shelter, knowing Swiss had no idea the amount of protection he'd provide for her by living on the other side of the duplex. If someone broke into her door during the night, he'd hear. If strange men cased the street looking for her, he'd see. If the worst happened, and the men after her attacked her as she walked to her car, he'd be the one to find her.

But Swiss turned out to be more than a totem security pole. She'd found an interesting man who shared more of himself in action than words.

Quiet.

Strong.

Gruff.

Learning he'd covered her with a blanket, let her borrow his couch, looked after her last night when she'd fallen asleep at his place, and even bought her a tire, fed her, and kept her company, she thought of other things all day instead of dwelling on her situation and feeling sorry for herself.

She wanted to know if he thought about her at all while he worked and if he looked forward to taking her with him to the clubhouse. Everything about her situation screamed for her to stay out of view of others, to not trust strangers. She definitely shouldn't be excited to go to his clubhouse, but she was.

Swiss's offer to go with him to somewhere that's a part of him, to share his time, and in turn, let her relax in the comfort of knowing she was safe had done funny things to her all day.

The nervousness.

The anticipation.

The newness.

She'd willingly concentrated on good things for a change, and maybe that was the biggest gift Swiss had given her since she pulled up to the duplex with a flat tire.

The water pipe connected to Swiss's shower vibrated in her bathroom, hammering against the studs in the wall behind the sheetrock. She crossed the room and stood outside her bathroom doorway. The sound soothed her, knowing Swiss was close and within yelling distance.

Only a wall separated them.

Her body tingled and goosebumps appeared on her arms and legs. She crossed her arms to contain the quiver that started her thoughts going to Swiss's naked, wet body less than six feet away from her. Now was not the time to think about sex.

Not with Swiss.

Not with anyone.

Everything she knew about him, which was more than he knew about her, warned her away. He'd been married. He'd had a kid. He lived a solitary life, only keeping in contact with his motorcycle club family.

And yet, she could easily rally against the negative and point out the positive.

He served in the Army. He supported himself.

He belonged to a motorcycle club. As a middle-aged man, he held a job, wasn't an alcoholic as far as she knew, and had lived most of his life in Haugan.

Most of all, he protected a woman who remained a stranger to him because he was the type of man who couldn't look away or ignore a woman who couldn't even supply enough food to live on.

The water shut off. She closed her eyes a second longer than necessary, shook the arousal out of her head, and walked away from the bathroom. In that instantaneous burst of sanity, she missed her parents more than anything.

She wanted someone to fall back on, to sit down in their living room and feel like she'd never left home. Except, her parents were both gone.

First, her father died of bone cancer after a short fight, and then her mother passed away from a stroke three years later and joined her dad in heaven. Luckily, they were both in their late seventies and lived a good life together. They were able to see her graduate high school, college, and get a job and become independent. That's all they wished for, and now she was thankful she could give that to them.

She rubbed her stomach. Her twenties officially sucked, and her thirties weren't heading in that great of direction either.

A knock came at the door. She sniffed and blew out her breath. Her excitement for the evening dashed by regrets and sadness.

Opening the door, she plastered on a smile to cover where her jumbled thoughts had taken her. "Hey."

The clean scent of soap off his warm body

wafted toward her. She inhaled through her nose and regretted the action immediately when her stomach warmed, and she caught herself leaning toward him.

"Ready?" His gaze swept from her face to her legs and back up again to her eyes where the slight lift of his brow and parting of his lips told her everything she needed to know. He approved of her outfit, and if he hadn't thought about her while he worked, he was thinking now.

She nodded and grabbed her purse off the back handle of the door. "Yes."

His hand stopped the door from closing. "Grab a sweatshirt. The ride back will be cold."

"I…" She scrunched her nose and put the long strap of her purse over her head and let her bag hang across her body to her hip. "I haven't done laundry yet, and I don't have a clean sweatshirt."

He lowered his hand, shut the door, and made sure it was locked for her. "Then, you'll wear the one I have in my pack on the bike."

She followed him out to his motorcycle. Both excited and nervous. She'd never rode one before, but it looked fun.

She stopped beside the bike and patted the back of the motorcycle seat. "What will I need to do so I don't make you crash."

"Hold on to me." He slipped a black helmet she recognized as the one from his television stand onto of her head. "Is your hair okay?"

She reached up and tucked the strands pushed out on her cheeks under the helmet. "I think so."

"Climb on the seat after I sit down." He walked around the motorcycle, leaned down, and pointed at the side of the bike. "Watch your leg on the muffler. It gets hot and can blister your skin if you lean against it. You should be wearing jeans."

"I don't—"

"I'm not worrying about your clothes tonight. We're not going far." He paused and tilted his head, looking at her face. "It's important to keep your feet on the pegs, sweet."

"I will," she said, warmed by his endearment. He never used sweetheart, which was generic and covered lots of people. He used 'sweet' as if he personally gave her a name only he was allowed to use, and she liked how he owned that right. It made her feel special.

He grabbed his phone out of the back pocket of his jeans and looked at the screen.

Waiting for him to get on the motorcycle, she gazed at the way the muscles on his bare arms bunched when he moved. She wondered what the odds of his phone being untraceable and if he'd let her borrow it.

She needed to check in with Bianca and find out if there was any more news and if it looked like she could go back home soon.

Once Swiss finished communicating on his phone, he situated himself on the bike, and the engine roared to life. She put her foot on the peg and wondered if she'd tip Swiss and the motorcycle over when she got on.

Swiss patted his shoulder. She put her hand on the broadest part of his body and stepped up, sliding her other leg across the bike and found the other foot peg.

He took her hand and lowered it to his waist and reached back for her other hand. She latched her fingers together around him, and he squeezed her hands. Before she could wonder if she was doing everything right, the motorcycle moved forward.

She held on tighter. Maybe at the party, she could use the clubhouse's phone without anyone knowing and call Seattle. That way she wouldn't have to ask Swiss and keep the fact she was even more useless than he already imagined.

Chapter Nine

Music blared out of the two-story clubhouse. Gia fingered her hair after taking the helmet off her head and hoped her makeup hadn't slid off her face in the massive amount of wind pressing against her during the ride. She'd expected something more bar-like for a clubhouse.

Everything from the shutters, hedges, and driveway made the Ronacks clubhouse look like any other house built in the seventies. A little outdated and worn, but homey.

Swiss placed his hand on her lower back and guided her to the front door. She gazed up at him, uncertain if she wanted other people around her. They'd ask questions about where she came from and who she was, and she hadn't prepared to lie. Unless all the Ronacks members were men of few words like Swiss and she could tell them the same short story—which was as close to the truth as she could get without digging herself into a bigger hole.

"When we get inside, you can make yourself at home. The downstairs is free range. Stay out of the upstairs. That's Battery and Bree's private part of the house." Swiss hesitated at the door. "If you need anything while you're here, ask me or one of the women."

"Okay," she said, growing more nervous.

"Another thing." He lowered his voice. "You can talk to the men, but they're off limits."

"Off limits?"

His squint became, even more, squintier. "It's

a party, sweet. Every man without a woman inside will be looking for a good time. They'll see you and want what you can give them."

"Oh," she mouthed. "Maybe it isn't such a good idea that I go inside with you."

"You'll be fine."

"Are you sure?" she asked.

"We'll leave before things get crazy," he said. "Let's go eat."

Swiss opened the door. She braced against the music, the smoke, the questionable people clustered into one large room with a pool table in the middle covered with bowls and plates filled with food. Stepping closer to Swiss, she noted that her outfit was fine compared to the other women. In fact, she could be overdressed because everyone else seemed to be in bikini's or cutoffs and bras, she couldn't tell.

"Swiss," yelled a man from across the room standing beside a table. "Bro, come here."

Swiss kept his hand on Gia and took her with him. Glad he wouldn't dump her at a party for his club after the warning about the men, she grabbed onto the bottom edge of his vest and made sure she stayed with him.

The man, another biker with a Ronacks vest on, pointed at Swiss. "Tell Sander about that twin cylinder you can hook him up with."

Swiss cocked his head in Gia's direction. "Gia, that's Rod, Ronacks Vice President, that's talking. The guy next to him with the black eye is Sander and the woman with him is Jana. Everyone, this is Gia."

Jana swung her blonde hair over her shoulder and smiled. "I'll show you where the food is and help you get Swiss a plate, too, while he bullshits with the guys."

"Thanks," Gia said, stepping away from the table.

"From past parties, I know Swiss can eat his weight in food. You'll need an extra pair of hands to fill his plate."

Gia's stomach growled. "Okay."

"I haven't seen you around Haugan before." Jana passed her a paper plate. "Or, at a Ronacks party."

"I just moved here last week." She peered down at the food. "Swiss is my neighbor."

"In the duplex?" asked Jana.

Gia's gaze snapped to Jana hearing curiosity in the woman's question. Was she one of Swiss's old girlfriends or a hookup at the last party?

"Yes." Gia shrugged. "It's a starting point for me at the moment."

"No, I don't mean it in a bad way. I was surprised because the last I heard nobody would or could rent that side of the duplex. It's been empty since I can remember, and I grew up here." Jana pointed to a bowl. "Oh, you have to try the seven-layer salad. Raelyn brought it for the first time. It's really good."

"Raelyn?" she asked.

Jana nodded and pointed to Gia's right. "See the woman holding the baby on the couch?"

She found the couch and spotted the woman with what appeared to be a little boy on her lap. The baby had fluorescent orange foam earplugs in.

"Yes, I see her. Her baby is cute," said Gia,

glad the mother was protecting the child's hearing with the loud music playing.

"She manages Pine Bar and Girl in town." Jana grinned. "When I'm not working at the bar, I babysit Dukie. Do you have any kids?"

Gia picked up a piece of cheesy bread and added it to her plate. "No, I'm not married."

Jana laughed. "Honey, you don't have to be married to have a kid."

"Sorry." Gia relaxed. "That came out wrong."

"Don't sweat it. I don't have kids either." Jana held up the plate. "Do you think this is enough for Swiss?"

"Uh…" Gia laughed. "I have no idea, but if he eats enough food to feed three people, I think that'll be plenty."

Jana grinned. "Come on. You can sit down at the table where Swiss is talking to the guys, and I'll keep you company. When bikers start talking about motorcycles, it'll keep them going for a while."

The other woman led the way. Gia concentrated on not bumping into anyone and not spilling her food. At the table, she sat beside Jana and glanced up at Swiss.

He'd taken his plate from Jana and dipped his chin at Gia in thanks. She smiled and rubbed her hands on her bare thighs. It felt good to have him pay attention to her when he was busy with his friends. It wasn't as if they were on a date and he was obligated to keep her entertained. Tonight was all about sharing another meal together, and nothing more.

Jana put her cell phone on the table and picked up a bottle of beer. Unsure of what to talk about, Gia ate from the plate and forced herself to take her time. The others had no idea how hungry she'd become and how wonderful real food tasted to her.

Swiss sat down beside her and leaned closer. "Eat up. It beats cooking and eating out."

She ducked her head and took another bite of macaroni salad. Of course, Swiss would understand her position. He'd seen her lack of groceries or at least her grab-and-eat selection of convenience food, plus he'd fed her last night.

Unable to follow most of the conversations around her, she enjoyed her meal and the comfort of having food in her stomach.

A woman with dark red hair approached the table. "Has anyone seen Battery?"

"He's out red boxing," said Rod.

"Figures." The woman smiled, and her gaze fell on Gia. "Hi."

Gia ran her tongue over her teeth to make sure her mouth was clear of food and then said, "Hi. I'm Gia."

"I'm Bree. Who did you come with?"

"I brought her," said Swiss.

"Ah…" Bree raised her brows. "Awesome. Well, I'm going outside to find my husband and then going to the pond, so if anyone wants to go swimming before it gets too cold, come on out."

"Swiss?" Jana scooted her chair back from the table.

Swiss lifted his chin. "Go. I'll stay with Gia."

Jana left the table. Gia's spine straightened, and she raised her hand to call Jana back and tell her she forgot her phone on the table and changed her mind.

"Swiss?" Gia wiped her mouth with a paper napkin. "What's red boxing?"

"It means Battery is outside having a cigarette."

"Oh." Gia turned in her chair. "You can go with the others to the pond. I'm fine waiting in here for you if you'd like to join the others. You don't have to babysit me."

All she needed was one short phone call on Jana's cell phone. She could call Bianca in Seattle, check in, and find out if there was any more news that would end her nightmare.

Swiss shoved the last half of a buttered roll in his mouth. "I don't swim."

"None of the members ever swim in the pond." Rod stretched his arms out to the side and joined the conversation. "We go to make sure none of the women drown. You never know when one of them could get a cramp or need to be pulled out of the water."

Gia laughed catching amusement in Rod's reasoning. "Don't let me stop your fun."

Rod smacked Sander on the back. "Grab a bottle of whiskey on your way out and let's go play lifeguard."

Gia inhaled deeply. Her stomach full and her plate almost empty. The others left in the room would assume the phone on the table belonged to her. She only needed to get rid of Swiss for a few minutes and make her call.

She leaned back in her chair, spotted a

garbage can for the used paper plates, and said, "Where's the pond at?"

"About two hundred yards from the east side of the house." Swiss wiped his mouth with the back of his hand. "Did you want to go out there?"

"Sure." She sat up straighter and grabbed his empty plate and hers. "Let me throw away our garbage. Is there a bathroom I could use before we go outside?"

Swiss stood. "Back of the room, go through the hallway. It's the second door on your right."

"Thanks." She stepped away and stopped. "Go ahead and go outside. I'll come out when I'm done."

Swiss nodded, falling into the universal man's code of manners of never questioning a woman's bathroom habits or why she needed privacy.

The door shut behind him. She threw the plates away and walked back to the table, aware of a dozen eyes in the room. Besides a curious glance, nobody gave her too much attention. She worried about her actions and tried to stay relaxed as she picked up the phone Jana left behind.

She tapped out a phone number she knew by heart and waited.

After the third ring, the call connected. "Hello?"

"It's me," she whispered. "Oh my God, it took me forever to find a phone I can use without any worry."

"Where are you?" asked Bianca.

"I'm with Swiss around, uh, the people he hangs out with." Her heart raced, and she watched the front door. If anyone came in, she'd put the phone down before getting caught. "I can't talk long, and I don't want to say too much. I'm using someone's phone without them knowing. Is there any news?"

"No. There's been nothing in the paper and the police even removed the crime scene tape from the building. The company hasn't reopened, but they're free to do so."

The muscles in Gia's neck tightened. "Stay away from there. You have no idea who could be watching, and they'll wonder why you're curious."

"I'm careful." Bianca paused. "How is everything there?"

"Okay." She glanced around the room before staring at the door again. "It's harder than I thought it would be."

"You're safe, though?"

"I think so."

"What do you mean? Has something happened?"

Gia swallowed, remembering her panic coming home from the grocery store and believing someone followed her. "I'm more paranoid than I thought I would be, but so far, nobody has questioned me, and the duplex seems safe."

"The living conditions are okay?"

"I'm dealing with them." She sighed. "Swiss is nice, and he's gone out of his way to help me on several different occasions."

Bianca's silence spoke volumes.

"I better go." Gia's gaze blurred and she blinked. "I'll try to find a phone faster next time."

"I worry about you. Maybe I should've had you stay in Wyoming or even here at the shelter."

"No, I think we did the right thing. The police weren't going to help, and you have other women staying at the shelter. It'd kill me to know I brought danger to their already perilous existence." Gia ran her finger under her eyelashes. "God, it's so good to hear your voice, though."

"Stay strong. This could all end soon, and the police will catch them and you can come back to Seattle."

"I hope so," she whispered, knowing she'd spent too long on the phone, and Swiss could come looking for her any moment. "Bye."

"Bye, Gia. Stay safe."

Gia disconnected the call, brought up the call log and deleted Bianca's number from the record before shutting off the screen and putting the phone back where she'd found it on the table. Her heart raced with a depressing thrum. So many lives changed from the act of a couple of men, and yet she wondered if everyone's path had already been decided. Something bigger was happening. Something she couldn't pinpoint. Something that had the power to change everyone involved.

Chapter Ten

Swiss stepped away from the window after observing Gia use Jana's phone. She hadn't gone to the bathroom and instead decided to use someone else's phone.

He wanted to know who she called and why she'd lied.

The fact she never asked to borrow his phone only brought more questions instead of answers. What the fuck was she doing in Montana?

She came unprepared to live on her own, and she accepted the condition of her side of the duplex without any concerns. Renters had rights in the lease. The owner was obligated under the law to provide a safe and healthy environment.

Rod jogged around the corner of the house and slowed to a walk until he stood in front of Swiss. "Did you see?"

"Yeah." Swiss had asked Rod to go through the back and keep an eye on Gia, knowing something was going on. She flipped from being there with him and enjoying the meal to using him, and he allowed nobody to use him.

"When she comes out, I'll need you to find out who she called on the phone." Swiss took out a cigarette and lit the end. "I knew something else was going on."

"I'll grab all the information from the phone and run the number of who she called through the system when I get it." Rod looked through the window and stepped away. "She's coming out."

Rod walked off toward the pond and ducked around the corner of the house out of sight. Swiss exhaled a cloud of smoke in the air when the front door opened, and Gia strolled outside.

"Sorry, it took so long." Gia gazed out across the yard and found the others at the edge of the pond. "The property is gorgeous. I can see why the others like to hang around the pond."

"Did you still want to go down to the water or are you ready to go back to the duplex?" Swiss rubbed the end of his cigarette against the thigh of his jeans, putting it out.

His gruffness rolled over her, and she frowned. "I'd like to see the water if you have time."

He put his hand on her lower back and directed her across the yard. His attitude sunk lower. Not knowing what happened when Gia was inside, he could only wait to find out if Rod found out anything by looking at Jana's phone.

Gia meant nothing to him. She could lie and make up stories all she wanted. She had no obligations toward him. He wanted her gone.

He never asked for a neighbor or the responsibility of making sure she had food inside her.

"Look." Gia pointed ahead of them. "They're going to jump in."

Raelyn and Bree stood at the end of the dock, prepared to go in the pond. All the men were at the bank or sitting at the three picnic tables close by in the yard. Not in the mood to be around the others, he guided Gia off to the side, near a pine tree, and sat down on the grass.

Gia lowered herself to her knees beside him,

picked up a pinecone off the grown, and rolled it on her hand while gazing out at the water with a smile.

He looked away from her. The less involved he became, the less he had to worry about what she was doing.

An orange glow had settled on the peak of the mountain and dusk already settled on the water. The outdoor floodlight at the end of the dock buzzed, growing brighter as it powered on.

A loud shriek drew his attention to the picnic table. Sander wrestled with Jana, picking her up and running down the dock with her over his shoulder. He turned his attention to Gia. She'd caught her lower lip between her teeth and appeared to enjoy the entertainment. Yet, she knew none of them, and he wondered what she was doing here with him.

He'd invited her, and yet she had other reasons for everything she'd done since she moved into the duplex.

"Swiss?" called Mel.

The prospect held up a bottle of alcohol. Gia glanced at Swiss, and he could feel her judging him on whether or not he drank.

He shook his head at Mel. He'd like nothing more than to drink the whole bottle and forget his reasons for bringing Gia. Since she lied to him about using the bathroom to nab Jana's phone, he only planned to stay long enough to give her a look at the pond, and then he was taking her back home.

He should never have brought her to the clubhouse without knowing more about her. In the meantime, he'd keep her away from the members and out of earshot of any conversations. Even being around the other women posed a risk until he understood what she was doing in Montana.

"You don't drink?" she asked.

He huffed. "I drink when I'm not responsible for getting a woman home on the back of my bike."

The disappointment in her eyes before she looked away pissed him off. Swiss gritted his teeth, recognizing a familiar look. One his ex-wife threw his way often when they were married. He'd also seen the same look in women around town who judged him. First for wearing a patch on his vest and second for his lack of commitment. He preferred the women who partied with the club and led an independent life with no desire to commit to any man.

"I'm getting pretty tired. It was a big deal." Gia stood. "You can take me back to the duplex and still return to party with your club."

That was the best idea yet. He followed her to his feet. "Let's go."

There was no more to do or say. Gia belonged on her own. She came to Montana to strike out on a new life for herself, and he needed to stay far away. Whatever she was up to, he wanted no part in her games.

Rod stood outside the front door when he reached the driveway. Swiss stopped. "Go ahead and wait for me by my Harley. You can put the helmet on."

Gia nodded and looked everywhere but at him, and walked off. He headed toward his V.P. Tonight, he'd put distance between Gia's need to be around him and all her problems. He couldn't risk getting sucked into being responsible for her.

"Did you find out anything?" he asked Rod.

Rod shook his head. "She either never made a call or she deleted the record of having made one. There's nothing on the phone, except calls from when Jana had possession of the phone. Jane uses one of ours, it's untraceable unless we put our own tracker on it."

"Fuck," he muttered. "You and I both saw her use the phone. I want to know what she's up to."

"Maybe you're too close to seeing what is going on. She's a beautiful woman." Rod shrugged. "If you want, I can watch her for a few days. The prospects are close to her age. I could send one of them over to friend her up."

"No." His cheek pulsed, uncomfortable with the idea of anyone else around her. "Can you take me off the work roster for two days. I rather get this problem settled before it turns into something bigger."

"Call it done, man," said Rod. "Anything else?"

"No. She'll slip up, and I'll be there when she does." He lifted his chin. "Thanks, brother."

"No problem." Rod strolled off toward the pond. "Are you coming back after you drop her off?"

He nodded. "Yeah, for a couple of hours. Save me a bottle of the good stuff."

Swiss shoved the conversation to the back of his head and walked to Gia. He could return to the clubhouse, loosen up, find a friendly woman, and stomp out his need to deal with Gia at the moment.

He sat his bike, put his hand out to help his neighbor on the seat, and rode away from the clubhouse. The warm body pressed against his back a quick reminder not to get involved. It would be too easy to take Gia to bed. He'd feel her out for any problems over the next couple of days, and be done with her.

Chapter Eleven

Swiss passed the duplex and continued riding down the street. Gia patted his stomach to get his attention. He had said he was taking her home.

His body taunt during the route back to Haugan, he ignored her attempt to get his attention and kept riding around the corner. She held on tighter, instantly alert that something was wrong. The motorcycle leaned further around the corners than before, and he was going faster than the speed limit.

She had no recourse but to cling to Swiss's back to keep her seat on the bike.

His sudden odd behavior at the clubhouse when she'd joined him outside, and the silent ride sent warning bells throughout her. Had he catered to her need for protection and made her blind to how he really was? Where was he going? Could he be working for the men who were after her?

She frantically searched the darkness for anyone on the residential street. Anyone who would notice the man on the Harley taking her away from the duplex and safety.

Swiss shifted the Harley and instantly slowed. The momentum pressed her against his back. Unable to right herself, she could only use his large body to keep her place on the back of the motorcycle.

The second the bike stopped completely, and her upper body rebounded. She pushed against Swiss and slid her ass toward the side of the seat to get off.

His hand clamped down on her leg. "Sit."

She barely heard the order through her helmet

and her adrenaline screamed for her to run. He'd taken her only a few streets away from the duplex, but she was lost. She had no idea which way to go.

Swiss removed his phone and put it to his ear without letting go of her leg. "I need everyone at the duplex. Ride in and secure the area. I'm three blocks west on Sycamore Street."

Gia tugged against the firm hold he had on her leg and failed to get away.

"Yeah, she's with me," he said into the phone.

She stilled, leaning back. Was the whole club helping him?

Swiss pocketed his phone and turned to her. "I need you off the bike."

She scrambled to her feet and moved away from him. "Wh-what do you want from me?"

"Gia, you need to calm down." He held his hands out at his sides and stepped toward her.

She backed away, keeping distance between them.

"Whoa, sweet." He stopped. "You're scared of the wrong person."

"You didn't take me to the duplex." She flickered her gaze around the area. "Who did you call? Who is after me?"

In the silence, the houses glowed with their inside lights on, and shadows dotted the areas where the streetlights failed to reach. Her heartbeat raced, thundering in her ears, and she swallowed, attempting to draw moisture into her dry mouth.

"We've got a problem." He softened his voice. "Give me twenty minutes to sort everything out, and I'll take you back to the duplex."

"Problem?" Her heel hit the curb of the sidewalk, and she sidestepped to keep away from his hands. "The problem is you told me you'd take me back to the duplex, and you rode right past it, and you're forcing me to stand outside in the dark. You called someone, and you're holding me here. That's the problem."

She turned and stepped up on the sidewalk, planning to walk until she found the right street, pick up her bag, and get out of Montana.

He grabbed her arm. "You need to stay here with me."

"Let me go." She jerked on her arm and broke free. "Don't touch me."

"Gia, Ronacks members are coming through to make sure everything is safe for you to return to the duplex. While we wait, you need to stay here with me so I can make sure no harm comes to you." Swiss hooked her neck and brought her forward. "You're safe."

Her whole body pulsed. She had no idea what he knew or what was happening. The only person she halfway knew in Haugan was Swiss.

"What do you mean Ronacks members are making things safe?" she whispered. "They're coming after me?"

His fingers kneaded her neck muscles. "No, sweet. Someone has been at the duplex and slashed at least two of the tires on your car, including the brand new one. That's what alerted me that something was wrong. It also looks like whoever vandalized your car also left you a message on the window. I didn't get a good look, cause it was more important to keep you away from any activity until we know what we're dealing with."

Her tires? She couldn't leave?

"Oh, God. You're not working for them but helping me," she mumbled, sagging forward in relief.

Her helmet hit his chest, and his fingers came up under her chin to unlatch the clip. She pulled back and shook her head to get the helmet off her faster.

As soon as she was free, Swiss pulled her against him, and she leaned against his broad chest, thankful for the strength to keep her on her feet. The men trying to kill her had found her. They weren't supposed to follow her. Montana was two states away from Seattle. How had they caught up with her?

Whether they wanted to warn her or kill her tonight, they'd done a good job of scaring her to death. Thank God, Swiss was with her.

"We need to talk, Gia." Swiss's hand cupped the back of her head, soothing her. "If you don't feel comfortable discussing what is going on with the club, then later you're going to talk to me. If you're in trouble, we can help."

He was right. She'd failed to outrun and hide the killers. Living beside Swiss had placed him in danger, and he had a right to know what she'd done. He was going to hate her.

She nodded, aware of what he was offering and knowing he would stand between her and the killers if she found herself in the predicament of needing him. That'd been her plan all along. She never expected the men to follow her or allowed herself to believe nowhere was safe.

She never expected the guilt of bringing

trouble to Swiss's doorstep to bother her or to ever tell him what she was going through. Her coming to Montana wasn't supposed to end this way.

She'd come to Haugan to be safe. Swiss was supposed to be her beacon of light in a world that scared her to death.

A slow rumble in the distance brought Gia's head off Swiss's chest. She gazed down the street in dread as the sound grew in intensity. She placed her hand on her chest to keep the fear buried deep. The thrum of the engines vibrated her inside and out, and she lost the ability to show no fear.

Swiss kept his hand on the back of her neck, and she was grateful for the support when it appeared as if every member of Ronacks rode down the street, two at a time, taking up the whole block and prohibiting anyone else from traveling by.

One after the other, the engines turned off. The residual noise hummed in her head. On top of the events that forced men to come after her, she had a biker club chomping to protect her.

Everything centered around her, and it was too much.

A biker strode forward and stopped in front of her. A member she couldn't remember seeing at the party. She stared up into a rough bearded face that focused over her head at Swiss.

"There's nobody around the duplex, and we cleared the block. I'll have half the members secure the area for the night, and you can get some sleep." The biker looked down at her, then up at Swiss. "All four tires on a Honda were slashed. They left a message in lipstick on the back window."

"Lipstick?" said Swiss.

"Yeah." The biker's gaze intensified. "We can throw together a meeting now or wait until tomorrow when the sun is up. Your call, considering it has to do with your girl."

His girl? Gia shook her head and looked up at Swiss. His hand tightened on her neck, reassuring her he'd hold to his word. She couldn't talk to the bikers. Only him.

Once Swiss found out the whole truth, she'd ruin his life. He never asked for her to show up on his doorstep, dogging his every step. The danger was real. The murderers were in Haugan, and she'd brought them.

"I'll talk with Gia tonight, and meet with the club in the morning." Swiss pulled her closer. "In the meantime, tell the others to watch for both males and females."

Gia pressed her hand to her stomach. He had no clue what he was getting into or who he would need to deal with if he aligned himself with her. The best thing she could do would be to find a way out of Montana and keep moving. The two men had taken over a week to catch up with her. Maybe Swiss could distract them while she got a head start.

Except, her stupid car wasn't moving away from the curb until she could purchase new tires and even if she counted the money she had left after paying the lease on the duplex, she knew it wasn't enough for four brand new tires.

Chapter Twelve

Gia sat on the edge of the couch, unable to sit still. Swiss put a tumbler of whiskey in her hands and ordered her to drink. It would do no good jumping up to look out the window every thirty seconds. He needed her to focus.

"Trust me, sweet." Swiss sat on the couch beside her. "The duplex is covered by Ronacks members. Nobody is going to get close to you."

"You don't know that." She drank from the cup, shuddered, and looked at him. "I'm so sorry."

"Stop." He lowered his voice to make a point. "Why don't you let me make up my own mind if I have an apology coming to me."

She shook her head. "I'm scared."

"About...?"

"If I tell you, I have to face the fact that everything I've done up until now was for nothing." Her forehead wrinkled. "That there's no way out and the police can't do a thing for me."

"The police are involved?" That information got his attention.

She showed up in town without food and any possessions. Either on the run or wanted by the police, she decided to hide out on the other side of the duplex. His duplex.

"It's an open case. The police and detectives know the reason behind the crime, but they have no proof to go after the person or people." She drank more of the whiskey, steadier that time. "The police, no matter what they tell me, can't protect me unless a crime has been committed against me and for that to happen, it'll be too late. I'll be dead. They've told me over and over, they are not a security firm. They don't guard people but come when help is needed. All I have to do is call 911 and wait for the policemen to arrive."

"Someone is after you?" he asked.

She nodded, sipping the alcohol. "L-law enforcement said they'd send extra patrol cars to my area as a courtesy. If that was true, their presence never stopped the men from breaking into my condominium or running me off the road. I thought if I left the state, the men after me would leave me alone."

"Men?" Swiss focused on the facts. Crime, killings, stalking.

She nodded. "There were two of them in my condominium. I have to believe those two men are the ones involved, or they were hired to take me out of the picture."

"Okay, hold on, now. I'm trying to understand, but you're only giving me glimpses into your life, and I can't put the pieces together." Swiss ran his hand across his jaw. "You mentioned a crime. Let's start there."

Gia put the glass down on the coffee table and folded her arms across her waist, leaning forward. "It's in the Seattle paper if you don't believe me."

"I'm not questioning your honesty, sweet. I need to know what the crime was and how you're involved." He softened his voice. "Can you start at the beginning?"

She moistened her lips. "I worked at Loans by

Day, it's a—"

"I know what it is." There were Loans by Day companies popping up all over cities nationwide. They specialized in secured loans, usually smaller amounts where customers handed over a title for a car or took a second mortgage out on their house, going more in debt than they'd started out. He suspected the company made most of their money going after the car or house the customer put up against the loan when they failed to make their high payments, coupled with high-interest rates.

"Right. Of course." She gazed at him and took a deep breath. "I enjoyed my job and loved helping people secure money and purchase their dreams. I know a lot of them came to see me because they were so far in debt, I was their last option. They borrowed money at a high-interest rate to keep their electricity on or make a car payment, but even more, people came in to purchase a house, a vacation, a wedding, and they walked out with a smile. I really felt like I was helping."

Swiss rubbed her leg. "What happened, Gia?"

She rotated her shoulders, working her neck. "I arrived at work about a month ago. The backdoor was unlocked, but that wasn't unusual. The manager was often there before any employees. I went down the hallway, and something was off. I don't know what clued me in, maybe the smell or the music wasn't on—there was always elevator music plumbed throughout the office. I walked into the lobby and…and I…"

He reached over and gathered her hand in his. She trembled. Whatever she'd walked in on left her petrified.

"The manager, Sean, and Trinity, a loan officer like me, were shot dead, laying on the floor," she said, gushing out the words. "I called the police from my desk. I was afraid to leave the office in case the killer was outside or in another part of the building, so I locked my office door and sat on the floor out of view—there was a window on the top half of the door, and I could see out. God, I was so scared. It was like a dream. I couldn't understand what I saw in the other room, but I had blood on my clothes and hands." She grabbed onto his hand tighter. "I-I must've touched them to see if they were still alive, but I can't remember doing so."

"Okay," he whispered. "What happened next?"

"That's all I did. I called the police, but I couldn't identify who it was that killed Sean and Trinity. I don't know. I just don't know."

"Sh." He brought her closer and held her to his chest. "You did the right thing."

She laid her head down on him. "I've told the police and the detective in charge everything I can remember. I even voluntarily took a polygraph test to prove I was telling the truth, and I didn't know anything else."

"They thought you killed two people?" He understood police procedure. They never polygraphed witnesses, only suspects.

"At first, I think so, or maybe they wanted to make sure I was innocent. I was the only one there, so I understand why they needed me to tell them everything. They asked me lots of questions about the business and wanted to know if I held a grudge against the manager or if I was involved in the Ponzi scheme that was going on in the company." She lifted her head. "I knew nothing about any scheme. That was the first I'd heard that word, and the officer had to explain to me how it was illegal. I only gave small personal loans to customers. I had no idea the manager was running something else besides business within the company. I still find it so hard to believe that Sean would do something like that. He was a nice guy, and I thought he cared about Loans by Day."

"Ponzi scheme?" He needed her to stay focused on the story. "That was the motive behind the killings?"

"That's what the police called it. I have no idea if that's true or not. It was about a week after the murders, and the detective working the case traced some of the money coming into Loans by Day to an underground organization in Seattle, but the paperwork at the office was all done to cover what Sean was really doing. Th-they said Sean was laundering money using the company's business, and yet they can't point to who was involved with him or his purpose for the Ponzi scheme." She lifted her head. "Everything I'm telling you has been on the news and in the paper. Like many murders in Seattle, if the police can't solve the case after two weeks, they move on and eventually it becomes a cold case."

He'd seen Ponzi schemes work before. Quick money for a few investors, while the main contributors investing the big money took a huge loss. A quick scheme that usually broke up after a few months, because those investing their money would start to demand why they weren't receiving their fair share of promised kickbacks.

"You believe whoever killed your coworkers is after you?" Now that he had the root of what she'd experienced, he still had no idea who was terrorizing her and had followed her to Montana.

"Yes. That's the only people I can think of who would want me dead." Her gaze pleaded with him to believe her, and he had to wonder what the cops put her through.

From everything he'd witnessed, Gia wasn't a woman who let her imagination take over reality. She was scared, and from the sounds of it, rightfully so.

"Was your name in the paper during the investigation?" he asked.

"No, but it wouldn't be hard to figure out I worked there during the time of the murders. For all I know, the people who were involved in the Ponzi scheme came in and met with Sean while I was there. I could've even talked to them because I still don't know who was involved." She inhaled deeply and shook her head. "I've thought of nothing else since it happened."

"I'll do some research and see what is printed in the papers during that time." He cupped the back of her neck. "Who were the police investigating?"

"Besides asking me questions, I honestly don't know." She grabbed his arm. "But while at the police department, in one of their back rooms, I heard others talking. I can't be sure if it was tied to the case at Loans by Day, but they mentioned Sparrows and Ponzi scheme in the same conversation."

"Sparrows?"

"They're bad people, Swiss. Everyone in Seattle knows they have their hand in businesses and work underground. There're even rumors that they have people in the police force." She pressed his hand to her face, holding it there. "That's all I know, and I can't be sure I've connected the right people to what happened to Sean and Trinity."

"What's the name of the organization?" He shifted to his hip and removed his phone from his pocket.

"Yesler Street Gang. They go by Sparrows on the street," she whispered. "Who are you texting?"

"Battery." Swiss glanced at her and sent the message with the name of the organization. "He's the one who talked to us earlier when the club rode in to clear the duplex. He's the president of Ronacks...Bree's husband."

She pushed off his chest. "I should leave."

"You're not going anywhere." Swiss set his phone on the coffee table. "He or she could be out there expecting you to go. It's better that you're here with me."

"She?" She stood. "I told you it's men after me."

Swiss got up from the couch, held her shoulders, and said, "The message on the car was done with lipstick."

"So?"

"Women use lipstick."

She sighed. "Then the men bought lipstick for the sole purpose of writing 'dead' on the back of my car. I don't know what to tell you, Swiss. But, the men who broke into my place back in Seattle were definitely men. It's not a woman behind everything. If it were a woman, I never would've left Seattle."

Swiss studied her. Adamant about who was behind tonight's attack, she became frustrated with his lack of understanding the situation. By morning, he would know every detail and have a plan on what to do to make sure she remained safe.

"They broke into your house? You've seen them?" His chest tightened. He instantly wanted to know who was responsible for taking care of her and making sure she was safe. Who failed?

"I've seen two men in my condominium. They were wearing masks. They also chased me when I was driving. I never got a good look at the, but it was a blue car. That's all I could remember. I got away when I drove through someone's yard," she said.

"Good girl," he mumbled, glad to hear she kept her head in the heat of an emergency. "What else has happened?"

"Little things." She shrugged. "Most of the odd things that had happened I excused as me being paranoid."

"Tell me. It doesn't matter if you can prove it or not. I need to know what we're up against," he said.

"I always placed my car keys on my nightstand at night." She groaned. "Now looking back it was silly, but living on my own, I thought if someone ever broke in I could push my car alarm, and someone would come running to help me."

"Your car doesn't have an alarm."

"No, not the car I have now. I traded *my* car to get the Honda so nobody would follow me to Montana." She closed her eyes, exhaled, and continued. "Anyways, I woke up, and my keys were on the kitchen table. I convinced myself that I did put them there, but Swiss, I know it wasn't me. I always made sure the keys were beside my bed."

"That explains why the piece of crap at the curb isn't in your name," he muttered.

"You checked up on me?"

"I knew something wasn't right," he said.

She waved her hand in front of her. "It doesn't matter."

"Anything else happen?

"The sliding door in my bedroom went out to a balcony overlooking a wooded area." She blew out her lips. "I lived in a gated community. After taking a shower, I found the sliding door open and blamed it on the wind."

"Not possible."

"I know." She shook her head. "Then, I started getting the sense that someone was following me. But, it was only when the two men broke into my condominium, and I faced them that I realized I couldn't make excuses anymore. Someone was after me. I had packed a bag planning on getting out of Seattle and the night before I was going to leave, I received a text on my phone."

"What did it say."

She stared at him with tears in her eyes and whispered, "Only one word. Dead."

"The same message outside on your car," he said.

"Yes."

"What's your plan?" he asked, changing the subject and distracting her from the real threat.

"There's nothing I can do. I've called the police when things were happening to me in Seattle. They take a report, pat my head, and send me on my way. I can't get a restraining order against men I can't identify. Haugan's police department will be no different, and if it's the men who killed my coworkers after me, which I swear it is, telling the police will only make them more determined to kill me," she said.

"That's what you believe they are here to do?"

"Why else would they follow me to Montana?" She stood, worn out from talking and bringing up every scary detail she'd lived through. "I was hoping I was only paranoid or the stress was making me crazy. The police said after a trauma, a lot of people will imagine someone is after them."

"It's not in your head." He stood up, dropped his chin, and looked her in the eyes. "In the morning, I'll meet with the club. We'll have a better understanding of what we're up against."

"I can't let you become involved. You've already done so much, and...I can't ask you for more." She stretched on her tiptoes and kissed his cheek. "You probably saved my life tonight by inviting me to your club. Thank you."

He held her against him. "You're not going anywhere. You'll stay here with me."

"I can't," she whispered. "I thought..."

"What?"

She sank down on her feet, and he let her go. "It's not important."

"The way I see it, you don't have many options that won't put you in more danger."

She blew out her breath. "Maybe I can contact the landlord and see about getting out of my lease, and hope that he'll give me back some of my deposit."

"You paid for a year in advance?" He rubbed his head, trying hard not to tell her she'd never see a dime of her fucking money back. The landlord lived in Florida. Repairs, complaints, and all inquiries into dealing with an absent landlord went unanswered. The only time you could get ahold of him is if you left a message wanting to send him payments in cash.

"No, he offered me a six-month lease if I paid in cash." She rubbed her forehead. "That's the only thing I can think of doing. I don't have enough money to purchase tires, and before you open your mouth, no, I'm not letting you buy anything more for me."

"Sweet, don't you have parents, a brother, someone who can help you and give you a place to stay?" The thought of someone else protecting and knowing how to deal with killers set him on edge. He had enough skills to do the job and yet it was her decision on who she wanted to help her.

"No, I'm alone." Her shoulders lifted, and she raised her hands before letting them fall to her sides. "I had a job, coworkers, a condominium, a nice dependable car, and I thought life was finally settling down after losing my parents one after another. Then everything fell apart the morning I walked into work and found Sean and Trinity dead."

So much of her story remained missing. A lone woman on her own with limited access to money made different choices than someone with a family and financial support. "Why come to Montana, sweet?"

Gia pressed her fingers to her forehead and moaned. He hooked his finger under her chin and raised her face.

He used his thumb to stroke her cheek. "What's wrong?"

She winced. "My head is killing me."

"There's Tylenol in the medicine cabinet in the bathroom." He turned her around. "Go take two and then crawl into my bed for the night. I'll bunk on the couch."

She glanced over her shoulder. "I can't—"

"Don't argue." He lifted his chin, setting her in motion. "I'm going over and grabbing your things from the other side of the duplex.

She turned around. "Why?"

"Until we have everything sorted, I want you closer to me."

She lowered her gaze and walked into the bathroom, shutting the door. He stepped outside, looked and listened, and took the fifteen steps to her door. Underneath the mat, he removed the spare key he knew he'd find. Luckily, the killers hadn't thought to look there, or Gia would be dead.

Chapter Thirteen

Inside the clubhouse, Battery slid a piece of paper across the pool table toward Swiss once every Ronacks member settled in for the meeting. Swiss picked up the paper and read through three copied newspaper articles regarding the murders at Loans by Day in Seattle. The crime barely covered by the reporters, all he got from each update were the facts.

When he finished, he nodded at his president.

While Battery filled his MC brothers in on the major details of why Gia came to Haugan and the trouble that came to the duplex last night, Swiss accepted what he'd read by the media. The specifics Battery provided to the club were ones Swiss handed over earlier and were exactly what Gia had told him privately.

A few phone calls to connections in Seattle came back with proof that Gia gave him all the information she had. Her name was nowhere in the articles, and the case was open for the time being with no suspects.

"A few years ago, the leader of Sparrows—a man named Vince Pladonta, was murdered and half the members of the Yesler Street Gang were put in prison when the FBI took out their prostitution ring. A handful of the members not caught went legit without their leader. The other ones tried to join other street gangs in Seattle and finding out they were tainted by bad blood, rallied amongst themselves and tried to rebuild under the Sparrows creed. Instead of peddling women, they went back to laundering dirty money." Battery thumped his knuckles against the table. "That's the men we're more likely than not dealing with here. Swiss has informed me that Gia overheard some talk while being questioned at the police department and the fingers were pointed at Sparrows being involved in the Ponzi scheme, but as of yet, there have been no arrests or any pinpointing on a suspect."

Rod whistled long and softly. "We're not talking a lone man bent on revenge or someone we can easily take out."

Battery shook his head. "Any action from us against Sparrows will bring more trouble down on the club. Don't let their location fool you. They've traveled from Seattle to come after Gia in Montana. They're not worried about crossing territories."

"What if it isn't Sparrows?" Swiss folded the papers and tossed them to the middle of the pool table. "Lipstick on the car…"

"Could be anyone," said Sander.

Swiss inhaled deeply. "Has anyone carried lipstick in their pocket in the off chance they wanted to leave a message?"

Dead silence answered him.

"Right." Swiss looked at Battery. "The night you went to Pine Bar and Grill, about eight days or so ago, there was a woman there that caused trouble for Raelyn."

"Yeah." Battery frowned. "She was looking for her sister."

"Gia doesn't have any sisters or brothers," said Swiss. "Can you remember any details about the woman?"

Battery ran his hand down his beard. "Fuck..."

Swiss kicked his own ass for not paying better attention. He'd gone into the bar knowing Battery and Rod were there to take care of the problem.

"She was about five foot, nine inches. About up to here..." Rod cut the air in front of his mouth with his hand. "She had a nice ass."

"She needed to get her hair dyed, cause there was brown up top, blonde at the shoulders. Not long, not short." Battery lowered his hand from his face.

"Hair can change," said Swiss.

"Her ass ain't changing." Rod grinned. "Long legs up to there. I noticed because when she walked in front of me, she was at the perfect height to fuck me standing up."

"Pull your head out of your ass, Rod. Do you expect us all to ride around the fucking town looking for a woman you'd be able to fuck without bending your fucking knees?" Swiss planted his hands on the table. "If we're done here, and all you want to do is throw bullshit down on the table, I'm out."

"Hang on." Battery pointed to Mel. "Prove your worth, Prospect. Wherever Swiss and Gia go, you're on their ass."

"Got it, Prez," said Mel, stepping forward.

"Rod, since you've got a good look at the woman's ass, you're staying in town." Battery's gaze intensified. "Pick a brother to go with you. I want your eyes everywhere. You see someone fitting the woman's description, you put a call out to everyone."

Swiss pulled out his pack of cigarettes and stuck a smoke between his lips, ready to leave and take Gia back to the duplex. He spent most of the night looking out the window, trying to piece together Gia's story. Hearing about Sparrows, he only wanted to go in the backroom where Gia sat with Bree while he met with the club, and make sure she was safe and not let her out of his sight.

"Everyone else, check the roster before you head out. Six people have been pulled off of working at the businesses that employ Ronacks members. That's the new crew that will keep two riders on the duplex and two on the clubhouse. I'm not taking another fucking chance of something going wrong." Battery held up his hand. "Meeting's over."

Swiss walked out of the room, down the hallway, and opened the backroom the members used for all kinds of business. Fucking, planning, talking.

Gia stood at the sight of him. His chest tightened. He hated seeing any woman living in fear, and she had a good reason to be afraid.

He held out his hand. "We can go home now."

Gia slipped her fingers into his palm and latched on to him. Swiss turned to Bree. "How are you doing?"

It wasn't long ago that trouble hit the club and everything centered around Bree. She'd almost lost Battery, and in the end, the club lost Duke, a brother, and Bree lost her father.

"I'm good, Swiss," Bree said softly. "You take care of Gia. Ronacks has your back, always."

"Right." He walked out of the room, taking Gia with him. Outside, he lit the cigarette he'd been holding between his lips and slowed his steps at the sight of Raelyn with her ass pointing out of the backseat of her car.

"Hang with me a second, sweet. I need to talk to someone." Without letting go of Gia's hand, he led her over to Raelyn.

Duke's widow straightened from the car with her baby and turned with a smile. "Hi there, stranger. You haven't come around for a drink all week."

"Been busy." Swiss let go of Gia's hand and held out his arms to Dukie, who pushed against his momma and stretched his upper body out toward him. "Come here, son."

He held the boy to his chest and let Dukie pull on his goatee. At one-and-a-half years old, the kid touched and climbed on everything. A regular brawler. "Everything okay at the bar?"

"Yeah." Raelyn continued to glance at Gia and answered Swiss. "I had Dukie's well-baby checkup this morning with the pediatrician, and Bree wanted me to stop by for a few minutes before I go back to town and open up the bar. Why don't you stop by for a drink later and we'll catch up?"

"We might do that." He shifted the kid to his other side. "This is Gia. She's staying with me for a while."

"Hi." Raelyn held out her hand to Gia. "I'm Raelyn."

"It's nice to meet you." Gia stepped back and pointed over her shoulder. "I'll wait over by the motorcycle and give you two time to talk."

"Hang on." He turned and held out Dukie. "Take him with you while I talk with Raelyn."

"Oh." Gia's head came back, and she scrambled to get a tight hold on Raelyn's son. "Okay."

Swiss waited for Gia to walk off before he turned to Raelyn, who grinned at him shaking her head. "What?"

"That was rude." Raelyn squeezed his arm. "You could've asked her to hold him before you threw my kid at her, and now she's going to think something is going on between us. I can *see* she believes something is going on, and she doesn't like it."

"So?"

"So..." Raelyn grew serious. "You don't do that to a woman if you're interested in her."

"Who says I am?"

"God, Swiss. Not every woman you meet is going to throw themselves at you for sex like the women who hang around Ronacks. She's interested in you."

He grunted. If Gia was interested, she had plenty of time to do something about it before shit went down at the duplex and he found out the truth.

"Who is she to you?" asked Raelyn.

"Nobody." Swiss lied, even though it was mostly true. "She moved into the duplex and is having a bit of trouble. That's what I need to talk to you about."

"Okay," said Raelyn, giving him her full attention. "What can I do to help?"

"A little over a week ago, I showed up at the bar to find Battery and Rod diffusing a situation with a woman who was looking for her sister." He paused. "Remember?"

Raelyn's brow wrinkled. "A week ago? Oh, I remember her. It was right at closing time. She made me nervous because it was late and I was getting the cash bundled for when you rode in."

"That's the woman I'm asking about." Swiss lowered his voice and turned to keep an eye on Gia. "Can you tell me what she looked like and any more details than she was looking for her sister?"

Raelyn caught her bottom lip between her teeth and stared at the ground in thought. Swiss's attention went back to Gia, who rocked side to side gently, swinging her hips and talking to Dukie. She was a natural with kids.

"I'd say the woman was about my age," said Raelyn.

Swiss snapped his attention back to Raelyn. "How old are you?"

"I'm twenty-six years old, and most days I feel fifty." Raelyn sighed. "You know, Swiss. I thought you were the smartest biker in Ronacks. But, dude, you need a woman to smooth the edges a little. You've been on your own too long."

"Do you remember anything else about her?" he asked, ignoring the advice and surprised to hear Raelyn was the same age as his daughter he'd lost twenty-two years ago.

Raelyn rolled her eyes. "She had ombre hair."

"What's that?"

"Two toned hair with the top darker than the ends, which are blonde. About my size, but taller." She laughed when he stared. "She was real pretty, but honestly Swiss, I've seen girls like her. She was a little too intense, almost in a panic. Either a man or drugs cause that kind of jitteriness."

"That it?"

Raelyn shrugged. "I guess. I'm not sure what you're looking for."

"Any accent?"

"No."

Swiss inhaled. "Okay. Thanks, honey."

"Can I get my son now?" She half hugged him. "Bree is going to wonder where we are, and I need to hurry. I'm cutting time close."

"Yeah, go get him, momma." He followed her to Gia.

Gia kissed Dukie's forehead and handed the kid back to his mom. Swiss took in her eyes, softened by her time spent holding someone who needed her. He understood the comfort a child brought when overwhelmed with responsibilities as an adult.

"It was nice to meet you, Gia. I hope to see you around more." Raelyn told Dukie to wave and laughed when he slapped her shoulder. "See you two later."

Swiss placed his hand on Gia's lower back to get her attention. She turned to him smiling and quickly lost all pleasure. He motioned with his chin at the bike, and she stepped in front of him to pick up the helmet.

He'd make sure the trouble hounding her stopped, and she could go back to smiling. The look was good on her.

Chapter Fourteen

Everything bothered Gia. She paced the length of Swiss's living room waiting for him to come inside.

The meeting about Gia at the clubhouse.

The shock of holding Raelyn's son.

The unease of knowing the men after her were in Montana.

Who was the woman Swiss talked to privately?

Was the baby Gia held while waiting for Swiss his son? He'd called him son.

She hated the way her mind worked and the disappointment that came when Swiss pushed her away to talk with another woman privately. Gia squeezed the skin at the base of her neck. Every day, more problems piled up around her.

She was the creator of the mess in her life.

The responsibility of coming to Montana and force feeding Swiss to protect her without his knowledge somehow convinced her that he was here solely for her. How selfish could she be?

She could never tell him the truth that he was the reason she moved into the duplex. If he never found out, it wouldn't matter. He'd already promised to keep her safe.

Guilt called her all kinds of names. She had no right to even think that Swiss was here because of her.

He had others in his life. Not only the club, but other women played a part as friends and probably sex partners. Maybe, he even had babies by those women.

She stopped in front of the television stand and picked up the only picture Swiss had in the room. He'd said it was his daughter.

God, he had a daughter.

She knew nothing about him, besides he was a nice guy toward her. He could be a horrible husband—ex-husband, and a deadbeat dad. Maybe he worked for the motorcycle club because he was a felon or got fired from every other job he tried to do. For all she knew, he could be totally different around others, and she hadn't seen his real side yet.

In the picture, Swiss's daughter was barely bigger than the baby she'd held today. His daughter held on to Swiss's pant leg wanting to be picked up, and the smile on Swiss's face made her want to cry. Every emotion ever known was reflected in his eyes. At first, she concentrated too much on his daughter and tried to imagine what she'd look like as an adult.

Then, she noticed the man in the picture was a younger version of Swiss. Hair buzzed, clean shaven, and wearing fatigues. He had the world at his feet, literally.

Had divorce split up his family or his commitment to the Army pushed his wife away? She'd lied when she shared she had grown up an Army brat. It was to make him want to indulge having her around. His tattoo gave him away, and she'd always heard men and women enlisted in the service never leave someone behind. Lying was the only way she could think to make him keep her around.

He never deserved her barging into his life.

"Gia?" said Swiss, walking into the duplex.

She put the picture frame back where she'd found it, wiped her cheeks off with her hands, and turned to face him. "I'm sorry," she whispered.

"I think we talked about you being sorry." His gaze softened. "I still can't see where you asked for any of this to happen."

"God, of course not." She sniffed.

"You're tired."

"I'm okay." She shook her head, disgusted at always pretending everything was okay when everything was not okay. "No, I'm not. I've been tired since the day I walked into work and found…nevermind."

He approached her and without asking, took her hand, and led her to the couch. She followed him down onto the cushion and found herself pulled over until her head landed on his thigh.

"Put your feet up," Swiss said, smoothing the hair off her face. "Close your eyes."

Her eyes burned, and she followed his order without question. She couldn't even find enough strength to feel self-conscious about laying her head on his lap or guilty because she enjoyed the way his rough, broad hands comforted her.

"Only for a few minutes," she mumbled

His strokes along her hair softened. "Rest, sweet. I won't let anything happen to you."

She let the full weight of her head settle on his thigh and pulled her knees higher on the couch. "I forgot to take off my shoes," she mumbled.

"Don't matter."

She sighed, and even the slight noise throbbed in her head. The thought of taking Tylenol when Swiss brought her back to the duplex after the meeting forgotten as more important matters filled her head.

The thought of Swiss having a daughter and at one time, he probably soothed her tears and comforted her until she slept warmed her. He'd be a good dad, which went against his answer he'd given her. She couldn't imagine the pain he lived with not having a close relationship with his own flesh and blood.

"Sh…," he said under his breath.

She smiled or at least inside she had. He couldn't get up with her on his lap. She'd relax for a few more minutes until the pressure in her head eased. Then she'd do something about trying to figure out her next step and how to stay safe.

Chapter Fifteen

Swiss checked his phone. Gia had been in the bathroom for an hour and a half. Granted, he understood women took a long time to get ready but she'd let him know exactly what she'd thought of his plan to take her to Pine Bar and Grill. After she had got up from her eight-hour nap, he'd spent a half hour trying to convince her she'd be fine surrounded by Ronacks members and she needed to eat a good meal.

Raelyn could provide the food. Ronacks had security down. Gia needed to get the hell out of the duplex for a few hours to relax.

And, he hoped Sparrows made a move in public, and he could take the assholes out.

He shoved his phone back in his pocket. If nothing else, while Gia ate, he could keep watch for the woman that'd shown up at the bar wanting to find her sister. His gut feeling leaned toward her being the one that would come after Gia. The street gangs in the inner cities often used women for their dirty work. He had no trouble dealing with a female. It'd be that much easier to have the woman lead him to the men threatening Gia.

The bathroom door opened, and Gia walked out with her hair dry and wearing a black dress that hugged her curves and gave him a flash of cleavage. He whistled softly. Her beauty always got his attention, but her outfit put everything out there for him to enjoy.

"I only have a dress clean. It was either wear this one or put on dirty clothes." She put a pair of black high heels on the floor and stepped into them.

"Or, if you think it's too dressy. I could stay here and do laundry while you go eat."

"Not leaving your side and I'm hungry." He walked over to the door with his dick throbbing. "You're actually safer with a crowd around you."

"I know." She picked up her purse and swayed her hips, strutting like a God damn supermodel in heels. "The nap seemed to only make me more irritable, but I appreciate you taking care of me. If nothing else, I needed to shut off my brain."

He inhaled the sweet, clean scent of her. "You look beautiful."

She scoffed and looked at him again, and when she met his eyes, she softened. "It's just a dress, Swiss."

"Hell of a dress, sweet," he whispered, wanting to kiss her.

Her eyes rounded, and she put her hand on his arm. "I can't go."

"You can."

"No, I can't. I won't be able to get on the back of your motorcycle wearing this," she said.

"Lucky for you, I have a car, too." He wrapped his arm around her and put his hand on her hip. The warmth of her body through the thin material had him tugging her closer.

She gulped at his touch. "You do?"

"It's Montana. I need some way to get around in the winter when the snow plow can't keep up with the snow." Amusement rumbled in his chest. The time it took her to get ready to leave was worth the wait. "I phoned Mel and had him bring my ride around while you slept. I usually keep it in one of the storage units across town in the summer."

He kept his left arm around her back, his hand on her hip, and scanned the area outside as he walked her out of the duplex and to the curb. Even with the armed escorts waiting at each end of the block, he wouldn't forget that his sole purpose was to protect Gia.

"Um, Swiss, that's not a part-time vehicle or one that fits in with the amount of snow I hear Montana gets in the winter." Gia stopped beside him and gawked at his car. "You own a Mercedes."

"If I'm forced to enclose myself, I'm going to be comfortable. Besides, the plows are good about keeping the streets free of snow in town." He hit the button on his keychain, unlocked the door, and opened the passenger side for her. Gia slipped inside, and he hustled around the back of the car and got in the driver's seat.

"Your theory is lame?" she asked, grinning. "You're picky about your motorcycle and car, but not where you live."

"Don't care where I put my head," he said.

"Oh. My. God," she whispered. "I can't believe you said that."

Her surprise over his answer made him chuckle. "You've got a dirty mind, sweet."

"You said it, not me." She laughed softly.

He exhaled in pleasure, pleased she was loosening up after her fright last night. They could enjoy dinner together and be one step closer to ending the bad business targeted at her back.

At the first stop sign, Gia said, "What happens if they show up at the bar?"

"Ronacks will contain the situation until we know they can't harm anyone, and you're safe."

"What's that mean?"

"It means what it means." He pulled out on Main Street. "Your job isn't to worry about what we'll do, but to keep your eyes open. If you see anyone you recognize or feel is a threat to you, tell me. I'll be right beside you every step."

He turned on his blinker, looked in his rear view mirror to see Rod riding behind him, and turned to park behind the bar at the closest spot next to the entrance where he wouldn't have to backup if he needed to get out in a hurry.

Choke and LeWorth walked out the back door of Pine Bar and Grill and headed to the Mercedes. He reached over and laid his hand on Gia's wrist.

"Hang on a second," he said, giving her a squeeze of reassurance. "Your door is going to come open in a few seconds, and LeWorth and Choke will stand with you until I walk around the car. There's nothing to fear, we're extra cautious in public."

LeWorth opened the passenger side door and nodded at Gia. "We're normally not fancy or hold ourselves to proper manners, but once in a while I like to brush up on the skills my grandma B. instilled in me. So, if you'd walk with me, you'd be doing my grandma proud."

Gia glanced at Swiss, unsure whether to trust LeWorth's smooth words.

"Go ahead. We're going to have you surrounded. It's only a precaution." He opened his car door and joined her outside the Mercedes on the other side.

He stepped around her, keeping her on his left side, and his non-dominate hand on her back. "Everything clear inside?" he asked LeWorth.

"Only the regulars." LeWorth walked on the other side of Gia. "All doors are covered, and there are four brothers inside, not counting Rod and us."

"Tell everyone on the outside to drop back." Swiss reached out and pushed open the back door. "Fuck, I'm starving."

Gia looked up at him, keeping pace in her high heels and studied him a bit longer than simple curiosity.

He rubbed his hand along her lower back. "What?"

"You've protected others before," she said, stating the obvious. "You're comfortable with the role of the other members making everything secure, and you have a routine."

He walked her the rest of the way into the bar, took a table at the back of the room, and sat so he could view the entire area. When she sat down, still studying him, he appeased her curiosity.

"Ronacks is a territorial motorcycle club, which means we take care of a specific area and make sure what happens in our territory is what we want to happen," he said.

"Like a street gang," said Gia, leaning further back in her chair.

Swiss caught Raelyn's gaze behind the bar and nodded for her to bring the food, and then directed his attention back to answering Gia. "In some ways, except we're not conducting illegal business. We all work to protect what is in our territory."

"What do you do?"

"A little of everything." He thumped his thumb against the table to keep from reaching across and touching her. "Right now, I'm working security at Watson's Repo and Towing, because they've run into a bit of trouble."

"Dangerous trouble?"

"No." He shrugged. "Nothing I can't handle."

Her lips pursed, and she watched his hand until he stopped all movement and forced her to face him. "Have you dealt with anything like I've experienced?" she asked.

More times than he wanted, he'd dealt with people where the end result ended up with someone dead. The reasons no longer mattered, it was what was better for the town, the people in the territory, and the club. He'd done the job without any leftover guilt. The way the Army trained him.

He nodded. "I've dealt and stopped trouble from happening that was at the level you're experiencing."

"Can you tell me what happened?" She leaned forward.

He cleared his throat. "The only thing you need to know is that the job ended the way we wanted it to, and those that needed protected remained safe. I will stop the men coming after you, Gia. It might not be tonight or even next week, but I don't walk away from a job until it's finished. Ronacks doesn't let shit like that happen in Haugan."

"That's why the woman at the shelter sent me to you," she whispered.

"Excuse me?" he said.

She never once mentioned a shelter or a woman sending her to him. She claimed to have ran away from Seattle and come to Montana to hide on her own.

Gia glanced around, leaned forward, and softly said, "I ran to a woman's shelter the night I received the text from the killers. The woman there helped me find a place where I'd be safe. There were two choices of places I could go. A rural farmhouse in Wyoming away from everyone or come to Haugan and stay by you at the duplex. I picked you because the woman mentioned you were a biker and in my head that meant you were tough enough to scare people away."

"Impossible." He looked over to see if Rod heard the conversation, but of course, the music and noise in the bar gave them privacy. "We don't work outside the club or with any shelter. We do what must be done for Haugan, that's good enough."

"I didn't know anything about all of that until tonight." She tilted her head. "I know the woman checked out the area. Maybe the phone conversation with the landlord brought out the kind of information she needed on whether the duplex was safe for me. Couldn't she have asked the landlord information about you?"

"The landlord only knows me by my real name."

Gia nodded. "Greg Jones. That's the name I was given on who would be living next door in the duplex."

Swiss's scar deepened and he squinted. "From there, anyone can get my military background. It's not something I can't hide."

Gia frowned. "Why would you want to?"

"Never said I do." He caught Raelyn carrying two plates to his table and leaned back bringing the conversation to a stop. "Food's here."

Gia looked over her shoulder and placed her hands on her lap.

"I hope you're hungry." Raelyn sat a plate in front of Gia, then Swiss, and stepped back and let Linda—the newest waitress—set two more plates in the middle of the table. "If you need anything else, you know where to find me. And, before you ask, Swiss. Dessert will be out by the time you take your last bite."

He flashed her a grin. "You take good care of me, Raelyn."

"Someone has to." Raelyn stepped forward, kissed the top of Swiss's head, and stopped beside Gia. Her smile slipped. "Enjoy your meal."

"Thank you," said Gia.

Swiss picked up the knife, the fork, and cut into his steak. "Eat up."

Gia glanced around at the others in the bar. Swiss, knowing she'd eat if he ate, put the piece of steak in his mouth. She copied his movements and took her first bite. From experience, he kept eating. The grilled food offered at Pine Bar and Grill was the best in the county.

While Gia ate, she couldn't talk, and he could think about everything she'd shared with him. The landlord had no business sharing any personal information about him. Even if it was only his name, there was a right to privacy act or some such bullshit in the paperwork for his rental lease.

After several minutes, Gia placed her fork on her plate, wiped her mouth with a napkin, and said, "You know, Raelyn doesn't approve of you eating dinner with me."

"She's fine with it." He dropped more butter onto his baked potato, realizing that Gia was trying to figure out how Raelyn played a role in his life.

Gia leaned forward. "She is not *fine* with me."

"Her attitude has nothing to do with you," he said.

"Well, it's certainly not you that caused her good mood to vanish."

He glanced over at Raelyn working behind the bar, unaware of being the subject of the conversation. Swiss took a few more bites of his potato, scooping the corn up with each forkful. Raelyn was a good girl. Her continued involvement with Ronacks showed how deep her feelings ran. She still claimed the club as family now that Duke was gone.

"You asked before if I've ever had to protect others. It happens more often than I'd like." He took another bite and swallowed. "About two years ago, Ronacks lost a good brother. That brother was Raelyn's man and her son's father. His name was Duke."

Gia put her hands under the table and closed her eyes an extra beat. When she looked up again, compassion gazed back at him.

"Two years ago?" The skin at the bridge of her nose puckered. "The baby isn't that…"

"No." He pushed his empty plate away. "She was pregnant when she lost her husband."

"Oh God," she mumbled. "That's awful. The poor woman."

"Yeah. It was difficult for her, and it continues to be hard when she's reminded every day of what she is missing. Every once in a while, like tonight, I can see her looking at me, looking at you, and wishing with all her heart it was Duke taking her out to dinner, instead of her serving everyone else while her baby is upstairs with the babysitter." He planted his elbows on the table. "The club has taken care of her ever since Duke died."

Gia swallowed. "I'm sorry. I never meant to pry. None of what you shared with me is any of my business."

"No harm in knowing." He pointed at her plate. "Eat up."

"I'm full."

Half the baked potato and two bites of her steak remained. She'd done a good job getting most of the food down.

"Sure?" he said.

She nodded, rubbing her bare arm. "Yes. That was a lot of food."

Swiss pulled her plate over in front of him, picked up his fork, and proceeded to finish her dinner, too. Aware of her watching him, he made sure that anyone observing them understood they were together, they came to eat, and by all appearances, he paid no attention to his surroundings.

The opposite was true.

While enjoying their meal, he became aware of how much he wanted Gia. She had him enjoying the meal with her and having her head on his lap and the way she continued to talk, even when he refused to reply. Those thoughts left him uncomfortable and wanting to do more than protect her.

Chapter Sixteen

The heavy meal Gia consumed sat at the top of her stomach. She couldn't look at Swiss. Not after feeling foolish over Raelyn's comradery with Swiss and finding out that their history went back years and involved a woman losing her husband while pregnant. The truth wiped out any uncomfortable jealousy she'd felt. Jealousy she had no right to feel.

She'd become flustered and blurted out about the woman's shelter. Now Swiss would believe she'd kept more information from him.

Swiss leaned back from the table having finished his meal and hers. Gia took a chance and glanced at him, amazed that through coming to the bar to try and bring the men after her out in the open, he remained calm and unworried.

"What?" she said, paranoid he could see what she was thinking about him.

Swiss wiped his hand across his mouth. "Just when I think I've figured out women, one of you comes along and kicks my ass."

"What do you mean?"

"Raelyn thought you were upset when I talked to her the other day out at the clubhouse," he said.

"Me?" She gulped and looked away again.

Upset wasn't the right word for the mix of emotions she'd gone through having Swiss talk to another woman he was more familiar with than her. Disappointed, maybe. Envious, definitely.

She had no right to be physically attracted to him. Even his personality pulled her toward him, and she found it almost impossible to push herself away when she wanted the security he gave her.

"I can see you thinking," he said, tilting his head to the side. "Whatever it is, you're probably wrong, and I swear to fuck, sweet, you better not try apologizing for how you feel."

She shook her head. "I wasn't going to."

"Good," he muttered.

She opened her mouth to reiterate and stopped herself. He'd think she was crazy. She'd lied to him already, and he'd voluntarily signed up to protect her. What kind of man does such a thing?

She was on the verge of losing all her composure. He turned her on. Plain and simple. What kind of woman fantasized about a man when the only thing she could think about was staying alive when killers were near enough to hurt her? She had no time for a personal life. The only thing she could do was let Swiss and Ronacks help her and try with all her power not to fall for Swiss.

At least the club members believed she was in danger, which was more than the police. All law enforcement could do was send a patrol car to circle the block or arrive after she needed help. The killers were smarter. The men never approached her with a cop around, and they never warned her before they showed up.

But, would they hesitate with Swiss nearby to protect her? Could she trust that Swiss could take care of himself? That nothing bad would happen to him?

She swallowed over the panic rising in her throat. She had no choice. Swiss was the only one who offered her help. Yes, she showed up with the intention of using him, but at a distance. She never expected him to set up, attack, and get rid of the men coming after her.

Raelyn showed up at the table. Gia wiped the worry off her face and smiled politely. The dynamics of the Ronacks Motorcycle club escaped her. Whether Raelyn and Swiss were together or friends or lovers, she had no idea, but what she knew was the woman was a single parent who had lived through heartbreak, and no matter how much she hoped Swiss was not involved with the bar manager, she had empathy for Raelyn.

"Ready for dessert?" Raelyn looked at Gia.

Surprised to find the focus on her, she blew out her cheeks. "I don't think I could eat anything more. Dinner was fabulous."

Raelyn leaned over and planted her hands on the table. "Whether you can or can't eat it, you need to take a bite. Whatever is left, the big guy across from you will eat the rest."

Gia laughed softly, knowing Swiss's appetite exceeded the normal limits.

"We have apple pie with vanilla ice cream and brownie delight," said Raelyn.

"Pie, please." Gia looked to Swiss when he nodded his approval. "Thank you."

"You're welcome." Raelynn reached out and squeezed her shoulder.

Stunned at the easiness of getting along with those involved with Ronacks Motorcycle Club when she opened her mind and pushed the doubt away, she gawked at Swiss. She'd assumed a lot from one private conversation and had jumped to conclusions to keep herself from getting hurt. A hurt she couldn't even validate, because she had no freedom to feel anything but grateful toward Swiss.

The seriousness etched around Swiss's eyes and his intense, predatory gaze watching her brought everything to the forefront. The truth had been in front of her the whole time. It was her imagination that had created a history between Swiss and Raelyn.

"You've never been involved with Raelyn," she said.

Swiss held her gaze, refusing to give an inch.

Her confidence in her ability to read other people beaten until she'd fabricated a history of Swiss's past in her mind that she could understand and grasp; she'd held him accountable for her feelings. Feelings he wasn't even aware she had for him.

She blew out her breath. "I'm sor—"

"Don't say it," he murmured, running his finger along the butter knife on the table. "We're not only here to make sure you eat and to draw whoever is after you out into the open."

"We're not?" She raised her gaze from his broad, rough hand to his face.

She was getting used to the way he squinted. No longer the scary expression she'd first thought, he studied her with warmth in his gaze and humor in his voice. The combination threw her off. He wasn't cold or unapproachable once she looked past his exterior.

He leaned forward and her heart almost skipped a beat at the sudden change he brought out in her. "You look damn good in that dress, sweet."

"Thank you," she whispered.

He continued gazing at her, and after a few seconds when she honestly thought she'd crumble in her chair at the hypnotic pull from across the table, he said, "You and your dress, and the way you're blushing right this second, has me thinking I'm going to kiss you."

She caught herself panting and closed her mouth.

"Not here." He straightened and looked around the room and mumbled, "Later."

"Later?" She ducked her chin. Oh God, she'd said that out loud.

He chuckled low. "Do you need a specific time?"

She looked through lowered lashes. "That might help because I can't even think right now with you saying everything you're saying and looking at me that way, and me being scared and not knowing what is going on with everything…and you. You scare me, Swiss."

He ran his thumb and index finger down the outside lines of his goatee. "All you have to do is tell me no."

"No," she blurted. "I mean yes. I want you to kiss me."

There.

She'd said it.

Her confession tumbled out of her mouth, and the relief at having it out in the open felt fantastic. She might not have known she wanted his kiss, but the curiosity was there from the first night she'd met him. Always hovering in their conversations and even when he was near and not saying a word, she wondered what he'd taste like and how he'd kiss.

The corner of his mouth lifted. She sighed in impatience over how relaxed and easy-going he could state he wanted to kiss her, and she was everything but calm.

"I don't know what I'm doing. You're like nobody I've ever known." She glanced around making sure they hadn't grabbed anyone else's attention. "I'm also feeling guilty."

"About?"

She sagged in her chair. "I came here with the intent to use you for protection like some big warning sign to keep the bad men away and instead…"

"Instead, you want me," he said, shrugging. "It is what it is, sweet."

She burst out laughing and shut off her nervous amusement instantly, mortified that she'd forget about everyone else in the bar and nodded. "Yes, I guess that's what I'm saying."

"Hold that thought," he said, looking away from the table.

She followed his gaze and found Raelyn approaching the table with their desserts. Grabbing the distraction, she pressed her hand to her fluttering stomach. Swiss's blunt way of talking and only saying what he wanted her to hear set her on fire. She rolled her shoulders to ease the crawling sensation in her spine. No stranger to flirting, she was out of her element with Swiss putting his cards on the table and telling her what will happen.

At least she understood where he stood and she hadn't imagined him looking longer, touching more, or standing closer lately.

Raelynn set the dishes on the table and plopped a can of whipped cream down in front of Swiss. Gia bit her lower lip, her thoughts going to what Swiss could do with the canister if they weren't sitting in a full bar in front of twenty-some strangers and a handful of Ronacks members.

"If you need anything else, let me know." Raelyn hurried away.

Swiss wrapped his hand around the can of whipped cream and rocked the container back and forth against the table. Gia raised her gaze, flushing at the arousal in Swiss's gaze directed at her.

"You have an easy face to read." He popped the top off and sprayed the whipped cream on his three-tiered brownie.

Gia picked up her fork and hovered over her piece of apple pie. "Maybe about certain things."

Swiss grunted in approval, making her stomach flutter even more, and dug into his dessert. Without anything else to take her mind off the man across from her at the table and her out of control libido, she lifted a piece of the pie to her mouth and practically moaned at the sweetness and cinnamon hitting her tongue.

Swiss's fist hit the table, rattling her pleasure. She caught movement in front of her and lifted her head, letting out a gasp at finding the bulk of Swiss's body leaning over the small table. Her surprise swallowed by Swiss's mouth capturing hers. Held captive by his large hand cupping the back of her head, she could do nothing but let him assault her senses.

Scrumptiously.

Dangerously.

His tongue contradicted the urgency behind him not waiting until later to kiss her. She lavished attention back on him, meeting him stroke for warm stroke.

Her back arched in the chair as she let him hold her head. Her taste buds stimulated, she hungered for more.

A lull in the music brought her back to reality. Swiss sensed her distraction and eased away without letting her go.

"Let's call it a night," he said against her lips.

She nodded, unable to speak.

Then, he pulled her from the chair, forgetting their desserts, and escorted her to the bar. He transferred her to his left side, and she grabbed his hand, aware of the others in the room staring at them.

Raelyn hurried over. "Rod is at the back door when you're ready."

"Thanks for dinner, Raelyn," said Swiss, leading Gia to the kitchen without stopping.

Before she could think about what waited for them outside, she was hustled into the Mercedes and surrounded in warmth from the heater and Swiss's hand on her thigh as he took her back to the duplex. Like someone starving for normal, she greedily concentrated on Swiss knowing the moment they stepped into the safety of the duplex, she'd be having sex with him.

Chapter Seventeen

Lost in the noise and general chaos of Ronacks members escorting her and Swiss into his side of the duplex to safety, Gia clung to Swiss's hand, though his possessive hold on her never wavered. He had held no fear going out with her, and she tried desperately to hold on to her sanity.

Swiss spoke with Rod and LeWorth, who followed them inside to the living room. She couldn't tell you what they spoke about. Her pulse drummed in her head, muffling their words, and her focus went to Swiss's rock hard body next to her.

His size never stopped intimidating her.

For how much he fascinated her when he moved with confidence and power, and the security he provided when he was near, it was his strength that made her nervous. Was it possible to fantasize and fear something at the same time?

The other two Ronacks members left, and the door closed. She gazed up at Swiss as he turned and put his hand on the back of her head, bringing her closer. Suddenly self-conscious, she wondered how she'd measure up. He had women all around him at the clubhouse. While she wasn't inexperienced in the sex department, the men in her life had always been nice. Too nice. They firmly believed vanilla sex was the only way.

Swiss had her thinking of all flavors.

His thumb rode her neck and tangled in her hair. "I want to feel what it's like to bury myself in your body."

Her heart beat erratically leaving her off-balance. She wanted what he wanted more than anything. To stay connected with him and forget what brought them together.

"Swiss…we need to be safe."

He tightened his hold on her. "I'm not going to let anyone hurt you or get to you when you're with me."

She placed her hands under his leather vest and sprawled her fingers over his chest. "No, I mean, you need to wear a condom. We don't know anything about each other's past and the women at the club…"

"I'll cover my dick." He bent his knees, holding her gaze. "No worries there. Not with me."

"Okay. You don't have to worry about me, either." She curled her fingers into his shirt and tugged him forward. "Thank you."

Swiss lowered his hand and fiddled with the material of her dress at her hip and walked her backward toward his room. "I can go slowly if that's what you want."

He swatted the wall, turning on the light outside the bedroom, and walked her inside. She hummed in thought, not sure slow was what she wanted.

In answer, she pushed his vest off his shoulders and took it from him. Then, she folded it in half down the back and laid it on the dresser in his room. When she turned back toward him, he'd removed his shirt, and his hands were working on his belt. Anxious to have his body against hers, she wiggled out of her dress.

Swiss halted with his jeans open and loose on

his hips. Conscious of him wanting to watch her, she slipped off her heels, wishing she had sexy lingerie to wear for her first time with him. Instead, she went braless and wore a pair of black panties that were neither sexy or small, but perfect to wear under a tight black dress. The sooner she removed everything, the faster she could forget about not being prepared for a night of sex with the most perfect man she'd ever met.

His boot hit the floor, followed by the other one, and he straightened, pushing his jeans down his legs. She blew out her breath, getting his attention.

"Commando?" Her lower stomach warmed in appreciation.

He glanced down and returned his gaze to her. "Hate anything tight."

Any kind of underwear would be tight on him in his current condition. She swallowed hard and whispered, "I can imagine."

"Fuck, sweet," he said, running his hand over his hard stomach. "Keep looking at me all hot and bothered, and I'll make sure my boxers never come out of my dresser while you're staying with me."

She moistened her lips. "I think I like that idea."

He growled stalking toward her. She met him halfway and pulled him down on the bed. Her lips parted, and he captured her mouth.

Swiss groaned, landing with his pelvis between her legs and his arms bracing his weight. Her pulse pounded. She could only imagine what would happen when he slid his cock inside of her, and she would get to experience the complete bulk of him.

Wet mouths, nips of teeth, and the sweet hint

of hardness hitting the inside of her thigh had her pussy throbbing to match her heartbeat. Lost in the overwhelming rush, she moaned.

Swiss eased away with short, soft kisses. She gazed up at him wide-eyed waiting impatiently. He traced his finger along her lower lip. "Slow isn't going to work, sweet. "

"I don't want slow. Not now. Not tonight." She caught her lip between her teeth.

He stared into her eyes. "Last chance, Gia. I can walk out of the room and sleep on the couch, and you can have my room. "

"That's not what I want." She planted her hand on his broad chest, caressing the light strip of hair down the center. "I like it fast…hard."

He covered her hand. "But, you haven't had fast and hard with me. It's going to be different with me."

Her mouth dry, she swallowed. Her pussy spasmed as he let her continue touching him and put his hand between her breasts. All she could manage to do was focus on the way his finger followed the line of her collarbone to the hollow of her throat.

"I need different," she whispered. "I need you, please?"

He dipped his chin in acknowledgment, moved his hand, and swept his thumb over the fullness of her breast. Her nipple constricted even more as if pointing toward his touch.

Unable to lie there and let him explore her body without having her hands on him in return was too much, and she pushed against him until he rolled to his hip and onto his back. She lifted her knee and moved over him to straddle his waist. "Different is good."

He slid his hands over her hips, her stomach, and cupped her breasts. She let her head fall back, all her strength leaving her body and a tremendous craving hit her. She squirmed on top of him. Swiss invaded all her senses, from the sweet taste of him, the rugged leather scent that clung to him after he stripped, to the gentle manipulation of his hands making her body sway and gyrate atop him.

His constant attention never wavered.

Even underneath her, he seemed to fill the room. She lowered her gaze. His ball sack sat high and tight, her fingers itched to cup the taunt skin and weigh its heaviness.

Swiss reached out with his right hand and opened the nightstand, removing a condom. She licked her lips as he rolled the protection over his hardness. Later, hopefully, she'd get a chance to taste him and run her tongue over every inch of his body. Not now, but soon when she had all the time in the world to show him how much he turned her on.

Swiss's gaze intensified. "Get on your back."

Something in his eyes warned her not to argue. Swiss was a man who led, never followed. Whether right or wrong, he stood behind his reasons.

And, that was good enough for her.

She shifted and rolled off him. He quickly followed and laid his body over her holding his weight with his arms. "Like that, Gia." He opened his mouth along the side of her neck and sucked. "Seeing you trust me. Hearing your breathing. Feeling your excitement."

Her legs widened, and she rubbed the sides of his hips. "I-is it wrong to ask you to hurry?"

His warm breath tickled her ear. "Like that, too, sweet."

He pushed back, shifted his hips, and teased her pussy with the head of his engorged cock. She arched and gasped as she stretched to accommodate his size.

"Gonna be fast."

"Yes," she said on a hiss.

He plunged into her pussy. She sank into the mattress under the pressure of his body. A squeak came out of her mouth from somewhere deep in her core. Wrapping her arms around his neck, she pulled him down. Skin to skin, as close as two people could be.

He held himself stiff above her. "You okay?"

She trembled, already used to the fullness turning her insides to a tightly wound ball. "Don't stop. J-just fuck me. Fuck me hard."

Growling, Swiss pulled out and slid back in her, then withdrew and plunged balls-deep. Each stroke faster and more powerful until they were both gasping and giving their bodies permission to do what comes naturally.

She squirmed, arched her neck, and urged him to go deeper. Her fingers dug into his ass, and her breath came hot and heavy. She moaned, and for the first time in a long time, she only cared about coming.

Coming hard.

Coming around him.

Coming and forgetting.

Escaping.

On the down stroke, Swiss arched his back making sure his cock rubbed against her pubic bone. Her inner muscles clamped down, and she bit her lip, stifling her scream of pleasure. Wired tight, she unraveled as her climax trickled out through the rest of her body.

"Oh God…Swiss!"

He added a deep groan and clenched his jaw. She gazed up into his face enjoying the way his expression changed from determined to blissful to possessive. His cock pulsed inside of her, and she trembled through the aftershocks of the high.

He collapsed to the side of her and dragged her into his embrace. She snuggled her head into the crook of his neck. So soon, the edges of perfection were marred by reality.

She held onto him tighter. Her feeble attempt to keep what they'd done and why they'd fallen into bed together on a night meant for catching the men who were after her played on her mind, poisoning what Swiss gave her.

"Thank you." She softly kissed the sensitive spot underneath his chin. "I appreciate what you've done for me."

He lifted his head. "What I've done?"

"Sex." She sat up and crossed her arms, cupping her shoulders to cover her bare breasts. "I know you did that to help me get my mind off of tonight and being here, living by you…"

He pulled her back down and held her against him. "I'm only going to say this once, but sex with you was not a job to distract you, sweet. Sex tonight was because you've been dancing around the idea since you pulled a fucking gun on me the first night you arrived in Montana. As for me, you're a beautiful woman. There was something in your eyes tonight that told me you were mine if I wanted you. And, I wanted you more than I wanted the rest of my dessert."

"But with everything going on and—"

"Drop it, Gia." His thumb strummed her bare shoulder. "No excuses."

She swallowed and stayed still. His words sunk in. Had he really confessed to wanting her more than he wanted to eat dessert?

A slow smile started in her middle and grew until her lips curled against his chest and her eyes closed. Somehow, that made her feel better.

Chapter Eighteen

The phone vibrated on the counter. Swiss set down the tongs he held above the skillet on the stove and picked up the cell.

Battery: All clear. Nothing.
Swiss replied: Ok.

The bacon sizzled in the pan. He stepped out of the kitchen nook and peeked into the bedroom. His gut warmed. Gia slept on her side facing the wall, buried neck deep in a blanket.

Returning to the stove, he yanked an arm-length worth of paper towels off the holder and folded them in a stack on the empty plate, picked up the tongs, and removed the bacon from the pan. He'd eaten breakfast at four o'clock in the morning when he'd gotten out of bed, unable to sleep.

He glanced at his phone. It was almost nine o'clock. He was hungry for more than the bowl of cereal he'd consumed.

The bedroom door creaked. He looked across the room, and his cock twinged in pleasure.

Gia stood in the doorway, wrapped in his blanket, her hair tousled from sleep, and her eyes barely opened, but warm. Warmer than normal.

He thought her beautiful before they'd had sex and even more so afterward. Gia stumbling out of the bedroom, worn out from having his dick in her, looking at him as if she would rather have sex with him again than have breakfast kicked his ass.

He turned off the stove burner and approached her. "Morning."

"Morning," she mumbled, leaning toward him.

He wrapped her in his arms and inhaled deeply, swept up in last night and her response to him. "Hungry?"

"Mm," she said with a sigh. "A little."

"Got breakfast done." He kissed the top of her head and stepped away, needing the space to get his dick under control, or he'd walk her back into the bedroom and slip between her legs. The only reason he kept from taking her more last night was she needed the sleep.

Exhausted and mentally beaten, she needed to be strong until the shit with Sparrows or whoever was after Gia ended.

He wasn't done with her by a long shot. He wanted her again until he got his fill.

Gia followed him to the kitchen and sat on the stool beside the counter. He swept his gaze over her again, appreciating a woman who was comfortable around him the morning after having sex to eating breakfast naked with only a blanket wrapped around her. It meant her mind was still on last night.

Hell, he couldn't remember letting any woman stay the night since he was married. He preferred to get what he needed from them and then send them away to avoid the awkwardness. Having Gia in his side of the duplex felt natural.

He put four pieces of bread in the four-slot toaster and grabbed the butter and jam from the fridge. While he waited for the toast to pop up, he watched Gia.

She stared at the bacon and for every blink, her shoulders rose under the blanket until she looked at him. "Nothing happened while I slept?"

"Nope. It's been quiet."

"Good," she mouthed.

"Hey." He waited for her to look at him again. "Everything will work out. Give me time to figure out what needs to be done, and in the meantime, you'll stay with me and be safe."

She stuck her arm out of her blanket, snapped off the end of a piece of bacon, and nodded. "Okay."

The toaster popped. He put two pieces of toast on a plate and set it in front of her. "Eat up."

She raised her brows and refused to make a move toward the food. He picked up the butter knife, put butter, jam, and three pieces of bacon on each piece of toast.

"Here." He held breakfast out to her.

She laughed softly. "You're serious? This is what you eat for breakfast?"

He nodded, seeing nothing wrong with the food. "Take it and eat."

She gingerly balanced the toast on three fingers and brought it to her lips. Swiss watched her lips part as she bit into the corner of the toast, then her tongue darted out to wipe away the speck of strawberry jam at the corner of her mouth.

Conditioned to hold back emotions, he forced himself to prepare another piece of toast for her and ignore the pulsing of his blood heading south.

"Oh," she said on a moan. "This is…"

He glanced up and chuckled. "Good?"

"Delicious." She took another bite, and her tongue came out again to catch the leftover jam. "Do you have any coffee?"

He laid a few strips of bacon on the extra toast he'd prepared and took a bite, carrying it over to the coffeemaker. Using one hand, he poured her a cup of coffee—adding three scoops of sugar, then set the mug in front of her.

He had finished his two pieces of toast before she took her first sip. "Will you need more?"

"Coffee?" she asked.

"No, breakfast."

She laughed softly. "Two pieces of toast is perfect, and the six pieces of bacon will hold me until dinner...or close to it."

Swiss studied her, wondering if she was joking, which made her laugh louder. "I'll take that as you're good to go."

Her smile came easily. "Yeah, I'm good. Thank you."

"No thanks needed. You needed to eat, and I was hungry again from breakfast."

"How long have you been awake?" She pulled the blanket around her tighter.

He tossed the dirty dishes in the sink. "I don't require a lot of sleep."

"But, you did sleep." She gazed down at his chest. "You went to bed after we..."

"Yeah. I slept enough." He leaned over the counter and kissed her soft and short. "You better get dressed. A couple of my MC brothers are swinging by, and they'll be here soon."

She slid off the stool and walked toward the bedroom, stopped, and turned around. "Can I use your washer and dryer, and some of your laundry detergent?"

He nodded.

"Thank you." She turned around but not before he caught her frown and slipped into his bedroom, shutting the door behind her.

He'd never met anyone who pleased and thanked him to death. For the simplest things, she acknowledged his part. He shook his head in bewilderment. Those manners went away in bed. Soft spoken and polite during the day, she spoke her mind at night during sex. If she gave that to only him, he appreciated it.

He loaded the dishwasher, wiped down the counter, grabbed his smokes off the television stand, and went outside at the same time he heard the rumble of his brothers arriving. Outside, he lit a cigarette and waited.

Rod and Sander walked toward him, followed by Battery. He'd expected the first two and having Battery show up meant something had happened.

"Where's Gia?" asked Battery, stopping in front of Swiss.

"Inside." Swiss held Battery's gaze. "What's up?"

"I talked to Bantorus Motorcycle Club over in Federal, letting them know we might have visitors here in Haugan and to keep an eye out over in Idaho for any travelers coming through." Battery glanced off at the smoke Swiss exhaled. "Within a half hour, their president called me back with information he got from the mother chapter in Pitnam with more information on the Yesler Street Gang."

"What about them?" Swiss flicked the coal off his cigarette.

"There's been a clean cut between the remaining Sparrows members. The arm of members who picked up where Vince Pladonta left off when he was murdered fell right into moving money. That part of Gia's story plays out, but we're not finding anything from inside the police division that they're going after Sparrows." Battery shrugged. "They might believe the dirty money comes from them, but unless someone comes forward wanting to know where their money is and believing they were scammed, legally there's nothing about the crime that points to Sparrows, especially since the police department knows their ringleader is dead."

"So, LE views the case as a double murder without probable cause or at least a closed case with all fingers pointing at the ones who are now six feet underground being the ringleaders of the Ponzi scheme," muttered Swiss. "Gia's not going to convince the police otherwise, and we all know how they view harassment and stalkers. She has zero protection and the police will be there *after* something happens, because their hands are tied behind the badge."

Battery nodded. "I understand you'll take her under protection regardless if Ronacks backs you, but I need to know how Gia showed up in Haugan. She's far away from Seattle. That sits wrong with me."

"She mentioned last night that she'd gone to a woman's shelter when the men broke into her place asking for help. They found her a place to live here, and she says while they were making sure the duplex would be safe, they got intel on me. Me being a biker and former Army meant safety to her, apparently." Swiss glanced back at the door before looking at Battery again. "I believe her. She's too scared to make up a story now that we've seen the proof that someone is here to do her harm."

"What's the name of the shelter she went to for help?" asked Battery.

"I don't know."

Battery nodded. "Get that information for me. In the meantime, Ronacks will continue to run protection twenty-four/seven."

"Will do." Swiss shook Battery's hand.

He stood with Rod and Sander while Battery returned to his motorcycle and rode away. Over the years, they'd dealt with other street gangs, motorcycle clubs, and even a branch off the Russian mob. Used to running security for the businesses around town, he dealt with stalkers, harassment, and it often broke out into physical violence. Gia's case was something he'd seen and done numerous times, but this time felt different.

He'd never had sex with a woman who he had under his protection before.

"Are you going to try and work the roster?" Rod leaned over and picked a weed out of the crack in the sidewalk.

Swiss shook his head. "No. I don't want to leave her alone."

"I'll make the necessary changes and bump you down a tier in pay," said Rod. "How will that work for you?"

"I'm good," he said.

He'd survive. Money wasn't a concern. Even going down to the fourth tier would give him enough to continue living at the duplex and food for the week.

"Let's ride out." Sander pulled down his beanie. "Swiss can catch us up later. You're coming around to the clubhouse tomorrow night, right?"

"Yeah, I'll be there." Swiss smacked Sander on the back. "Catch you later."

He walked to the door and let himself in. The whir of the washing machine filled the duplex. Gia sat on the couch in a pair of shorts and a tank top, watching him for any hint of bad news. The situation thrust upon her unfamiliar and scary, she only had him to rely on.

She'd need to learn fast to trust him.

Chapter Nineteen

Swiss sat on the couch, his feet on the coffee table, and his eyes on Gia. She walked a three-foot path in front of the television, pushing and pulling the vacuum over the carpet in Swiss's side of the duplex. The lines on the carpet made by the beater bar on the vacuum abusing the already cleaned carpet filled her with happiness knowing the surface was free of dust and lint.

She'd found the vacuum earlier while switching the last load of laundry—consisting of Swiss's cut-off flannel shirts and her Tees— from the washer to the dryer.

To keep herself busy and to pay Swiss back for letting her stay in his side of the duplex, she'd found cleaners, rags, and the vacuum. His living space now smelled pine-fresh and not a dust particle floated in the air.

Reluctantly, she turned off the vacuum, cutting off the white-noise she'd surrounded herself in for the last ten minutes. She could no longer ignore Swiss.

"There you go. Now you don't have to do any chores for a couple of days." She unplugged the cord and wound the length back on the handle of the vacuum.

"Appreciate it," said Swiss.

Truth be told, Swiss was a clean freak.

There wasn't a stray whisker on the bathroom counter, and the only dust she found was on the back of the flat screen television. She'd looked everywhere and called it cleaning when what she was doing was snooping. Since Swiss worked on his motorcycle outside and gave her time alone, she'd found his medicine cabinet bare of everything except extra shampoo, a bar of soap, deodorant, toothbrush, toothpaste, and a small bottle of Tylenol.

No signs of a woman anywhere—no tampons, hairbrush, or earrings. He was also not on any medicine for a mental disease or suffered from a sexually transmitted disease—not that she suspected anything wrong with him.

She might've gone too far in her panic to know more about the man she'd had sex with for the last week.

Sex.

Great sex.

She wheeled the vacuum back to the closet where she'd found it and inhaled a deep breath. No matter how busy she kept herself, she couldn't forget how quickly Swiss made her feel like she belonged to him.

Her willingness to listen and follow his orders when it came to her safety followed her into the bedroom. He orchestrated her body into doing wonderful things, and she willingly let him do whatever he wanted. She couldn't stop, because she'd become addicted to what he gave her.

He'd offer. She'd accept, and then she took everything he gave her to escape thinking about what she was doing and what she was living through. Sex with Swiss was the first thing that worked to distract her, and she found herself relaxing as long as they stayed inside.

She'd formed a habit.

Sex meant feeling good. Feeling normal. Feeling safe.

She returned to the living room area of the duplex. Swiss hadn't moved and continued to sit there with his focus on her.

It hit her that his attention to everything she had done around the duplex could be because he hated someone else touching his stuff. She hadn't asked him if she could tidy up the place. The urge to clean had come swiftly and she'd ran with the idea.

"I think I screwed up," she said softly. "I should've asked to clean. I'm so sor—"

He held up his hand. "You can clean all you want without asking."

She swallowed and nodded.

"I get it." He patted the couch for her to sit.

She walked around the coffee table and sat beside him. Close enough to touch, but keeping her thigh away from his thigh, her arm away from his arm.

"I hope you don't think by my cleaning your place that I believed your side of the duplex was dirty." She crossed her legs and shoved her hands between her thighs to keep from touching him. "It's just that…staying on the other side without proper cleaning supplies drove me mental. Even laying on a blanket on the floor made me feel gross. When I noticed everything you use to clean your place, I wanted to use them. It felt good to make myself useful, and I can't tell you how much I appreciate you letting me stay here. I know the last week has been about keeping me safe, and sex was a bonus. Please, don't think I'm making it out to be more by going all domestic or I believe your place is dirty—it's impeccable. I just like to clean. I'm weird."

He slipped his hand between her legs and pulled out her left hand, keeping it in his grasp. "My mother believed a clean house meant a clean soul, while I grew up with little in the form of possessions, she made sure my dad, brother, and I understood how to clean and the responsibility of taking care of what we owned. The Army reaffirmed that lesson by proving I could survive off little and demanding order. I get your need to clean."

She shifted sideways. "You have a brother?"

"One."

"Does he live near you?"

His eye twitched. "He's no longer a part of my life, and my parents are dead."

She stared down at their linked hands, trying not to pry and wanting to know more. Swiss gave her little in the sense of how he lived his life, his childhood, and even his adulthood. Sure, he was easy to get along with, so she concluded that whatever happened to break the bond of a family was out of his control.

To keep him from dwelling on what could be a painful subject and to let him know she appreciated the information he volunteered, she said, "I keep thinking that when this is over, you'll be glad to get rid of me."

"How so?"

She looked up and smiled. "You'll have all your free time back, and Mel can actually come inside instead of walking past the duplex every forty-five minutes."

Swiss chuckled. "He's on foot patrol. The kid takes his job seriously considering the vote is coming up."

"Ah, the mysterious motorcycle club vote." She leaned her head back on the couch while continuing to look at him. "It's a good thing. Soon, I'll be able to go home and…"

"Gia?" he said, rubbing his thumb against the back of her hand.

"Yes?"

He looked at her. "Don't pretend everything will go back the way it was and being with me meant nothing to you. What you're going through will change your life, and I know you're not a woman who accepts sex as something to pass the time."

She tried to pull her hand away, and he refused to let her go. "Hey, I know having sex with you helps us pass the time, and we're two adults who are attracted to each other. With everything going on, I should never have let myself get distracted. But, shit happens, right? When this is all over, I'll go back to Seattle, and be forever grateful for the help you've given me."

"Sweet." His scar deepened until only one of his eyes remained opened. "We come from two different worlds. Sex between us is good."

"Yeah," she said, inhaling swiftly. "I mean, I'm okay if you want to keep having sex with me. No big deal. Sex is sex."

"Hold on." He raised his hand and stroked her cheek. "This is where that whole other world part comes in, cause I have you pegged as someone who will think there's more involved than having sex because it feels fucking good. That's not how I live. I'm careful when I do have sex, but that's all it is for me. I'm not looking for anything more. I don't have it in me to share my life with anyone else, and if you can handle that, then yeah, we're going to have sex while you stay with me. If you can't, I'll still protect you and respect the line you drew in front of me."

Her heart raced. Warmth filled her face. Besides the obvious way they'd met and his assumption that she was scared of her own shadow—she was, he thought of her as a prude.

Okay, she'd had two long-term relationships—both men lasted almost five years with her before the relationship became stagnant. In-between relationships, she'd dated when asked, which was at least once a month because she believed in love.

But, she wasn't foolish or immature.

She could appreciate sex for the simple act of feeling good with another person she found attractive and respected. When the circumstances changed for her, she could walk away without falling in love.

"I have men after me who want me dead." She worked her lips. "The last thing I can or will do is believe there is more to having sex with you. My brain can't process more about my situation right now, and you give me something that requires no thinking. I'm not normally like that, but I am with you. You don't have to worry about me fantasizing that staying with you, having sex with you, is anything more than what it is. Trust me, I just want my life back, and while I'm with you, the constant worry is easier to handle. I've slept better this week than I have in a month, and that's because of you."

He leaned over, kissed her forehead and left his lips on her and said, "You need to trust me to see that you remain safe, and between Ronacks and me, we will make sure the men after you stop, and you can go back home."

She closed her eyes an extra beat and sniffed. It felt wonderful to have someone who believed her, even if she failed to understand her feelings. She also loved being close to Swiss. The rugged smell of leather light in the air, she wanted to rub against him.

"Thank you."

"I need to ask you a couple more questions." He sat back on the couch, squeezed her hand, and said, "What exactly did you do when you left your condominium for the last time?"

"I already told you."

"Sweet, there's things that you might not be aware of even knowing and the more you talk, maybe new information will show itself and help me figure out how to stop the men from coming after you."

"The first thing I did after I ran from my condominium was go to a woman's shelter. They fed me, let me sleep in the building, and helped me figure out my next step in the safety of their building with others around me. The employee who worked with me found two places away from Seattle and out of Washington that was feasible places for me to go to seek safety with the money I had saved up. I wouldn't and couldn't stay at the shelter. I feared anyone else getting hurt." She glanced at his chest and thought back to the conversation. "The first place that was offered was in Dubois, Wyoming and the woman at the shelter talked me out of going there, because the safe house was too rural. There were no neighbors within five miles, and she thought I'd feel more secure with others around me. The second choice was Haugan, Montana and I could share a duplex with a man from a motorcycle club who had skills from being in the Army. You."

"And, the landlord told the crisis worker that?" he asked, his body stiffening.

She shook her head. "I don't know. I can only guess that's what happened."

Swiss grunted in displeasure. "That's all assumptions then."

She inhaled deeply and blew out her breath, to slow down the disappointment she got from Swiss's remark. "At the time, I couldn't even make the simplest of choices. I had no idea what to do and tried to convince myself that two men hadn't been in my place trying to harm me. I latched on to what made me feel safe, and that was the description of Haugan, knowing you'd be here in the duplex with me. I thought if there was a slim chance of the men following me that far away from Seattle, I rather have a man who lived on the other side of the duplex than be stuck by myself."

Her voice gave out. Her throat spasmed. She trusted Swiss, but what could she say to convince him that she'd come here simply because to her, he was a man that could protect her?

She'd taken off and drove almost four hundred miles away from everything familiar, trusting that a woman's shelter had her safety in mind. Maybe she should've asked more questions, but at the time, she couldn't even remember the password to the gate at the front of her condominium or her pin number for her debit card, and she was grateful someone else helped her.

"What was the name of the women's shelter and the employee who helped you?"

Feeling foolish, she shrugged. "The shelter was on Tenth and Parkway, or maybe Belmont. I never paid attention to the legal name. They had a big sign on the building, and I went by there every day on my way to and from work, never thinking I'd need to use them. The woman who helped me set up a pay-as-you-go phone to give me when I left. Her name is Bianca. I know she set up the lease for me under the name Lisa Graham, and she gave me a driver's license with that same name. It's also the name I used when I traded my car for the Honda."

"Gia." She whispered, "Gia Lorenz."

"Okay." He stood up, pulling her to her feet. "That helps."

"I don't see how." She leaned into him, frustrated from seeing how he viewed the situation compared to her living through the fear. "I wish I could tell you more or at least give you the answers you're looking for. I don't even know what you think you'll find."

"You're doing good." He tilted her head and kissed her lips. "We're going to leave for the clubhouse in twenty minutes. If you got anything you need to do before, you better get to it. I'm going to step outside and make a phone call."

She grabbed his wrist, stopping him from moving away. "Please, don't."

"Step out?"

"No, make a phone call." She swallowed her panic. "Not if it's about me or about the situation. I was told not to use any phones, except ones that can't be traced back to me and since I'm staying with you…"

"I'm not going to let anything happen to you."

"You can promise, but you can't control other people. P-people can get information from phone calls and pictures from Smartphones that can pinpoint exactly where I am." Her head pounded. "Please, if you're calling your club, can you wait until you're there and then talk to them about me?"

"The club doesn't use phones that can be traced." He slipped his phone back into his pocket. "But, I'll wait until we get to the clubhouse."

"Thank you," she whispered, stepping away. "Let me go grab my sweatshirt, and I'll be ready to go."

She walked into the bedroom and rubbed her face. Numb and confused, she second-guessed her decisions. She trusted Swiss. She had to trust him.

Chapter Twenty

Raelyn, Jana, and Bree surrounded Gia inside the clubhouse, keeping her entertained and managing to bring her out of the funk his questions had created before they'd left the duplex. Swiss's gut tightened, knowing he was the reason she had added stress in her life.

He assumed her quick stance in how she only viewed sex with him as a need he was filling had gone against everything she believed in. Her words failed to reassure him. It was the sadness in her eyes she couldn't hide and the way her body stiffened beside him while she tried to make him feel better that bothered him. She wasn't handling sleeping with him on top of dealing with the fear she lived with since walking in and finding her co-workers murdered.

Maybe if the situation was different and they'd met under different circumstances, she'd be able to handle having casual sex with him, or maybe she wouldn't have anything to do with him at all.

The later thought bothered him. He wasn't a corruptor of women. Hell, he worshiped women.

The right type of women.

Normally, he stayed away from women like Gia who had a handle on their life and planned for the future. Women who put every thought into others and invested in sharing their emotions when it came to spreading their legs for a man. Gia looked for long-term relationships, proven by her track record.

Yet, damned if she wasn't there one-hundred

percent in bed with him, taking and giving.

Rod lined up four phones in front of Swiss on the table and tapped the middle one. "Give Gia this one. LeWorth and I programmed it to the club's computer. That way we can find out who she calls and see if anyone else is reading her data."

He wanted to believe Gia's fear of him using the phone would keep her from contacting anyone, but after witnessing her snatch Jana's phone to make a private call, he understood baiting her would get the answers he needed. Proof that she was in contact with someone else created a weak link in his plan to protect her.

If she hid the truth or one small detail, it put her at risk. Hell, it put him and each member of Ronacks MC in danger. They needed to know everything and go in armed with information to catch the men or person after Gia.

"The other phones you can use. They're throwaways." LeWorth lowered his voice. "Encourage her to learn more about what is happening in Seattle. If she wants to call the detective in charge of the case, let her. At this point, if she raises questions with anyone from the outside, we can use that to our advantage because eyes and ears will be off Ronacks, and hopefully, it'll draw us that much closer to Sparrows."

"If it *is* Sparrows," muttered Swiss.

He still wasn't positive a street gang from Seattle would leave their territory, come to Montana, and risk being connected to a crime they wanted to bury deep within the legal system.

"We're keeping all possibilities open." Battery

gazed across the table at Swiss, blocking his view of Gia. "You need to stay focused."

He knew better than most how to shut off outside influences. Trained to take out the enemy, he could put the club and Gia out of his head at a moment's notice.

He ran his finger over the scar on his cheek. Only once had he let his attachment to others distract him from what was important, and he wouldn't make that mistake again.

"How is the new lineup on the roster working out?" Swiss pocketed the phone he'd give to Gia and picked up the rest of them. "No trouble at Watson's?"

"The court date got moved back six weeks." Battery stuck a cigarette behind his ear. "Mel's teaming with Grady, and they've got a good handle on Watson's. It's working out well."

LeWorth smirked. "Mel has something to keep his mind off why the women who come to the club parties aren't hanging on him."

The dedication and loyalty amongst his brothers relaxed Swiss. The last couple of weeks before being patched in fucked with everyone's head. The club used the prospects for entertainment until they became a lifer. While the deviant acts kept the prospect guessing at the outcome of the vote, the way Mel handled the burdens said a lot about what kind of brother he'd make each one of them. So far in Mel's two years of tests, he'd performed fine for someone his age.

"Keep me notified on what happens here." Swiss stepped away from the table and walked across the room toward the women.

Bree continued talking to Jana when he approached, and Gia stepped away from the group and came to his side. He piled the phones in his right hand and placed his left on her lower back. Her gaze questioned him, and the darkness under her eyes gave him a hint at how she was handling the stress level.

"Come outside with me." He led her through the crowd of bikers and out into the night air.

She rubbed her bare arms. "What's with the phones?"

"For us to use. They're untraceable." He motioned with his chin. "Let me go put them in the bag on the bike, and we can grab your sweatshirt. It's getting cool already."

"The temperature is different here than in Seattle." She walked beside him. "I can't believe how it can be hot during the day and chilly as soon as the sun goes down."

"It's the mountains and higher elevation." He stopped beside his Harley and put the phones in the bag, then opened the other side and grabbed Gia's sweatshirt. "Here you go."

Gia slipped the sweatshirt over her head and wiggled her arms into the sleeves. He reached over and gathered her caught hair and pulled it out from under the material. Recognizing the scent of his shampoo in her hair, the freshness of his detergent in her clothes, he held her close liking the way it appeared as if she belonged to him.

Another reminder that she had given him permission to continue having sex with her. He could seek relief, and she could grab comfort.

"Open your mouth." He pressed the pad of his

thumb against her chin and then kissed her.

A slow stroke of her tongue and he kissed her deeper, lust tightening his balls. He couldn't remember how long it'd been since he'd wanted to protect a woman. Keep her with him and hide from the world, and selfishly keep everything about her to himself. He hated sharing.

He never tolerated letting others take what he had until he no longer cared and gave everything away or threw what was important out of his life. The worst moment of his life, he'd walked away from the chance at making himself happy because of his strict need to keep what was his.

Maybe he never fought hard enough.

In the end, nothing mattered. He'd lost. And, that loss about killed him.

Gia moaned and pulled back. "We should stop."

Caught in another time, he stepped away. What was he doing?

Sex was all that he was after. His need to possess Gia, to make sure she stayed safe was only the protection he could give her as a Ronacks member. Nothing more.

"Right." He ran his hand over his mouth, staring down into eyes that refused to leave him alone. Digging in his vest pocket, he pulled out his pack of cigarettes needing to get rid of the hunger for her taste off his tongue. "I'm gonna have a smoke before we head back. Do you want to wait inside for me? I'm going to walk out on the dock."

She glanced around the yard. A few members stood outside. Choke and a woman—Candace, he believed, were talking by Jana's car. "Is it okay if I stay by your motorcycle?" she asked.

"Yeah, you're safe here on club property." He stepped away and lit the cigarette, and kept walking.

It was only natural that he'd want to touch her, kiss her, and keep her near when they were together all day long. That's what happened when he was around the club. The women who wanted to hook up with him hung around and were glad for the attention he gave them.

There was no need to discuss what came after. He knew what was expected, and the woman never asked for more. Hell, they never wanted more.

They knew bikers were fun to party with, but none of them wanted to be held back by the governing laws of Ronacks. To claim one woman, it was as good as being married.

He inhaled deeply and let the smoke out slowly. He needed to keep his distance from Gia. Her resolve to take their living conditions for what it was and accept that he only wanted her for sex meant more to him because he couldn't make himself believe it was what she wanted.

She'd expect some kind of commitment or at least responsibility, and she fucking glowed after they had sex. He'd never seen such a thing. That kind of gratitude fucked him in the head something good.

He'd had that.

He'd lost that.

Instead of going out on the dock, he stopped at the bank and finished his cigarette. From a distance, he could barely make out the music playing in the clubhouse. Refusing to turn around and check on Gia, knowing every Ronacks member had an obligation to look out for her, Swiss took time to remember how much it hurt to believe in a woman. To love. And, how painful it was to lose his whole life when he watched his baby wave goodbye to him over her mom's shoulder.

He put the cigarette out on the thigh of his jeans.

There was no way he'd put himself through that shit again. Sex was sex. Gia would have to figure that out on her own so he could go back to having his quiet life back with no responsibilities once he made her world safe again.

Chapter Twenty One

Chilled to the bone after riding home from the clubhouse in the cool night air, Gia snuggled down underneath the covers seeking warmth while Swiss finished talking outside to the two Ronacks members patrolling the duplex for the night.

A shiver rolled over her spine. She brought her knees up to her chest. Riding the motorcycle, especially at night, always made her nervous that someone would shoot her. An open target to anyone driving by, she'd clung to Swiss's back and kept her eyes closed.

As if no warning of her demise would be better than knowing what would happen a few seconds later if she found a gun raised in her direction, she willingly tried to live in the moment and take her cue from Swiss.

The wait for something awful to happen was driving her crazy and yet Swiss's calmness and experience at protecting others helped her. Just as sex with him helped her calm down and find enough strength to stand her ground.

He'd assured her he had her covered, and the riders in front of them and behind them provided that added security. At night, alone with him, he assured her again with sex that he would take care of her. Never before had she been needy to the point of desperation, but she found herself looking forward to letting Swiss take care of her.

Maybe sex with Swiss let her have an excuse not to think too deeply. She exhaled harshly. She was so full of it. Since coming here, she'd reevaluated her whole life. From her dissatisfaction continuing in the same kind of work she'd done in Seattle to what she wanted for her future, including what type of man she wished she had.

Swiss fit everywhere in her life. In bed and out of bed. She wanted him.

The front door shut. She moistened her lips. Today, while talking to Bree and Raelyn, she realized that she envied what they both had in their lives. Not the hardships, but the sense of family they each found within Ronacks Motorcycle Club. While she imagined they both struggled with outside stresses—Raelyn being a single mother and Bree being the wife of the president—they were strong women. Much stronger than her.

How many times in the past had she wanted to step out of her comfort zone and enjoy the sexual side of her, but something always held her back. First, taking care of her parents had put any kind of sex life on the back burner. Then lately, she looked for a relationship and refused to settle for one night stands. Here she was in Haugan, out of her area, scared of being killed, and the sexiest man she'd ever met is offering her exactly what she'd always wanted.

She'd be a fool to turn him down and waste the energy to fight her attraction to him.

He was perfect for her. No obligations and free to leave at any time.

Their sexual chemistry was mind-blowing and wonderful, and to deny them both would only make her more miserable.

Swiss walked into the bedroom and stopped at

the sight of her already in bed. A smile tugged at her lips. Was he really surprised?

On the way home, when they hit Main Street, he'd reached back and rubbed her thigh. She'd propped her chin on the back of his shoulder and enjoyed the way he drew circles on her leg as he cruised down the street.

That one finger touching her was enough to get her blood pumping. By the time she walked into the duplex, she was ready to strip and have sex. Until two Ronacks members stopped by and wanted to speak with Swiss alone, and the chill in the air permeated her skin.

"Tired?" Swiss took off his vest and set it on the dresser.

She watched him from her pillow. "Not really. I was cold."

He grunted, bent at the waist, and took off his boots. She removed her arm out from under the blanket and propped her head up with her hand to watch him. Age wise, he was older than her by at least ten or fifteen years, but he was in better shape. Her stomach warmed. If only she could eat the same diet as him and look so good.

"How old are you?" she asked.

Swiss's gaze went to the ceiling before he answered. "Forty-five."

Swiss removed his clothes without any modesty, almost proud of his body. She moved her gaze up to his face and caught him looking at her. That same intense expression aimed at her melted her insides because she now recognized his interest. The same one that made him squint.

He stalked to the bed, crawled under the covers, and his cold hands found her hip. She yipped, jerking away, and he pulled her back along his length.

His fingers kneaded her curve. "Warm me up."

She willingly rolled with him until she was on top, her legs sprawled alongside his hips, and her breasts pressed against his chest.

"The rest of you is warm," she whispered.

"Bet your mouth is hotter." He lifted his right eyebrow.

Her breath hitched on a reply, knowing she had nothing to say because she was open to anything he suggested. Instead of answering, she squirmed down his body until her head disappeared underneath the blanket.

She kissed his chest, his abdomen, each hip, and settle between his legs. In the dark, blind to his body, she had to use her hand to find his cock. The moment she wrapped her fingers around his girth, his dick pulsed harder. The heady masculine scent she concluded as musk, outdoors, and leather filled her nose.

She moistened her lips and then lowered her head and licked the underside of his cock, from balls to head, and then circled around the rim of his dick.

Swiss's thighs hardened against her. She bit down on her lower lip to keep from smiling in satisfaction. He'd done more to her last night with his mouth, and if she gave Swiss half the pleasure she'd received, he was happy.

Opening her mouth, she encompassed his cock. A soft moan escaped her throat, and she slid down on him. His legs flexed, and she slowly pulled back, sucking harder until she reached the head of his dick and went down again.

Up.

Down.

She slipped her hands under his ass, holding him in place while she lavished him with her tongue. The power and confidence she craved from Swiss was given to her freely. He let her have her freedom to play with him. Anything she wanted to do to him, he'd allow.

The blanket slid down her body, and a rush of cool air flowed over her. She opened her eyes and gazed up Swiss's body to find him holding his head up with his hands and peering down at her.

His oak brown eyes appeared almost black with arousal.

"Get on your hands and knees." His deep voice rolled over her, and she gently let go of his cock and crawled over his legs and assumed the position he wanted.

The sheet under her knees warmed from his body only heightened her arousal. Swiss got behind her and pulled her back until her feet hung off the edge of the bed. She widened her knees and laid her head on the blanket.

Propped up, open to his view, turned her on.

He ran his finger over her slit, spreading her wetness. She sucked in her breath, electrified by his touch. He made everything seem simple. One touch, one look, one word, and she practically orgasmed.

"Hard," she said with a gasp.

"You want me to fuck you hard?"

"Yes." She fisted the blanket and hissed. "Please…"

His hand at her hip disappeared. She turned her head and found him grabbing a condom off the dresser and rolling it on his cock. Her legs shook in need.

He returned to her with his hand wrapped around his hardness and positioned himself at the opening of her pussy. "Hold on, sweet."

She turned her head, facing the headboard, and stretched her arms above her on the bed, grabbing the sheet when he plunged inside her. The fullness took her breath away, and her eyes rolled back behind her lids.

"God, yes." She held her body stiff as he withdrew, plunged, and owned her.

He took everything away from her and controlled how she thought, felt, and even how she accepted him. Free from constraints and worries, she soared.

Each stroke took her higher. She pushed back against him, rocking on her hands and knees, and arching her neck. He held her hip and grabbed a fistful of her hair, holding her in front of him, banging against her.

His balls slapped her clit. She bucked, panting for the ultimate pleasure that hovered at the edges of her senses.

"That's it," he said, groaning.

Her pussy constricted, and deep inside of her tightened until she let go with a muffled scream. Then her release hit her, flooding her body with pleasure. Her thighs quivered. Her breath whooshed out of her.

Her head fell forward as he released her hair.

Swiss grabbed her hips, made three more thrusts, and he planted himself fully inside of her and shuddered with his climax.

Weak and semi-unconscious except for what came natural—like breathing, she closed her eyes. Glad that Swiss held her hips or she'd flop down on the bed spent and ungraceful.

Suddenly, he slapped her ass. She jolted and sprung forward on the bed, turning to land on her butt.

She spotted his grin and gaped at him. "I can't believe you did that."

He chuckled and removed the condom, putting it in the small wastebasket at the side of the bed. "It was a good fuck, Gia."

She raised her brows and reached for the blanket to cover her body and her shock. "Wow, I can't say anyone has ever told me that before, Swiss. At least, not using such delightful terms."

He flung himself down on the bed, pulled her to his side, and covered them both. "Just telling you what I'm thinking."

She lay stiffly beside him. Fine, he wanted to prove a point. He'd succeeded. She heard him loud and clear.

"It was good, but…" She turned to her side, facing away from him. "I've had better."

Dead silence filled the room. She sighed quietly, already feeling guilty for being rude. She couldn't even remember all the times she'd had sex or her previous relationships. Swiss had wiped her mind of everything, except what happened in the last half hour.

The light beside Swiss's side of the bed went out. He rolled closer and spooned her. "You're so full of shit," he mumbled against her ear.

With cold reality swiftly sinking in came their agreement and the reason why she was sleeping next to a man who'd used her for sex.

She stared into the darkness of the room. A terrible flood of homesickness hit her.

She missed her bed, her home, her job.

She missed her coworkers who she'd called friends.

She missed going to sleep every night looking forward to tomorrow.

"Stop thinking, sweet," whispered Swiss. "I'll stay right here with you, and you can sleep."

At least she had Swiss.

Chapter Twenty Two

Gia woke with a start. The pitch dark room greeted her. It wasn't morning waking her up but a dream that the killers had broken in and stood beside the bed.

She reached out for Swiss seeking his comfort, found his side of the bed empty, and sat up fully awake. It wasn't the first night or the second that she'd found Swiss gone from the bed. He had a habit of getting up after she fell asleep.

She grabbed the throw blanket from the floor, wrapped it around her chilled body, and went looking for him.

In the living room, Swiss stood in front of the partially closed window staring out into the night. She approached him from the back, opened the blanket, and wrapped them both in the warmth. His nude body hot to the touch, she kissed his back.

"Is everything okay," she whispered, surprised that after having sex with her he'd still have the energy to stay up through the night.

His upper body expanded with air. "Yeah, you should go back to bed, it's two in the morning."

"Why don't you come with me?" She moved around his large body and stood in front of him.

His muscles remained tense. She rubbed his bare sides. He made no move to leave his perch at the window.

"Please?" She stepped away, trying one more time, and glad when he turned and followed.

Back in bed, she snuggled against his side and

covered them both with the sheet and blanket. Swiss's body remained tight, and he stayed quiet. Normally not a talker, his silence wouldn't have bothered her if it was the middle of the day.

At night, his lack of words and distance only made her want to get closer. He seemed to shed his loner status and welcome her closer. It was one of the reasons why they got along so well. He never demanded answers she wasn't prepared to hand him, and his quietness soothed her in her current frazzled state.

"Swiss?" she asked.

His hand came down to claim her hip, and she took that as a reply.

"Do you ever wonder what it'll be like when everything is over, and we both go back to our real lives?" She rubbed her hand in a circle on his hard stomach, suspecting he wouldn't tell her what was bothering him, but she'd try her best to distract him from his solemn mood.

"It's easier if you don't think about what will happen tomorrow," he said after a few seconds. "Just concentrate on making it through each day."

"That's impossible," she whispered, knowing she'd never forget Swiss. Not in a month, a year, a lifetime.

She refused to believe that he never thought of the future and what'll happen when she goes back to Seattle. The top of her head tingled, and she shivered.

He pulled her closer. She stretched her neck, needing to know every single thing about him before she was gone. "Why does everyone call you Swiss?"

"Short for Swiss Army knife. Got the name

when I prospected for Ronacks and it stuck." He inhaled deeply and let the air out.

"How did you get your scar?" She gazed up at him in the dark.

"That's enough talking." His chest hardened underneath her hand.

"One more thing." She softened her voice, lowering her head to his chest. "Can I text you? Maybe call you a couple of times once everything is over, and I go back to Seattle?"

The seconds ticked by in silence. Gia's heartbeat echoed in her ears. Until she'd asked, she had no idea how much she worried about never hearing his gruff voice again or being able to touch him. She already missed him.

"Yeah," he whispered. "You can call."

Her breath whooshed out of her, and she closed her eyes in relief. She wouldn't say thank you. Not this time. She'd give him no reason to change his mind.

The ground she'd broken and the huge step Swiss gave her, energized her. She couldn't go to sleep. The unknown time she had left with him too important to waste.

She hovered her hand over his stomach, skimming the short trail from his navel to under his boxer shorts and let the hair tickle her palm. His body fascinated her. All hardness and bulging strength, unlike her lower stomach which was soft and bare.

Over time, and during their nightly habit of sleeping with each other, she'd lost her hesitation on touching him. She loved to explore and find out what he enjoyed. Time worked against her, and she needed to know everything about him.

Slipping her hand inside his boxers, she cupped his balls and marveled at the way they drew up against his body. His skin tightening and protective. She gently scratched his sack and smiled against his chest when he widened his legs and sighed in contentment.

She'd never known a man who liked his balls scratched as much as Swiss. A delightful secret she'd found out a few nights ago when he'd softened and grunted his approval when her fingernail had scratched him. Not sure if she had read him right, she down swept her fingernails against the skin holding his balls and he practically sighed in pleasure.

Swiss's breathing deepened and lengthened. His body relaxed. She continued lazily scratching, glad to have something to do to help him. He was getting antsy cooped up in the duplex with her, knowing the other Ronacks members worked during the day. It was the least she could do to help him adjust to the many changes she'd brought into his life.

"What woke you up?" she whispered, unable to stay quiet.

He yawned. "Couldn't sleep."

"Is it because I'm here?"

"Just not a big sleeper." He patted her hip.

She stopped scratching. "What about when you were married?"

Ever since she'd spotted the picture of his daughter and him in the living room, she'd wanted to ask him questions about his family. She knew he was divorced, but he avoided any talk about marriage in general or any kind of family life.

"Like I said, I don't need much sleep." He rolled over to his side. "I need your pussy."

"Oh?" She laughed softly, lifting her leg and putting it on his hip. "You needed it earlier, too."

He growled into her neck and slipped his hand between her legs. His finger slid along her wetness. "It doesn't matter if I need you, or you need me, your pussy is wet, and my dick is hard."

She caressed his head, holding him to her, and pressed against his hand. He was right, she wanted him. She loved the connection when they had sex. Everything else ceased to exist.

"God, that feels good." She squirmed.

He slipped a finger inside of her and used his thumb to caress her clitoris. She shuddered at the contact, still sensitive from earlier.

"Let me feel you come, sweet." He pressed up inside of her and her legs shook at the instant jolt of pleasure tightening inside of her.

He stroked her G-spot and had her quivering, every nerve in her body tightening and reaching. She rolled her hips, unable to think or participate. Swiss took charge, and her body willingly bowed to him.

"Oh, God." She panted, clutching his shoulder with one hand afraid he'd stop and holding his head in the other, holding him close.

"That's it," he whispered through his harsh breathing.

Her body overheated and pleasure hit her hard, throwing her into an orgasm. She fiercely rippled against him, pure joy emitting from her with her release, and she laughed softly in his ear as she curled around him.

He continued stroking her softly, barely touching her clit, and soothed her down from her high. She reached down between their bodies and wrapped her fingers around his hardened cock.

"My turn with you," she whispered.

He removed his hand from between her legs and rolled onto his back. She stroked him firmly and slowly. The biggest man she'd ever been with, he also had an impressive dick that loved attention.

Swiss stretched his legs and reached over for her breast and rolled her nipple between his finger and thumb. She laid her head on his chest, kissing a path down his body.

His breathing grew heavier, and she scooted down in bed and held his hardness, aiming her mouth—

A banging echoed in the duplex. Swiss's body slid off the bed and away from her. She sat up, scrambling to her hands and knees.

"Swiss, open up," said a male voice.

"It's Grady." Swiss pulled on his jeans and grabbed his pistol off the nightstand. "Get dressed and stay inside the bedroom."

She nodded, not realizing that he couldn't see her in the dark, and hurried out of bed to grab her clothes. Her body clumsy, she tripped getting her foot in her jeans and hit her hip against the dresser.

Pain ricocheted down her leg, and she muffled her groan. Ronacks members had never visited in the middle of the night. Something had to be wrong.

Once she was fully dressed, she went to the bedroom door and listened. The murmured voices too low for her to hear.

The light from the living room came on. She stepped away from the doorway and a few seconds later Swiss came back into the bedroom.

"What's going on?" she asked, moving toward him.

He cupped the back of her head. "You need to come out to the living room."

She followed him, anxious to know what happened. Grady stood by the window and closed the drapes all the way. When he spotted her, he dipped his chin.

"Grady's going to stay inside with us until the sun comes up." Swiss set her down on the couch. "A car rammed into Mel's motorcycle at the end of the block when he walked away to take a piss behind a tree."

She pressed her hand to her chest. "Is he okay?"

"Yeah, he's fine. His bike is toast." Grady stood guard at the window. "The car that hit and sped off was a blue sedan."

"Th-that's the car you're looking for that you think the men are driving." She swallowed hard and looked at Swiss. "They came back?"

"They are not near the duplex." Swiss sat down on the coffee table and faced her. "Two other Ronacks members took off chasing them, while Grady came here. It's better if both of us are here with you while Mel waits for the tow truck to come and haul his bike back to the clubhouse and the others are preoccupied."

"We should call the police." She rocked back and forth on the couch. "This isn't harassment or stalking, a hit and run is a crime, and Mel witnessed it."

"Ronacks doesn't use the police." Swiss caught her look of disbelief. "Trust me, sweet. The police around here are good at catching speeders and the occasional drunk who needs a night in jail to sober up. Beyond that, the club takes care of club business."

She looked up at Grady. "I'm so sorry."

"Not your fault," said Grady.

The problems were escalating. The knowledge of a biker gang protecting her hadn't dissuaded the killers from coming after her. They could've killed Mel tonight if he had been on his motorcycle when they hit his bike.

She leaned back on the couch, pulled up her legs, and held her stomach. The two men in the room remained silent and waiting. All she could hear was the clock on the kitchen stove tick.

Tick.

Tick.

Tick.

Chapter Twenty Three

Swiss walked into the duplex. A wall of dead air hit him, and he whistled softly, reaching to reopen the door, letting out the heat Gia trapped inside the four walls. It had to be over a hundred degrees inside the duplex

He stepped over to the window.

"Don't." Gia rushed into the room. "You can't open the window."

He ignored her request and slid the glass along the track and let the fresh air inside. "Why not?"

She worked her hands in worry. "What if they're out there?"

It'd been a week since the people after Gia ran over Mel's motorcycle and there was no sign of anyone making another move toward her at the duplex or in town. While he never let down his guard, there was no reason for her to suffer through a hot, miserable day when he was outside to protect her.

"I've been at the curb all afternoon working on my bike. It's eighty-five degrees outside. I wanted you to stay inside, but I never meant you couldn't have the door and windows open. It feels like a fucking sauna in here."

"It's…hot, but not unbearable," she said, wiping the back of her hand across her forehead. "It'll cool down soon."

"A bullet can go through the glass as well as the screen." He instantly regretted his logic when Gia flinched.

He walked the distance separating them and

hooked her neck, bringing her to his chest. "Grady and Choke are nearby. Mel was out at the curb with me until noon. The only people driving down our street are those who are locals. They wouldn't let strangers get near you or the duplex."

"I know." She sighed and leaned her weight against him. "Sorry."

He gritted his teeth. She wasn't the only one who woke up in a bad mood. He'd taken himself out to work on his bike to get some space. His frustration level rising every day that passed without the killers caught. He kept hoping Gia would use the phone he gave her and the information they collected would move everything forward and he could put a stop to the threats against her life.

Distracting them both with sex only made it more difficult to wait. He found himself trying to figure out how to work around Gia staying indefinitely with him without any obligations on his part instead of actively pursuing the killers.

He kissed the top of her head. He was addicted to sex with her. Not fucking. He could get that anywhere. Gia fed off his moods, and it was a powerful drug he couldn't stop.

She wanted fast and hard, he gave it to her. She wanted slow and lazy, he'd spend all night touching her.

"Whoa, holy shit, am I glad to see you," said Mel behind Swiss.

Swiss pivoted, not letting go of Gia, and glared at Mel. "Ever hear of knocking?"

"The door was open, man." Mel thrust his fingers in his hair. "I came back and thought someone had broken in."

Gia stiffened in Swiss's embrace.

Leaving his hand on her lower back, he faced Mel. "And, what was the first thing you did when you saw the door open?"

"I called Rod," said Mel, holding up his hand. "Fuck. I better call him back."

Swiss nodded and watched the kid walk away from the door of the duplex. In an emergency, Mel understood that you call the club first before approaching.

"I'm sorry, I overreacted." Gia stepped away from him. "I need to trust Ronacks to watch the duplex."

"What you need to do is stop apologizing for every damn thing you do." Swiss walked into the kitchen, poured a cup of coffee, and put it in the microwave. "It's better to be safe. Just know that you can open the front window when I'm outside. I can hear you if you needed me."

Gia followed him and sat on the stool. "There's a couple of sandwiches in the fridge for you."

He glanced over at her. "You made me lunch?"

"I didn't know when you'd be finished working on your bike, so I made you two sandwiches and put them away for when you came in." She chewed on her bottom lip and ran her finger around the edge of the cell phone on the counter.

Her noticing the phone kicked him in gear, and he grabbed the sandwich, the coffee, and escaped the obvious. "I'll eat outside."

She slid off the stool and stopped him from leaving. "Can I go out and watch you?"

"You want to watch me do maintenance on the Harley?" All he wanted her to do was use the damn phone when he was out of the duplex.

"I'm getting antsy inside, and I've dusted twice. You said it was safe with Ronacks watching the block."

Fuck. Why wasn't she taking the bait and using the phone?

If she made only one call, he'd have more answers to who she was in contact with and how they helped or if they put her in danger.

"I'll leave the door open. You can watch from inside." He walked out, taking a bite of his sandwich, without giving her the option to argue with him.

So far, she'd always followed his instructions and never put herself at risk.

Mel sat on the curb by Swiss's motorcycle. Swiss popped the last bite of sandwich in his mouth, set his coffee on the ground, and pointed to the seat. "Go ahead and take the seat off."

Mel followed his orders. Swiss dug out his tools and kneeled on the asphalt.

"What do you want me to do?" asked Mel.

Swiss loosened the throttle cable. "Start up the bike and let me know when the tension feels right."

Mel stood. The engine turned over. Swiss gave a quarter turn, tightening the cable, and Mel shook his head. Two more notches and Mel nodded.

"That's good," yelled Mel.

Swiss motioned his finger across his throat to cut the engine and caught sight of Gia standing in the open doorway of the duplex. He looked up at Mel. The kid was learning. He wasn't so quick to talk everyone's ear off, and he took any job Swiss threw at him seriously.

"Hey, do me a favor," said Swiss, low enough Gia couldn't hear.

Mel let go of the Harley and leaned forward.

Swiss kept Gia in sight and spoke with his mouth below the seat of the bike. "Go keep Gia company. She's feeling cooped up this afternoon. Maybe see if she's missing any friends back in Seattle and make her feel better."

Mel nodded. "I can do that."

"And, Mel." Swiss leaned closer. "I don't want her finding out you're giving her a mercy talking."

"Gotcha."

Swiss stood. "Also, keep your hands off her. She's mine."

Mel chuckled. Swiss pointed at the kid, drilling his point home and then put his tools back under the seat. Once he was alone, he sat on the Harley with his back to the duplex, coffee in one hand, phone in the other, and called Rod.

His Vice President answered on the second ring. "You've got me."

"Anything?" asked Swiss, getting right to the point of his call.

"I'm getting off work in ten minutes and will swing by the clubhouse. Sander has been monitoring things from there, and I can double check, but so far I haven't heard anything."

"Damn." Swiss peered up the street. "It's been over two weeks since I gave her the phone, and she hasn't used it yet. That doesn't make sense, considering she lifted Jana's phone."

"Maybe she needs a little incentive," said Rod.

Swiss grunted. They'd had fucking every spare minute. The only thing sex accomplished was making Gia hornier, and he had a hell of a time limiting himself.

"That doesn't work," he said.

Rod busted out laughing. "Fuck, man. I'm not talking about screwing her brains out. Women lean on others when they're upset or need to talk. Make it so she wants to talk to someone else besides play with your dick."

Swiss dug the heel of his boot into the ground. "Yeah, maybe."

"No maybe about it. We need answers, or you'll be off work indefinitely." Rod paused. "Bring her to the clubhouse. That seemed to get her to use Jana's phone before. Whatever happened there, might tempt her to use the phone you gave her."

"I'll see if she's up to going out tonight."

"Okay, I'm going to go lock this joint up. See you later," said Rod.

"Later." He disconnected the call.

Rod made a good point. Gia talked to him a lot. Even when he never joined in the conversation, she seemed content to speak her thoughts to him whether in bed or out. His silence never stopped her, and he usually found himself listening intently trying to figure out what she was really thinking.

He glanced over his shoulder. The open doorway to the duplex empty.

If ten minutes with Mel couldn't send her

straight to the phone to call a girlfriend, nothing he tried would work. Unless he got her pissed off and she refused to talk to him.

He stretched his neck. Fuck.

The last thing he wanted to do was start a fight.

Chapter Twenty Four

Swiss walked Gia into the clubhouse. She grabbed his hand, not wanting to get lost in the crowd of people packed inside, and Swiss shook her off and left her standing at the edge of the room without saying a word.

He left her alone.

The shock stunned her.

He hadn't left her side since she'd moved in with him. She clasped her hands in front of her and her vision blurred as she stared at the spot where he'd disappeared into the crowd.

Normally, she'd be okay. As a single woman living on her own, she went wherever she chose because that was her only option. She was perfectly capable of standing in a clubhouse by herself. But Swiss's quiet attitude before they'd left and his lack of reassurance on the ride over here had already warned her something was wrong.

And, he left her.

He'd never left her before.

She looked around for Bree or Raelyn, two people she'd feel comfortable going up to and talking with while Swiss did whatever he had to do, but she couldn't find the two women.

The loud music thrummed in her chest. A man she couldn't remember seeing before thrust a beer bottle at her and walked away.

She clutched the unopened drink with both hands and stepped back to the wall out of the way. It was unlike Swiss to leave her by herself. She tried to understand why and came up empty. She already missed his hand on her hip, reassuring her that he had everything under control.

Standing out among the bikers and the women, she wanted to slip outside but knew Swiss would want to be able to find her when he returned.

The Ronacks members ignored her. She picked at the label of the bottle. Always grateful for their help, she wondered if their openness came with stipulations or if taking Swiss away from his job with the club put added stress on each of them.

The thought of what she'd put on the club, not only Swiss, entered her head and she wondered if she'd overstayed their charity. She peered around the room, feeling guilty.

A woman tottered over to her on high heels and a tank-dress she had to tug down with every other step. Obviously looking at her, Gia smiled back and then gazed down at the drink in her hand. It'd be rude to guzzle the beer before the man came back for his drink.

The woman stopped in front of Gia and adjusted her breasts and cocked a hip out. "Who are you here with?"

"Swiss." Gia glanced around the room looking for a reason to escape.

"Ah, the big guy." The woman hummed in approval. "I'm Darcy."

"Gia," she said, introducing herself.

"This is my second Ronacks party." Darcy leaned in. "I haven't been with Swiss, yet. I don't think."

The overpowering floral perfume wafting off

Darcy snapped Gia into the present. She sneezed, barely covering her mouth in time. The slut either knew or wanted to throw Swiss in Gia's face. All she knew for certain was that Swiss hadn't been with any other women since she moved in with him.

"Where's your guy?" asked Darcy. "Is he lining up the backroom for you?"

Oh God. After tonight, she couldn't speak of Swiss's sex life with confidence. He had plenty of time to get it on with any of the women at the party when he walked away from her.

"Talking to his president," Gia lied. No way would she give Darcy the satisfaction of winning one over on her. "Hey, have a beer. I need to go talk to someone."

The hell with Swiss, she was out of here. She gave Darcy the unopened beer bottle and left the house empty handed. Outside, she inhaled the night air deeply and paced through the excess energy the other woman had created in her.

There were other members outside. She scuffed the bottom of her sneaker against the pebbles on the asphalt driveway. Swiss went out of his way to guarantee her safety on property owned by Ronacks Motorcycle Club. She'd be safe as long as everyone else stayed outside within her view.

She pursed her lips, growing angrier. Expecting to try and distract Swiss while she snuck a phone call to Bianca, he'd totally thrown her off track by leaving her inside by herself.

Goosebumps broke out over her arms. She rubbed her skin, wishing she had her sweatshirt from the Harley.

Mel jogged toward her. She exhaled in relief. Finally, someone she knew and was comfortable being around without Swiss nearby.

"Hey, Gia." Mel stopped in front of her and grinned. "You never mentioned coming to the party earlier when we were talking."

"I didn't know myself until after you'd left Swiss's place." Gia cupped her elbows and looked at his patchless vest.

"I'm always here." Mel chuckled and rocked back on the heels of his boots. "It's pretty much required of me until I get my patch."

"You're single, right? It can't be that hard to hang out and party all the time." Her teeth chattered, and she snapped her jaw closed.

Mel shrugged. "It'll be more fun when I'm a full member."

"Ah…" She understood from their conversation earlier that there were many things he still had to learn about Ronacks. In some ways, he was an outsider like her.

"Where's Swiss?" asked Mel.

She shook her head. "Inside. He left me as soon as we arrived."

"Do you want me to get him for you?" He cleared his throat. "He might be in the back room."

"No, thanks." She turned to him fully. "Can you do me a favor?"

"Sure."

"My sweatshirt is in the leather bag on Swiss's bike. Can you get it for me?"

Mel clicked his tongue and shook his head. "Prospects can't touch a member's bike. I'll go get

Swiss to get it for you."

"No." She reached out and grabbed his arm before he could leave. "Don't bother him. Whatever he's doing is probably important. He'll probably come out any second."

Mel leaned to the side, looked past Gia, and held up two fingers in the peace sign. "Prez...Bree."

Gia turned and found Bree hurrying across the lawn beside Battery. She waved. The few times she'd spent with Bree, she found herself liking the other woman. She was down-to-earth, and her calming personality put Gia at ease.

"Hi." Bree waved back, separating from her husband, and came to Gia's side. "Are you leaving?"

"No. I'm waiting for Swiss. He's inside." Gia shivered.

Bree frowned and cocked her head. "Come on in and wait where it's warmer. It's practically freezing out here tonight."

"Thanks. I'd like that." Gia walked beside Bree.

"It's almost too cold to walk to the pond after the sun goes down and we haven't even entered fall yet." Bree swung the front door and held it open. "The weather is crazy. I went swimming earlier to cool off, and now everyone is trying to warm up. Someone needs to punch Mother Nature in the face."

Gia laughed. "No kidding. I can't get used to the dip in temperature at night, but I'll take it over sweating to death during the day."

Inside, Battery came over, whispered in Bree's ear, and then walked across the room. Bree motioned for Gia to follow and led her to the couch. She sat down, glad to have someone to sit with her.

"Raelyn was asking about you today when I dropped off Dukie at the bar." Bree turned sideways on the couch. "She thinks you're good for Swiss."

"Oh." She leaned back in surprise. "I don't know about that. I'm mostly a pain in the ass. I think he'd like to have his regular life back."

"How are you doing with everything?"

"Okay." She wrinkled her nose. "I spend half my time wishing everything was over and the other half wanting the problems to disappear without any more trouble. I hate what's happened, and it makes me angry that I've involved other people."

Bree's gaze softened. "Don't think that way. I've had my own trouble in the past. Trust me, when it's all over, you'll be glad that you came to Swiss."

"Maybe." She gazed around the room. Swiss still hadn't appeared, and her stomach tightened.

"Hey, don't worry about him. The guys disappear and talk all the time. Swiss knows you're safe here, and everyone will look out for you." Bree leaned forward. "If Battery suspected anything happening, he wouldn't allow me to be around you."

"You're sure?"

Bree nodded. "One-hundred percent."

The music changed. Gia looked out at the others. Most everyone had coupled up, except for a few men who stood around the bar on the other side of the room. She couldn't find Darcy and wondered where she'd gone.

At the level of flirting and touching happening in the room, she suspected the backroom that Darcy and Mel mentioned was where couples went to get some privacy. Boundaries seemed unimportant to the others. There were even two women hanging on one biker in the corner and neither women wore any kind of top. Their bare breasts out in plain sight and enjoyed by more than a few men who kept ogling them.

"This all must seem a bit much for you, huh?" said Bree. "The later it gets, the wilder the party. A few years ago, I used to hang out and drive Battery crazy by being down here. Now, we usually stay upstairs when everyone starts getting…friendly."

Gia looked down at her hands in her lap. "It's a little awkward. I keep telling myself it's no different than a club scene in Seattle."

"I wouldn't know about that. I've lived with Battery since I was sixteen." Bree waved her hand in front of Gia's shocked expression. "No, no…don't think what you're thinking. It's a long story. But, I grew up around everyone here. They party hard. They enjoy women. But, you won't find more loyal and dedicated men anywhere."

"Swiss is like that."

"They're all that way. A few are a little rougher around the edges, but when it comes down to it, we're all family. The best family I've ever had." Bree smiled gently, and her attention was dragged away to the area behind Gia. "Ah, there's Swiss now. I told you he wouldn't leave you for long."

Her rapid heartbeat at Swiss's name gave way to irritation. She had no right to be upset that he'd left her alone at the party or that Darcy practically staked her claim on Swiss. But, she was hurt.

Chapter Twenty Five

His plan to make Gia want to reach out to someone in the form of a phone call failed when Bree brought her back inside the clubhouse. Swiss walked back into the main room. Time was running out.

He understood her way of thinking enough to know asking her outright who she called would make her retreat. Loyal to a fault, manners that verged on too polite, Gia would do something reckless to protect someone else or if she believed a friend was in danger. Coming straight out and confronting her about the phone call she'd made could push her away and he needed her close to protect her.

If he didn't need more details, he'd admire her for standing strong and protecting those close to her. But, he needed names and connections. All he needed was a definite subject to point him in the right direction. She couldn't go on living each day not knowing if something would happen or not.

She also couldn't return to Seattle without proof that she was safe.

Gia looked at him approaching her. His gaze connected with her, and she turned her attention back to Bree. He growled. She gave him nothing, except a snub.

No interest, no lingering look, no warmth.

He'd succeeded at pissing her off.

Bree glanced between Gia and Swiss, and then raised her brows in curiosity. Swiss veered from going to the couch and instead walked over to the men gathered around the counter. The last thing he wanted to do was answer questions from two women. Neither one of them would want to hear what he had to say tonight.

LeWorth held up a bottle of whiskey. "You in for a shot, Swiss?"

He shook his head. The second he sent Gia home to Seattle he planned on taking his good friend Jim Beam to bed with him.

"Did you hear there's a new business opening up off of First Street?" Grady flicked his hair behind his shoulders. "An outdoor supply store. I ran into the owner when he was coming out of the shop after picking up his car. He says he's going to carry a whole line of rifles and pistols, plus dish out hunting tags."

"Who's supplying the weapons?" asked Battery.

"I asked him." Grady took a drink. "He's getting most of his inventory from the Lightfoot Militia and getting the rest from wholesalers."

"So, Bantorus Motorcycle Club will be supplying the arms to the militia, and they'll transport to Haugan." Battery stroked his beard. "Why don't you make contact with the owner again, Grady. See if you can get Ronacks in to cover the business and stress how the territory works. That way we can keep the lines between Bantorus MC and Ronacks from blurring. I'd like to keep our relationship with them friendly."

"Will do, Prez," said Grady.

Battery stood from the table, paused, grabbed his phone out of his pocket, and read the screen. "Everyone, hold on. It's Raelyn."

Swiss stepped forward. If Raelyn needed anything at Pine Bar and Grill during working hours, she was to call Rod. She was only to call Battery if it was an emergency.

"Slow down, Rae." Battery held up his hand and put his finger in his other ear. "How long ago? Which direction?"

Swiss looked over at Gia and found her in conversation with Bree, unaware of anything else going on in the room.

"No, keep the men with you in the bar. I'll take riders out with me and have a look around." Battery pointed to Sander, LeWorth, Grady, and then pointed at the door.

Swiss moved out of their way to go to Gia, knowing he wasn't needed, and Battery grabbed his vest.

His body hardened at attention.

"Okay, got it." Battery lowered his voice into the phone. "Keep your eyes open, Raelyn, and be smart."

Battery disconnected the call and turned to Swiss. "The woman came back to the bar, stepped inside and spotted Raelyn, and took off. She sent the prospect and Choke outside to follow her. Apparently, the woman took off in a navy colored sedan with Washington plates. They didn't get a read on the plate."

Swiss balled his hands. "This could be it."

Battery planted his hand in the middle of Swiss's chest. "I need you here to take care of your girl and Bree. Don't let them go outside."

He gritted his teeth and nodded in acceptance.

For how much he wanted to find the woman in question, he wouldn't allow anything to happen to Gia. For all he knew, the woman was a ploy in a man's game and the first chance he turned his back, the killers would get to Gia.

"I want in on it if it turns into something more," said Swiss.

"I'll call when I know something." Battery hurried over to Bree, whispered in her ear, and kissed her forehead.

Bree looked to Swiss and stood from the couch. He walked over before Bree could get the idea to find out more details. He'd need Bree to keep her head and help him distract Gia.

"Do you know what's going on?" Bree's eyes bore into him.

He recognized more than concern. It wasn't long ago, the Russians came after Bree, and her life was in danger.

"Raelyn wanted someone to come over and check the place out. She's fine, and business is open." Swiss pointed at the couch. "Visit with Gia. Battery will be back in a half hour, tops."

He sat down on the arm of the couch beside Gia and put his hand on the back of her neck. Her muscles constricted from his touch. He leaned down and kissed her temple.

"Everything okay?" he said against her skin.

"I'm fine."

She never looked up at him. He gave her a squeeze. Mindless rock music blared in the room. He gazed around at the others. Chuck and Jana were getting hot and heavy against the wall. Sander never seemed concerned that his ex-girlfriend played with every member of the club.

Roller, a newer lifer, already had Bethanie's shirt unbuttoned. JayJay entertained Charlene with shots at the table in the corner. Three women he never could remember their names danced for Lug and Round.

Gia remained stiff under his touch beside him. All he could do was wait to make her feel more secure. Hopefully, with the new development tonight in town, and he continued to keep Gia pissed off enough to reach out to her contact, he'd have enough information to end the problems.

"You two hungry?" he asked, thinking of ways to beat time.

Bree laughed. "Is that a hint?"

"Nah, I'm good." Swiss patted his stomach. "Gia made burgers before we came over."

"I bet it's nice to have someone living with you who will also feed you." Bree's teasing smile grew bigger. "Though Raelyn better hope she picks up more business without you coming into the bar three times a day."

"I'll be back to my normal schedule soon." Swiss chuckled. "I miss Rae's desserts."

Gia's shoulders slumped forward. He removed his hand and stood up. If he stayed beside her, he'd make things right.

He hated upsetting her, but it was more important to get closer to fixing her life than for her to enjoy a night out with him. She'd already proven she had a jealous streak.

"I'm gonna grab a bottle of water. Bree? Do

you want one?" he asked.

Bree said, "No, thanks."

He walked a few steps and turned around, "Oh, fuck. Forgot. Gia? How about you?"

Gia shook her head. He'd reduced her to not talking to him. Good.

He strolled over to the refrigerator. The guilt knowing he'd put her in the position of relying on him being around and her disappointment in something as simple as staying by her side, which obviously meant a lot to her, wasn't sitting well with him.

He understood her reasons. But, he refused to take responsibility for the situation they were both in. One of them needed to break, and it sure in the fuck wasn't going to be him.

Swiss opened the fridge, took out a plastic water bottle, and drank half the contents. It only took ten minutes to ride to Pine Bar and Grill. Ronacks should be there by now.

If they found the unknown woman who had visited the bar, he could ease up on Gia. He wouldn't need her making a phone call to find out more. A simple interrogation and he could have the woman blabbing who she worked for and why she was in town.

He sniffed and wiped his mouth with his forearm. Fuck, he needed a drink stronger than water.

"Yo, Swiss." JayJay leaned against the fridge. "Where did the others take off to?"

"The woman we've been looking for showed up at the bar and then took off. Prez took the others to see if they could find her."

"Good deal, man." JayJay nodded. "How's

your woman taking the news?"

His woman.

Swiss tossed the water bottle into the trash. "Keep your voice down. She doesn't know."

"Yeah," mumbled JayJay. "I'm toast, anyway."

"Crash in the backroom." Swiss eyed Charlene. "Take Char with you."

JayJay grinned. "That's the plan. Catch you tomorrow."

"Right," muttered Swiss, watching his MC brother lumber off.

Before Gia arrived, it would've been him borrowing the backroom and taking one of the women for a few hours of fun. He gazed at Gia, who also watched JayJay half-carry Charlene across the room while his sloppy attempt to undress her left both of them laughing.

His stomach tightened. The unmasked longing on Gia's face hardened his resolve to keep everything within boundaries for both of them. The last thing he needed was a woman wanting in his life and Gia would be better off without him. Her life was in Seattle, not Haugan.

His phone vibrated. He put it to his ear. "Yeah?"

"No sign of her," said Battery.

"Fuck," he muttered. "How can she get away?"

"You know as well as I do that the interstate makes Haugan vulnerable. I've sent LeWorth and Grady east and called Kurt with Bantorus Motorcycle Club to watch the west side of the interstate. They're going to be on the lookout for the car and meet with our members later if they arrive. Until then, all we can do is wait," said Battery.

"I'm going to take Gia home. Maybe the mysterious woman is hiding until she can get her opportunity to approach Gia." Swiss cupped the back of his neck and stretched his back.

"There's always the chance we're running toward a dead end."

"Let's hope not." Swiss exhaled loudly. "I rather get this settled sooner rather than later."

"Tell Bree I'm heading home. You can go ahead and leave. I double checked with the others who are on guard duty tonight, and it's been quiet at the duplex since you left. Before you go, speak with Roller and tell him he's to stay with Bree until I get back."

"I'm on it." Swiss disconnected the phone.

With nothing nailed down, anything could happen. He'd be alert and on guard, not knowing if the woman was a distraction to thin the club or if they were all on a wild goose chase.

"Roller?" He motioned his MC brother over.

"What's up?"

"Prez wants you to stay here and keep Bree inside," said Swiss. "I'm taking off with Gia."

"No problem." Roller lifted his Red Solo cup and spit the juice from his chew in it. "I was going to stick around longer anyways."

"Good. Before you go entertain Bree, gather two members who are sober to escort me home." Swiss slapped Roller on the arm and walked over to Gia.

Once the women said their goodbyes, he led Gia outside. Without saying a word, she climbed on behind him, and he rode back to the duplex. As usual, he took a couple of different side streets and made sure the only one following him was a Ronacks member. He also checked on the two other members who were close enough to have the block covered before he parked at the curb in front of the duplex.

Gia walked beside him to the door. He was no closer to bringing her situation to an end, but one thing was for sure. He'd succeeded in pissing Gia off.

Chapter Twenty Six

When the loud rumble from the biker riding past the duplex on his nightly watch failed to wake Swiss, Gia slid out of bed, grabbed one of Swiss's T-shirts, and hurried into the kitchen to grab the cell phone Swiss had given her a few weeks ago. Tonight would've been the perfect time to use someone's phone at the clubhouse, but Swiss leaving her to her own company had distracted her.

She stepped over and glanced back in the bedroom. Swiss continued to sleep. He rarely slept for more than two hours at a time. She'd need to hurry.

Going quietly into the bathroom, she shut the door and turned on the light. Her hands shook as she slipped the shirt over her head. She looked forward to hearing Bianca's voice. Lately, everyone in Ronacks, including Swiss, seemed to keep her on the outside.

They dealt with the situation privately, never including her or letting her in on what was going on. Earlier—last night, she suspected the men had come looking for her again. Even Bree couldn't cover for her husband's quick exit or Swiss hovering when he was perfectly fine leaving her alone earlier during the party.

Swiss had acted strangely all day. He remained quiet, refusing to talk, when they got ready for bed, and when she laid down naked beside him, he ignored her. She'd told him good night, and he'd grunted in reply.

She looked all over the phone for anything that stood out as being a traceable phone. It was a cheap one, probably bought right off the shelf. To be safe, when she finished the call, she'd run it under the faucet and then put it in the trash. She trusted no phone, not even one supplied by Ronacks for her use only.

If they wanted to keep secrets from her, she wouldn't feel guilty about keeping her one contact to Seattle to herself. Bianca couldn't help the club, and she had an invested interest in finding the killers. Trinity had been her coworker and Bianca's best friend, a fact that neither one of them knew until she'd blabbed everything at the woman's shelter.

She tapped out Bianca's number and put the phone to her ear. It was the middle of the night. Bianca had to be home.

"Hello?" said Bianca.

"It's me. Gia." She forced herself to whisper through her spike of adrenaline. "I am so glad to hear your voice."

"Oh my, God. Where have you been? I've been worried sick not hearing from you."

"With Swiss. The men after me are here. They found me and slashed my tires and left a message on my car, and ran over one of the Ronacks member's motorcycle." Her voice trembled. "Ronacks are protecting me, but they haven't seen the men after me in over a week."

"What? The men are in the same town?" said Bianca, louder and more awake.

"Yes." Gia paused to calm down. "Are the police saying anything in the papers or on the news?"

"No. Nothing. I hoped since I hadn't heard from you that nobody followed you. You're okay, right?"

"Physically, yes. But, I'm scared and frustrated. I don't know what to do. Swiss swore he'd take care of everything and make the men stop, but you and I both know what they've done and what they tried to do to me before I ran to the shelter." Gia sat down on the edge of the bathtub.

"Listen to me, Gia. You have to think about if you're better off by yourself or with Swiss." Bianca paused. "I'll help you any way I can, but the shelter's funds are limited. We have a network we work with, and you're the first woman we've helped financially to be placed in a private home out of state. I can go in front of the board and request a transfer to another shelter and try to get you farther away, maybe D.C. or Chicago. But, the chance of it happening is slim if not impossible."

Moving was not an option. The first step out the door, the men would follow her.

"I don't understand why they want me dead. I don't know who they are, and I never witnessed them killing Sean and Trinity." She leaned over and cradled her forehead in her hand. "Maybe I should go to the police here in Haugan. Maybe they'll help."

"What they'll do is listen, and then they'll convince you to take out a restraining order, but you don't have the names of the men." Bianca's voice hardened. "We've gone over your options before, and nothing has changed."

"I know. I know." She glanced toward the door. "I should go. Swiss could wake up at any time and wonder who I'm talking to. I just…I needed to talk. You're the only one who understands what I'm going through."

"You haven't told him who is helping you?"

"Yes." She sighed. "Swiss knows everything. I even told him the name of the shelter that sent me here, but I don't know what else to do...you're my lifeline to what is going on back there. You understand, and Trinity was your friend, too. I might not have known you before, but I value our friendship now."

"How are you calling me?"

Gia wrinkled her nose, knowing she took a big chance to reach out to Bianca. "Swiss gave me an untraceable phone, but I'm going to take the battery out and put it in water after I'm done. I won't take any chances."

"Will that work?"

"I don't know. It's the only thing I can think of doing without waking Swiss up."

"Gia..." Bianca softened her voice. "I know you don't want to, but I think it'd be better if you keep the phone and tell Swiss who you called."

"But what if he tells me to stop calling you?"

"Do you trust him?"

"I guess." She rubbed her hand over her eyes. There was more to the situation than she could confess to Bianca. Swiss had become everything to her, and her private relationship muddied everything.

"Who can help you more, Swiss or me?"

She closed her eyes. Admitting that Swiss was doing more than the police, Bianca, and even herself, put everything in order of importance.

"He moved you in with him. He gave you a phone. Use your head, honey. He's not going to be upset that you contacted me. You need to work with him and if there's anything you're keeping from him, tell him, so he can end this nightmare for both of us," said Bianca.

Her head pounded. After Swiss's indifference toward her last night, she dreaded talking to him. She'd thought having sex together meant something more. Not that she expected him to treat her like they were together, but at least friends.

"Are you still there?" asked Bianca.

"Yes." She opened her eyes. "I'll talk to Swiss."

"Promise me."

"I promise you," said Gia.

"Good." Bianca exhaled over the phone. "Call me back as soon as you can. That way I know everything is okay."

"I'll try." She stood. "Thanks for talking me down."

"That's what I'm here for."

"Okay, I'll let you go. Bye."

"Bye," said Bianca.

Gia disconnected the call and walked out of the bathroom. Wide awake, she turned to go into the kitchen where using the faucet with the quieter plumbing would hopefully not wake Swiss, and she almost ran into him. She pressed her hand to her chest to stop her sudden fright.

"I didn't see you standing there," she said, gasping. "Did I wake you?"

He held up his phone. "Got a call."

"Oh?" She smoothed the front of Swiss's T-shirt down the front of her. "Is everything okay?"

"Why don't you tell me?" Swiss stepped back, motioned toward the couch, and turned on the light. "And, before you start, I'll go ahead and tell you the phone you're holding onto tightly is untraceable to everyone, except Ronacks Motorcycle Club. Every time you make a call, the phone number you're dialing shows up on a computer at the clubhouse. Whatever you say during that call is recorded. Now, I'm expecting Rod to call me back any moment with all the details, but I'd like to give you a chance to tell me yourself who you called and what was discussed before I hear it from someone else."

"You tapped the phone you gave me?" she whispered.

He sat down on the couch. "I promised to keep you safe."

She looked down at the phone in her hand and set it on the coffee table. He'd asked her to trust him, and the whole time, he never believed her. He never trusted *her*.

Chapter Twenty Seven

Gia stood stiffly in the middle of Swiss's living room staring at him blankly. He gave her time to wrap her head around what she'd done by using the phone. What *he'd* done by giving her the phone.

In a few minutes, Rod would call him and play her conversation over the phone and give him the details of who Gia called. He wanted to believe she had a female friend she missed or an elderly neighbor she checked up on every month.

His gut had told him he was wrong. It's why he'd asked Battery for the traceable phone weeks ago.

She stepped to the side, sank down in the chair opposite the couch, and curled around herself, hugging her middle. "You don't believe me."

"That you're in danger?" He stayed calm. "I believe someone slashed your tires and wrote 'Dead' on your windshield. I know for a fact that two people were murdered in Seattle where you claimed you worked. I know Mel got his bike ran over."

"But, you don't believe the killers are after me," she stated.

"Someone is fucking with you, Gia. I've seen the proof." He slowed down in an attempt to get her to talk. "Why don't you tell me who you called?"

She closed her mouth and stared at him. He leaned forward and braced his elbows on his knees. Trained to wait out the enemy, he could sit here until the sun came up waiting for her to answer, and she would answer. He'd make sure of it.

Except, she wasn't the enemy.

He cared about her. He wasn't judging.

He rubbed his hands together watching her, waiting for her to trust him. At the moment, she wouldn't believe he was on her side. Everything he'd done, he'd done for her.

The phone rang. He gazed at Gia giving her the chance to come clean, knowing whatever she hid would come out into the open and change everything. Until now, he never realized how much weight he put on her being honest with him.

She stared at him without saying a word, challenging him to pick up the phone. To go over her head and find out what she'd done. To prove she was like his ex-wife and to admit that he'd thought of her more than someone who shared his bed for sex.

He looked away, unable to test her, and let Rod's call go to voice mail.

Gia exhaled audibly in the small room.

He'd made his choice.

"Sweet, talk to me," he whispered.

"I trusted you."

Without breaking their standoff, he said, "You can still trust me."

She shook her head slowly. He leaned back on the couch. It'd been twenty-four years since he'd pushed for answers. Out of practice at being close to a woman and agitated that his feelings for Gia had stepped between his need to protect her and his desire to have her, he couldn't go back to gambling with the life he'd set up for himself. He wasn't willing to compromise.

"Fuck this," he muttered, picking up the phone.

He called her bluff and put the call into Rod.
"Are you ready?" said Swiss into the phone.
He stared at Gia, wishing she'd stop him.

"Yeah. I was going to give you two minutes and put out a call for the club to ride over there and find out why the fuck you weren't answering your phone," said Rod.

Swiss paused, hoping Gia would stop him. She remained silent. He couldn't delay any longer.

"Do you have the recording?" asked Swiss.

"Yeah. All six and a half minutes of the conversation."

"I'm going to put you on speaker. Go ahead and play it." Swiss lowered the phone, tapped the button, and set the cell on the coffee table between him and Gia.

"Hello?"

"It's me. Gia. I am so glad to hear your voice."
"Oh my, God. Where have you been? I've been worried sick not hearing from you."

"With Swiss. The men after me are here. They found me and slashed my tires and left a message on my car, and ran over one of the

Ronacks member's motorcycle. Ronacks are protecting me, but they haven't seen the men after me in over a week."
...

    Intent on listening to every word, he stood and stared down at the phone. His heart thundered in his chest the further the conversation went. Gia never spoke of a woman named Bianca, and yet, the woman knew about the situation in Seattle and urged Gia to trust him.
    Who was the other woman?
    Where was she?
    Could she be the female that kept showing up at Pine Bar and Grill?
    The phone clicked, and Rod said, "Did you hear everything?"
    He sat back down on the couch, glanced at Gia sitting stone still in the chair, and rubbed the back of his head. "Yeah."
    "I've trailed the phone number, and we've got a couple red flags," said Rod. "I'd suggest taking me off speakerphone, walking outside, and letting me talk to you in private."
    Swiss stared at Gia. She stared back, formidable in her stance not to talk.
    "No, go ahead. I want Gia to hear what you found out." His cheek twitched, and he wanted to reach up and rub the scar.
    "Swiss, brother, that is not a good idea."

"Just fucking do it." Swiss reached for his pack of cigarettes and realized he only had on his jeans and hadn't taken the time to put on a shirt or his vest.

"Okay." Rod paused and cleared his throat. "Gia called the woman Bianca. The phone number goes to someone else."

Gia frowned and shook her head. "That's not possible. Bianca gave me the number to her private cell phone because her work phone is traceable."

"Swiss, I want to ask you again if you'd like to take this conversation somewhere private?" asked Rod.

Swiss fisted his hand. "Go on."

"I did some digging with the name of the shelter you gave me in Seattle and searched for an employee named Bianca, last name unknown, and there are no female employees with that name or any variation I could come up with in two minutes."

"Could it be a new hire?" asked Swiss.

Gia inched to the edge of the seat. He took in the way her legs shook, and her bare feet bounced against the floor.

"Possibly." The sound of paper crinkling came over the speaker. "But I doubt it. The name registered on the phone matches an employee at Inner Seattle Woman's shelter. Same woman, and I believe it's the woman Gia worked with to come to Montana."

Swiss ran his hand over his whiskered jaw. "What's that lady's name?"

"Heather Jones."

Swiss flinched, a jolt pierced his cheek, and he shook his head. "Repeat the name."

"Heather Jones," said Rod.

Sweat broke out across Swiss's back, and he stood running his hands down his face. Impossible.

Gia got to her feet. "Swiss?"

He held up his hand. "Don't."

"What's going on, brother?" asked Rod over the speaker.

He shook his head. There was no way. No fucking way.

Gia touched his arm. He jerked away, staring at her as if he hadn't been between her legs every fucking night since she moved in. That the woman who made him meals, cleaned his living quarters, and sighed after he gave her an orgasm was the same one who had lied to him the whole time.

"Swiss, talk to me," ordered Rod.

"I'll call you later." He stepped over to the phone and disconnected the call.

Gia hugged her middle. "I don't know who—"

"Don't say it." His harsh breathing filled the room.

"But, I don't know who—"

"You know fucking well who she is." He stepped in front of her. "What I want to know is what in the hell are you doing with my daughter?"

Gia's head snapped back. "Your daughter?"

His head pounded, and he clamped down at the roar building and pressing on his chest to come out. The loss he thought he'd lived through was reborn and took him to his knees.

Chapter Twenty Eight

Swiss's big body crumbled in front of Gia. She covered her mouth and reached out for him without breaching the space he created around him with his painful gaze. Kneeling, Swiss slumped forward, his arms hung uselessly on his thighs.

The last hour a nightmare she failed to understand. She'd talked to Bianca, not the other person Rod mentioned over the phone. She could prove it.

No, she couldn't.

None of the Ronacks members knew what Bianca looked like, but she'd met Bianca when she'd ran to the shelter for help. Bianca was the woman who'd comforted and helped her. Bianca helped her finance the trip and found the duplex for her. Bianca was her anchor when the world seemed to be attacking her from all sides.

Had Swiss thought Bianca had his daughter's phone?

"Where is she?" said Swiss, his monotone voice dragged down with emotion.

Gia took a step forward and dropped to her knees in front of him. Afraid to touch him in his unreceptive condition, she rocked back and forth.

"Bianca?" she whispered.

His head snapped up, and his angry gaze met hers. "No, my daughter."

"Swiss, I don't know your daughter." She inhaled deeply. "The conversation you listened to was between the woman who helped me at the woman's shelter and myself. I swear on my life. Her name is Bianca."

"There's no Bianca who works there."

She shook her head, frustrated over all the confusion. "I don't know. Maybe the workers go by different names when they're helping others. They do their best to protect women who are in danger. It could be that Bianca isn't her real name, but if that's so, I wasn't aware of it."

Swiss pushed to his feet, strode to the television, and picked up the picture she'd studied many times of him and his daughter from years ago. "Do you recognize her?"

Gia stood and accepted the picture. All she could see was a little girl who loved her daddy.

"Does she look like someone you know?" said Swiss harshly.

Wanting to help Swiss, she studied the picture again for his sake. The child was a normal little girl with long dark hair and a round face. She had a button nose, and her eyes were lit up with a smile.

Gia shook her head. "I'm sorry, but I don't know any children—"

"She's not a child anymore. She's twenty-six years old."

"I know. I'm listening to you, Swiss." Gia softened her voice. "It's just that in the picture, she looks like a child to me, and it's hard to imagine what she looks like today. If you could describe her mother to me, maybe I could—"

His hand sliced the air.

Tears welled in her vision. "I'm sorry, Swiss. I wish, I understood what you needed from me, or you could explain what I've done."

"Done?" he said, calm and scary. "You have no fucking clue what you've done."

"Then enlighten me."

He ignored her, grabbed his phone, and tapped out a message on the screen. She stood by helplessly. He walked past her to the bedroom and returned fully dressed. She had no time to ask him what he planned to do when a knock came at the door, and Mel stepped inside the duplex.

"Watch her," ordered Swiss before he walked out and the door slammed shut.

Mel grimaced and looked at Gia when the roar of a motorcycle started up outside. "Uh, do you know what's going on?"

"No," she whispered, reaching out for the chair and sitting down. "He's upset."

"Shit." Mel blew out his breath. "He's breaking code."

Tired of not understanding Swiss or the dynamics of the club, she snapped, "What code?"

"Ride with purpose." Mel sat down on the couch. "He's only supposed to ride for a reason. Anger isn't one of them."

A weight settled down on her shoulders. The whole night her fault, and yet she couldn't understand what she'd done. Swiss gave her the phone. He had to expect she'd use it. The only thing she'd done was keep her contact with Bianca secret. Her conversations with Bianca never put her at risk or she would've cut ties when she left Seattle. The woman's shelter was helping her.

"I've gotta call Battery," mumbled Mel,

pulling out his phone. It was as if she'd stepped into a different life. Swiss blamed her for something to do with his daughter. Rod tapped her private phone call. Ronacks had rules, and now the bikers were going to invade the duplex, and she had no answers for anyone.

Chapter Twenty Nine

One after another, Ronacks members cruised by Swiss as the sun rose below the cutting edge of the Bitterroot Mountains in the distance. He sat sideways on his Harley and counted eleven riders, which meant Mel had called an emergency in on him, and his brothers were marking off a circle of safety around him.

The excess anger and panic that had overtaken him in the duplex at hearing his daughter's name had worn off five minutes ago. Swiss crossed his ankles and lit a cigarette, glancing at his raw knuckles. After he'd left Gia, he'd gone three miles to the river and let out his anger on a Tamarack tree until he realized fear was what pounded in his head, not anger.

Fear for his daughter.

He had no right to Heather, but hearing her name come from Rod's lips brought out what he'd struggled to tamper down for twenty-two years. The hope that she'd seek him out. The fear that she hated him. The anger that his hands were tied when it came to his flesh and blood.

The rumble of motorcycles invaded his peace again. He sucked on the cigarette, tilted his head, and sent the smoke in the air.

Battery arrived first and instead of getting off his motorcycle, his president leaned forward and braced his forearms on the handlebars. Without saying a word, Battery questioned Swiss's state of mind.

Swiss shrugged. He had no idea if he was

okay. The pain in his chest held the tension in his shoulders. Tied up in a knot, he could only sit and accept what he'd heard.

The other riders shut off their bikes and joined Battery. Each one assessing Swiss.

"Mel called, believing you needed some help." Battery pulled a cigarette out of the pocket of his vest.

"Mel only wants to earn his patch." Swiss rubbed the end of his cigarette against his jeans and pocketed the butt.

"Rod put everything together, because of your last name, and filled me in, brother," said Battery. "What can we do?"

Swiss inhaled deeply. "I need to know if the woman who keeps showing up to the bar is my daughter."

Battery stood, straddling the motorcycle, and extracted a folded piece of paper from his back pocket. "Rod already solved that question. He found a picture of your daughter on Facebook and linked it to the employee picture at the woman's shelter. Rod and Sander both verified that your daughter and the woman at the bar are not the same person. I printed out a picture of Heather if you'd like it."

His lungs seized, and he coughed, grabbing for the paper. Refusing to look at the proof of his grown daughter, he slipped the paper into his vest pocket.

"Talk to me, Swiss." Battery sat back down. "Put the pieces together for us, so that we can help you."

He'd joined Ronacks a year after leaving the Army. A year after Anita took Heather away from him and he'd hit rock bottom. He fingered the scar on his cheekbone. A year after he got shot and almost died trying to keep his family together.

He inhaled deeply, and his chest only hurt more. "I've rented the duplex since I was twenty-one years old, newly married, and my then wife was pregnant with my baby. Four years later, I lost my family and haven't seen my daughter since. Until Rod told me the woman's name at the shelter, I never thought twice over who sent Gia to me. It could be my daughter helping Gia. Heather could be the one working at the shelter, though after everything that'd happened between her mom and me…I don't know. I fucking don't know anything else or the reasons why she'd even think of putting a woman in my life."

"Why would your daughter call herself Bianca?" asked Rod.

Swiss gazed at his vice president. "I don't know. Maybe she changed her name or…"

"She didn't want her dad to find out," said Battery, finishing Swiss's thought. "Swiss, I know what you must be thinking, man, but you've got to keep your head."

"I'm okay." He swallowed. "Not feeling much right now."

"That might have something to do with your bloody knuckles. Who did you beat up?" asked Sander.

Swiss curled his fingers, taking pleasure from the tight stinging skin. "Since your ugly ass wasn't around, I used a tree."

Sander dipped his chin in admiration. "Next time, let me know in advance, and I'll hold Mel for you to beat."

The comradery between him and his MC brothers eased the pressure in Swiss's chest enough for him to take a good-sized, much-needed breath. "I need to get back to Gia."

"The rest of the club is outside the duplex." Battery glanced at Rod. "We weren't sure how many of us we'd need to take you down."

Swiss stood, threw his leg over his Harley, and said. "A half hour ago, it would've taken more members than we have."

Battery straightened his beard and lowered his voice. "What are you doing with Gia?"

Swiss stared out into the street. Sometime between busting the skin open on his knuckles and dragging his ass back on his bike, he realized Gia stopped being the answer for sex while they worked to keep her safe.

"Depends on what she's going to do with me." Swiss started his motorcycle before Battery could ask any more questions and headed home.

Gia only knew what he'd given her, and it wasn't a whole hell of a lot. He sped up, taking the corner and pulling the bike up straight. They had a lot to work through, and he needed to find out more about Heather.

Afterward, he'd have to wait and see how things would turn out with Gia. It could be that Gia would decide he wasn't the type of man to plan tomorrow with, and she'd leave.

Chapter Thirty

Swiss sat at the two-person dinette inside the duplex. Gia's legs shook, and she held on to the back of the chair opposite of him, unable to sit down and face whatever decision Swiss had come to when he'd left the duplex. He'd returned with both of his hands raw and bloody and ignored her need to clean up his wounds. Instead, he ordered her to sit.

Sit at a table they'd never used before as if she was now a guest.

"Let me at least get you some ice," she said.

"My hands are fine." He lifted his chin, motioning toward her chair. "We need to talk."

Oh, God. He was going to kick her out. Where would she go? How could she leave him?

He needed her. She needed him. For whatever reason, her calling Bianca had set him off, and she needed to fix what she'd done. The men were still out there trying to get to her, and she still had so much to learn about Swiss. She wasn't ready to leave.

She sat down and grabbed the edge of the seat under her thighs. Mel's uneasiness while staying with her while Swiss left the duplex only heightened her anxiety. She had no idea what was going on or why Ronacks members remained outside in the small yard. Probably to escort her out of town.

"My tires are slashed. I can't go anywhere," she said, hoping it was enough to keep her in Haugan.

Swiss frowned. "No use buying new ones until we catch whoever is after you."

"You're going to let me stay and continue to

help me?"

"Gia." Swiss sprawled his hands on the top of the table, framing a folded piece of paper. "Nothing has changed. You've still got people after you who want to hurt you, and I'll continue protecting you. But, we need to discuss a few things. I've got half a story, and you've got the other half. Somehow, we're both mixed in this shit together."

"Okay," she whispered.

She'd tell him anything. Everything. Keeping Bianca from him was never meant to hinder the plan to stop the men from coming after her.

He stood and walked over and picked up the picture of him and his daughter where she'd replaced it after he'd stormed out of the duplex. Returning to the table, he set it in front of her.

"Open the paper on the table and then tell me if you recognize the woman." Swiss sat back down, planted his elbows on the table, and clasped his hands.

She watched him carefully as she followed his request. He kept his eyes averted and on his hands.

Carefully, she smoothed the paper with her open hand and looked down. The close-up of the woman smiling back at her got her full attention. She exhaled her relief.

"Do you know her?" asked Swiss.

"Yes." She sagged forward and leaned against the table. "This is Bianca, the woman who helped me get to Montana and you. She works at the woman's shelter in Seattle."

Swiss opened up his hands and cradled his face. She reached across the table and cupped his hand. "She's not a bad person, Swiss. She helped me. I'd swear on my life she's not mixed in with the men after me. My co-worker—Trinity, one of the two that were murdered—was Bianca's best friend. The night I showed up, pounding on the shelter's front door, Bianca let me in. I told her everything. I had no idea that she was friends with Trinity. But there was an instant bond between us. She understood what I was going through, and she went above her job to help me get out of Seattle."

Swiss pushed away from the table. "I need a drink."

"I'll make you a coffee," she said, standing.

He shook his head and rummaged through the kitchen cabinet and retrieved a bottle of whiskey. Gia had heard him say that he'd like some booze in the past and when she'd offer to pour him a glass, he always refused. He had stated he wanted nothing to cloud his awareness while protecting her.

Swiss drank straight from the bottle, wiped his mouth with his arm, and looked at her. "Ronacks is outside. They'll stay until I tell them to leave."

She held up her hands. "I'm not questioning you. I just don't understand what you're thinking and what you're going through."

"Hell," he mumbled, putting the bottle to his lips again.

He screwed the top back on and set the bottle in the cabinet. His hand shook, and she stepped over and put her palms on his stomach.

Swiss stiffened. A lump of emotion choked her, seeing him obviously upset. His usual immovable stance on everything from the way he lived his life to how he enjoyed sex with her had her believing he was untouchable. But, something had touched him deeply.

"Talk to me," she whispered. "This isn't about me, Bianca, or my situation. Let me help you."

He cupped the back of her head and brought her to his pounding chest. She wrapped her arms around him and absorbed his trembles.

Swiss kissed the top of her head. That one, little sign of affection fortified her.

"I think Bianca...I think she's my daughter Heather," he whispered as if afraid to admit it to himself.

She pulled back, and Swiss held on tighter. "You don't know?" she asked.

She felt him shake his head. "I haven't seen her since she was four years old."

Her heart raced. She'd assumed he'd been a part of his daughter's life. Phone calls, pictures, and maybe his ex-wife lived in a different country or the other side of the United States, and visits were far and few between. The Swiss she knew, the man who honored his Motorcycle Club family, his loyalty to his country by serving in the Army, would never walk away from his child.

"Why not?" said Gia.

Swiss let her go and walked back to the table. Without looking, he turned over the adult picture of Bia—Heather.

Gia followed him and sat down, weakened from the news. A whole new allegation toward Bianca/Heather came to her. Had his daughter sent her to Swiss? Why?

Gia had no idea anymore. She'd believed and

put her faith behind Bianca helping her. Not only because she worked in a woman's shelter, but because she was personally connected to Trinity and had wanted justice served to the men who killed her.

"Why would she send me to you?" she asked.

Swiss sat down opposite of her and picked up the picture of his baby girl that he remembered. "I don't know what it means."

Gia bowed her head, overwhelmed with the direction the conversation was going and how it involved her. She pressed her lips together as the realization that Bianca wasn't Bianca and her interest in helping Gia, seeing that Trinity's murderers were arrested, might not have been in Gia's best interest. That she could've been played.

The trust between them broken, she jumped to the obvious conclusion. "Does your daughter hate you?"

Swiss exhaled heavily and fingered the scar below his eye. "If she listened to her mother growing up? Yes."

She stood from the table and paced. "What have I got myself into," she muttered.

Gia's situation wasn't a joking matter. There was a street gang after her and planned to kill her. Now Swiss's daughter was mixed up in everything.

She turned to Swiss. "Does your daughter belong to Yesler Street Gang? Did I just walk into a trap?"

"Don't know," said Swiss.

He stared down at the table, thumping his fist against the surface. She sat back down in the chair, grabbed his hand, and forced him to look at her.

"She's the only one who can give us answers. We could sit here all day and never know why she sent me here," she said. "We need to call her."

"You're here because you'll be safe with me."

She snorted. "You don't know that. I don't even know that anymore. Maybe I should get my tires fixed and take off where nobody knows where I am. Sh-she could've sent the killers here, Swiss. Have you thought about that?"

The scar below his eye deepened until it appeared as if he looked out of only one eye. "All I know is you're not going anywhere."

"But, if it isn't safe anymore, I can't stay," she whispered.

Swiss shook his head, cleared his throat, and pulled away from her. "I need a cigarette."

"Now?"

He headed toward the door. "Give me ten minutes, sweet, and then I'll tell you the rest of the story about my daughter. Maybe then, you can figure it out for me."

The door shut.

Gia stared at the empty room.

Swiss's abrupt turnaround scared her. She wasn't sure she wanted to know, or if learning more about Swiss's past would help. Dread settled over her. Not knowing what happened years ago to break up a family, she could only go off the information Swiss gave her and the absolute pain he was going through.

She flipped over the picture of the adult Heather and slid the picture frame of Swiss's daughter next to her daddy. She studied each face, side by side, and finally recognized Bianca in the face of the child.

His daughter had Swiss's eyes.

Chapter Thirty One

Battery and Rod stood in the front yard of the duplex. Swiss puffed on his cigarette, stomping out second guesses. If he told Gia some bullshit story to appease her, he'd have a chance at keeping her in his life.

He couldn't face watching her walk away. He couldn't lose another person he loved, and he *was* falling in love with Gia. He never had to admit it to himself or face his feelings, because he lived for each day.

She woke up in his bed, and that was good enough for him.

Every night, she cuddled against him, and that felt right.

He never let her situation put fear in him because he had no doubt he could keep her safe. Nobody could take her away as long as she needed him.

But the truth punched him in the throat, and fear gripped him when he was faced with losing Gia. The distress in her eyes and the unasked questions, judging him for being a man who walked away from his child.

He was afraid of losing her.

"If you could keep five or six brothers around the block, I'd appreciate it." Swiss rubbed out the lit coal on his thigh.

Battery dipped his chin. "We'll always have your back."

Swiss looked out at the men. His family. His

brothers. They meant more to him than anything.

He'd stood beside them against others. Fought, bled, killed.

In return, they never judged, questioned, or demanded anything from him except for his loyalty.

He'd die for them.

All through the years, he'd kept his secret, preferring to have a clean slate with Ronacks and leave the past behind him. Whether Gia stayed or left him, he'd still have Ronacks, but over the last twenty-four hours, he knew deep in his soul, Ronacks wasn't enough. Not anymore.

He wasn't getting any younger. Until Gia moved in, he'd walked through each day with nothing to look forward to but the next party, the next woman, the next situation to hit the club. Gia made him look forward to what made him happy. He faced the part of himself that he'd ignored for twenty-two years.

Battery reached into his pocket, removed his phone, and put the cell to his ear. "Yeah?"

Swiss turned away to go back inside, and Rod slapped his shoulder and motioned toward Battery, who held up a finger wanting everyone to stay.

"When?" Battery looked to Swiss. His gaze intensified. "Do. Not. Let him leave the bar. I'm on it."

Battery circled his finger in the air to the others. Every member of Ronacks Motorcycle Club moved to their bikes. Swiss looked to Rod. "I can't leave Gia."

Rod nodded. "You'll stay."

"No, we're on it. Lock the building down. I'll stay in touch." Battery shoved his phone in his pocket and pointed at Swiss. "That was Raelyn. Two men and a female in a navy colored sedan parked a block away from the bar. Sander spotted them and went inside the bar without tipping them off. He can see them from the office window, and it is *the* woman from the bar, and the car's front fender has a hell of a dent from Mel's motorcycle."

Swiss changed his mind, knowing Rod would protect Gia with his life. In return, he'd protect Gia by getting rid of the threat. "Can you—?"

"Go. I've got Gia covered. Take care of her business." Rod stepped backward toward the front door of the duplex.

Swiss strode out to the curb with Battery. "I want them."

"You got it," said Battery. "Enter on Third Street. They shouldn't see you coming. I'll hold the others off. You've got two minutes from the time I lose sight of you before we all move in."

Swiss slipped on his gloves and yelled over the roar of engines lining the street. "Wait two minutes, and then follow me. I want an escort out of town. I don't care where the fuck we go, but they're not leaving the territory alive."

He rode off. His adrenaline kicked high, and he tuned into everything around him. The slight pine scent in the air. The beeping of a garbage truck on the next block picking up the morning garbage cans at the curb. The noxious diesel smell left behind by an old school bus heading to the high school. He focused on the cars around him in case the men he was after tried to leave.

On Third Street, he spotted the sedan and

shifted into neutral to quiet the engine, and rolled to the curb with at least two hundred feet between him and the men he wanted. On foot, he removed his pistol and carried it close to his thigh. While the residents of Haugan understood Ronacks position within the territory, there were tourists who wouldn't view the situation the same way.

He navigated between four parked cars and self-talked over the voices in his head while he inhaled four seconds and exhaled four seconds to steady himself. Running over the worst case scenario of these men touching, hurting, killing Gia the way they had her coworkers in Seattle, he focused on every possible outcome of what they'd do when he had them within range.

The driver gazed out the front windshield. The male passenger looked out the side. The woman in the backseat sat with her head against the side window.

None of them watched behind the car.

He rounded the back fender on the left side, raised his gun, and opened the back door. He slid into the seat behind the driver. "Nobody move."

The woman beside him remained leaning against the window, her eyes closed. Swiss made eye contact with the driver through the rearview mirror as the passenger stared at the driver in fear.

"Raise your fucking hands, real slow, and put them on the steering wheel. One wrong move or you go for the weapon you're carrying, and I have no problem putting a bullet in the back of your fucking head," said Swiss, keeping his pistol steady.

The driver put his hands on the wheel. Swiss tensed. The man had a sparrows tattoo on his right hand.

"You, in the passenger seat, put your hands on the dash," he said, looking for a tattoo.

Motherfuckingbingo.

Two inked Sparrows proclaiming their loyalty to the Yesler Street Gang. Beside Swiss, the woman was still out cold.

In the distance, the low rumble of motorcycles filled the car. Swiss stuck the end of the pistol at the back of the driver's head.

"Who do you answer to?" he asked, gazing in the rearview mirror at the driver's face.

"No one." Sweat ran down the man's temples.

"Tell me another fucking lie. Are you claiming the job in Seattle when you took out two people at Loans by Day?" He watched the passenger flinch out of his peripheral vision at the mention of the name.

The men gave him silence as an answer. He leaned forward and lowered his voice. "I do believe we have some more things to discuss. In about sixty seconds, there will be some bikers rolling down the street. You're going to let them escort you out of town. I'll take you somewhere more private where you can piss your pants when you decide it's smarter to open your mouth."

Battery, LeWorth, and Grady rode alongside the car and stopped in the middle of the street at the end of the block. The other Ronacks had the other end of the street blocked. There was nowhere for the man to drive, except forward.

"Start the car and follow those riders." Swiss scooted back, kicked the back of the passenger's seat.

"You, put your fucking hands on the top of your head."

The car rolled forward away from the curb. Surrounded by his club, Swiss reached over to the unconscious woman beside him and put his index and middle finger over her carotid artery. Her pulse was slow. Damn. The woman was his ticket to finding out if he had the right people.

Going on Gia's theory behind the crime—which was good enough for him—he had the killers of the Seattle murders in his hands. But, the club would want more. He needed solid proof.

Battery led them all onto Interstate 90. Ten minutes out of town, the caravan escorting the Yesler Street Gang members took a now defunct rest-stop-only exit that stated it was closed. Swiss flexed his left hand. The outbuilding had been closed for at least two years. The grass overgrown, the asphalt parking lot was breaking up from neglect and full of pot holes.

There wasn't a car or person in sight at seven o'clock in the morning. Swiss gazed out the side window satisfied with the location. Unseen from the interstate, the closed rest area was the perfect place to conduct business.

"Pull over at the end of the lot," said Swiss.

The passenger glanced at the driver, shook his head. Swiss kicked the seat.

"Turn off the engine and set your keys above the visor." Swiss opened the door and left the vehicle.

Keeping his pistol trained on the driver, he motioned with the gun for them to step out of the vehicle. With over a dozen bikers surrounding the car, he wasn't worried about either one of them going for their weapons or running. They'd have a bullet in their chest before they could raise their arm.

Battery walked up to Swiss. "How's everything going?"

"Put them on the grass and have them wait." Swiss slid his pistol into the back of his jeans.

When the car was clear and the two men contained, Swiss returned to the car and rummaged through the woman's purse. Her driver's license, if it was real, stated she was twenty-five years old, and her name was Sue Dillon from Seattle, Washington. He dumped the contents of her purse on the seat and found two empty plastic sandwich baggies, a used syringe with heroin residue, and a dirty spoon.

At least he understood how the Yesler Gang worked. They used female addicts to do their dirty work. He squeezed between the two front seats, opened the glove box—nothing, and being careful in case there were any needles, he went through the side pockets on the front doors.

His fingers felt around a circular tube and pulled it out. He tapped down his anger. An empty lipstick container stained red on the inside. A perfect match to the color of the message written on Gia's car.

He extracted himself from the vehicle and removed his pistol. Walking toward the men laying on the grass, face first, he said, "Someone needs to dump the car and the unconscious woman in the backseat over the state line, and then put a call in with the location. The rest of you can get out of here."

"Swiss?" Battery stepped up beside him. "I

recognize the tats. The license plate is out of Washington. Are you running on gut?"

Swiss tossed the empty container of lipstick in the air.

Battery caught it, opened it up, and whistled low. "Everyone ride out. LeWorth, take the car. Choke, you follow, and give him a ride back to the clubhouse."

Swiss stepped closer to the men while Battery finished orders. He squatted down at their heads. Fear had already planted itself in them. The passenger had pissed his pants. The driver hyperventilated, laying soaked in sweat.

"You've got one chance to save your lives." He reached out, grabbed a handful of hair from the driver, and lifted his head. "I'll make it real simple. Yes or no? Did you kill two people in Seattle at Loans by Day and plan on taking out the woman living with me?"

When the man refused to answer, Swiss shoved the pistol under the man's chin. "You've got three seconds, or you're a dead man."

The man grunted. "Fuck you."

Swiss backhanded him with the butt of the pistol. "Yes or no?"

"Yes," said the man with a grunt.

He kept tension on the trigger of his gun, sighed over the knowledge that he had the right men, and let the man's head fall forward to the ground. Swiss looked at Battery, who nodded. He had everything he needed.

Swiss lowered his voice. "In a few minutes, I'm going to put a hole in the back of your head. It's not going to do either of you any good to talk, so listen closely. You've come after my woman, and that's enough for me to bury you. But, if I find out you've touched my daughter, I swear to the motherfucking devil that I will take out every single member of Sparrows and kill them. Your crimes will fall back on them."

The air around Swiss quieted. One man prayed. He stood and backed away ten steps. Aware of Battery standing beside his motorcycle out of fire range, covering Swiss's back, loyal to the death, Swiss pulled the trigger and shot the driver. Before the passenger could move, he pulled the trigger again, taking him out.

His hand squeezed the grip as he waited for any sign of life. He inhaled four seconds and exhaled four seconds. He settled. Glad for the training he'd received in the Army.

He put his pistol away, took out his smokes, lit a cigarette, and walked over to Battery. His president watched him carefully, and he nodded to let him know he was fine. The job was done.

"Gia's safe," said Swiss.

"Unmarked pistol. No witnesses. Two men tagged as Sparrows. I think we can save our energy and leave them laying in the grass. We can let the state patrol do their job." Battery stroked his beard. "Looks like you're riding back to Haugan behind me."

"Fuck," muttered Swiss. "At least drop me off at my bike. I'll ride my Harley back to the duplex."

Battery grinned as he straddled his motorcycle. "Just watch your hands. Bree gets jealous."

Swiss eyed the sissy bar at the back of the seat. "When in the hell did you put that on?"

"Shut the fuck up and get on."

"Jesus…" Swiss lifted his leg and squeezed between Battery and the backrest. "Scoot up."

"I am."

His legs wouldn't bend far enough to use the pegs, and he strained to keep his boots off the ground. He kept his gaze on the dead men as Battery rode out and waited for a break in traffic before getting on I-90. The situation with Gia wasn't over by a long shot, and the worst case scenario played in his head, preparing him.

Chapter Thirty Two

Swiss sat on the couch beside Gia. She held his hand. By the time he came back to the duplex, talked to Rod outside, took a shower, and returned to her with his hair still damp and smelling good, insecurities she had no idea she owned hit her hard until her stomach threatened to revolt.

"Rod wouldn't tell me where everyone went and when you came back, you sent everyone home." She brought his hand to her chest and held on to him tightly trying to understand how everything changed from the time he left and the time he came home. "Even Mel left."

"It's over, sweet." He let his head fall to the back of the couch and turned his gaze to her. "When I was outside cooling off, a call came in. One of my MC brothers spotted the vehicle and the men not far from Pine Bar and Grill. I took care of the problem and now you don't have to worry about anything, anymore, and you're safe. They won't be bothering you again. They're gone."

"Gone?" She pressed his hand against her cheek, afraid to believe he was telling her the truth. "Gone, as in back to Seattle?"

He wiggled his hand free, put his arm around her, and tucked her against his bare chest. "I took care of them. They can't and won't threaten or hurt you or go after anyone you know again. Ronacks made sure that everything ended."

"What's that mean?" She angled her head to look at his face and panic caused her voice to grow higher. "Are they dead? Did you kill them?"

"Do you trust me?" He spoke calmly. There was no anger or tension coming from him.

She nodded.

"They're gone, sweet. There is no chance of you seeing them or being the subject of their threats every again. Let's leave it at that." Swiss cupped the back of her head.

"Oh my, God, Swiss. What have you done?" Her heart raced. "Do the police know?"

His silence destroyed her.

"I never asked you to kill them," she whispered. "I never thought…"

"Gia." Swiss held her firmly. "The men were from the Yesler Street Gang and admitted their role in killing your co-workers and coming after you. These are not normal men."

"But, you could get arrested," she said.

His gaze burned hot. In that second, she understood how Ronacks Motorcycle Club worked. Whatever he'd done, whatever happened, he'd regained the confidence, his rock status he'd lost when he found out Bianca was his daughter Heather. He held up his promise of protecting her.

"What Ronacks does when trouble hits someone we're protecting and what I do when I promise someone protection is dealt with through the club. The club doesn't discuss business with anyone, including you. All you need to know is it's over."

"God, Swiss." She swallowed hard. "This isn't real."

"It's real."

She looked up at him. "It's over?"

He nodded. "You're safe. Nobody is ever going to hurt you."

She closed her eyes, letting everything sink in. It was too soon. She was disgusted and yet relieved. She wasn't sure how she was supposed to feel.

"There are some things about my past that I need to talk to you about." Swiss cleared his throat.

She opened her eyes and whispered, "Heather?"

All morning while Swiss was gone, she'd had time to think about Bianca lying to her about her name and her relationship with Swiss. The hurt Bianca or Heather, whatever she wanted to call herself, caused Gia couldn't compare to what Swiss was going through. She failed to understand the depth of his pain. It was as if Swiss had wanted his daughter out of his life.

"I married young. Too young." Swiss stroked Gia's cheek with his thumb. "Anita, my ex-wife, was fresh out of high school. She had big dreams for herself, and those dreams included me. I was more than happy to make her smile, and I think I did when she found out she was pregnant."

Her chest constricted. Drawing air into her lungs hurt, and she held her breath until she couldn't any longer and then, she held on to his words.

"Around here, jobs were…are few and far between, especially for a young couple with a baby on the way. Once Heather was born, we struggled like most couples do when money is tight and things are stressful in the home with a new baby that equally captivated us and frightened us at the same time. After two years of marriage, I could see that our whole relationship was about fighting and making up. There wasn't much middle ground. I decided to do what I could to make our marriage better. So, I followed my big brother's footsteps and joined the Army. I could see how my brother had gone into the service, and he'd came back to Haugan smarter, more mature, and he had a reliable income he could count on. The day I joined was one of the best days of my life, and I expected Anita to be happy for us."

Gia studied Swiss preparing herself for heartbreak. "She wasn't proud of you?"

"No." Swiss's cheek twitched. "After boot camp, I was stationed at Fort Lewis in Washington and came home to Haugan every weekend to spend with Anita and Heather, plus I had the last week of every month free to be with them. Compared to every male civilian in Haugan, I was home more with my family, even being stationed over in Washington. I thought it was enough considering we finally had some money to live on and no worries when Heather needed to see the doctor, because for the first time in our life together, we had insurance. After a year in the Army, we'd been married three years by that time. I could tell things weren't good between us. She'd find excuses to stay away from the duplex when I was home, leaving me with Heather. I thought if I gave her space and time, prove to her that I was going to be a good husband and father, she'd come around."

He fell silent. Gia kissed his chest. Having never been married, she couldn't imagine the disappointment of loving someone who distanced themselves.

Swiss cleared his throat. "On Heather's fourth

birthday, Anita invited a bunch of people here, and I overheard one of her friends talking about how she's playing me over, and she couldn't believe that I had no clue that my wife was sleeping with my brother."

Gia raised her head and sat up beside him. Caught up in his story, Swiss wasn't aware that he'd dropped his hand from her head.

"I waited until the party was over and everyone went home, and Heather was asleep before confronting Anita about having an affair with Brad." He leaned forward and braced his elbows on his knees. "She owned right up to cheating on me, and I was angry."

"Of course, you were. Anyone would be," she said softly, but Swiss never acknowledged her.

"I had to get out of the duplex. The anger I felt over knowing my wife was fucking around and with my brother of all people…I'd never felt anything like it. I went looking for Brad and found him at his house. We got into a scuffle." Swiss rubbed his hands over his face. "Somehow—and I play that day through my head all the time, and I can't remember who picked up the pistol first."

She gasped and covered her mouth.

He glanced at her. "I had a concealed weapons permit and always carried to protect my family. All I can guess is the weapon came off me in the fight with my brother, and I got shot."

"Your brother shot you?" Gia wrapped her arm across his stomach. She'd known his scar came from a gunshot wound, and she'd assumed it happened in the Army.

"I was unconscious at the hospital for two

days while they dug the bullet out and kept me medicated. The lead lodged in my sinuses and shattered my cheekbone." Swiss lowered his head. "When I did wake up, Anita was in the hospital room with Heather, telling me she wanted a divorce. I told her I wouldn't give her one, and she said she was moving in with Brad, taking Heather, and had already told her lawyer and the police that I had pulled the gun on my brother, and while my brother was trying to remove the weapon, I was shot. She stated that I was a danger to our child. She said she was signing a restraining order against me as soon as she left the hospital. I begged her to wait until I got out of the hospital before she signed anything. I'm not sure why or even what I thought I could do. In my frame of mind, I wasn't even sure what the fuck I wanted from her."

Gia leaned her head against his arm. Everything she knew about Swiss and going from her instincts, she'd never believe that he would be a danger to his child or any woman he loved.

"Next thing I know, I was slapped with a civilian restraining order while still in the hospital, and that was enough for the judge to give sole custody to Anita. With my background in the Army and having weapons at my disposal, I was high risk." He paused and blew out his breath. "I sat in court when my wife divorced me and watched my life get stripped away by legal statements, and nobody gave a damn about me losing my daughter. The only thing I had left was my career in the Army. I was already on shaky ground because of the charges, but the Army was the only thing that held me together. Anita got her divorce. I went back and finished another year in the Army before I could leave. I never saw my daughter again."

Gia's thoughts overwhelmed her. "How long did she leave the restraining order on you?"

"I checked every year until Heather was ten years old, hoping she'd forget to go in and sign another one, and she never forgot. After that, I gave up. Heather was growing up and wouldn't even know me. Besides the affair, what did I have on them? Anita was a good mom. Being a bad wife wasn't a crime. She loved Heather. My brother…he loved Anita and obviously made her happy if she stayed with him. When Heather was in her teens, I found out my brother had passed away when the Sergeant my brother and I both had in the Army sent me a condolence card with a hundred-dollar contribution to cancer research."

"What about your parents? Couldn't they help you get even supervised visitations with your daughter?"

He shook his head. "Once I got shot and lost my family, my parents wanted nothing to do with me. Brad was the first born son, their golden boy. They passed away a few years after the divorce. Dad of old age. Mom of congested heart failure. I stayed away from the funerals because I knew Brad would be there, and I was unable to be close or talk to Anita because of the restraining order."

"Even after your brother died, you never tried to contact Anita or your daughter?"

Swiss stood and shoved his hands in the pocket of his jeans. "No."

"But, she's your daughter." Gia heart twisted, and she pressed her hands to her chest. "She needs to know the truth about why you weren't part of her life."

"Why? As a teenager, Heather had already gone through enough shit. Her parents were divorced. My brother, the one man Heather thought of as a father and got to raise her, had died. Heather probably grew up hearing how I pulled a gun on Brad and ended up getting shot myself. To top it off, what was I supposed to tell her? That I was proud of being a member of Ronacks Motorcycle Club, that I live off splitting a pot of monthly wages for doing security work? That I don't always follow the law and the patch I wear profiles me as a questionable character anywhere outside of Haugan?" Swiss slapped his chest. "Look at me. One look at the scar on my face would remind her of how my anger ruined my chances at being a father to her. She'd be scared of me."

Gia stood and shook her head. "Oh, Swiss. No. She'd never think that."

"Yes, she would." His voice deepened, and he continued. "It's the truth. She had a better life with her mom, with Brad."

Gia went to him. He stiffened, and she ignored his nature to pull away from her and wrapped her arms around his waist and peered up at him.

"Listen to me. I'm looking at your face." She licked the stray tear that ran over her lip. "I see a man who has been unfairly judged."

"Don't say it," he whispered on a croak.

"I see a man that I'm falling in love with and

he hurts because he's hurt for too long." She blinked to clear her vision. "I see a man who loved his daughter more than he loved himself and only wanted the best for her. I see a man who was scared of losing his family, who almost died fighting for them. I see a man who had no reason to protect me and did without any thought to himself. I see a man too strong for his own good. Too proud to admit he hurts. Too loving to admit that he needs more than sex in his life."

His chin came down, and he pressed his lips against her forehead. "You fucking scare me, Gia."

His confession meant more than his decision to share his past with her or his chivalrous attitude toward her since arriving in Montana or the sweet way he held her close at night after they'd had sex. Swiss was not a man to show weakness.

An expert at hiding his feelings and consciously taking responsibility where it wasn't due, he gave her the weakest part of him and trusted her to take care not to hurt him.

She swore on her life, right then, right there, that whatever happened in the next twenty-four hours and what had happened to both of them in the past, what he'd done for her to make her safe, would never be forgotten or used to hurt him.

Even though he promised her that she was safe and her troubles were over, he continued to protect her from the truth. In her heart, she understood what he wasn't saying. The Sparrows members who were after her were dead.

For him, she wouldn't question him more. For his loyalty to his club, she would respect his wishes.

For her, she understood and accepted that the

only way for Swiss to save her was to kill the killers. She was safe.

He'd opened up and let her into his life. A life he'd hidden for too long.

Slipping her hands up his chest, she stopped when she reached his face and held his head. Her thumb stroked the scar she would always view as bravery. "Let me make love to you."

Swiss closed his eyes an extra beat. She understood what asking him meant. He always took control and made sure she ended up satisfied—more than satisfied— before they fell asleep. She wanted to comfort him and make him feel loved.

He opened his eyes and kissed her gently for an answer. She slipped her hand into his and led him to the bedroom.

Chapter Thirty Three

Gia pushed Swiss's jeans down over his hips. He had no plans to let her make love to him. That was his job and one he wasn't giving up because she'd spoken about loving him.

Fuck, she loved him.

His chest warmed.

Even after hearing about his past, she stuck by him and believed his intentions and not the results. No questions, only pure strength as if she could see inside his head and feel inside his heart.

Gia stood, inhaled deeply and crossed her arms in front of her, lifting the hem of her shirt over her head. She shook her head, spreading her hair over her bare shoulders, and his balls tightened. Then, she wiggled out of her jeans, adding more enthusiasm into her moves with a smile of temptation that left him dealing with the need to take control.

"You're enjoying yourself," he mumbled.

She laughed softly. "Oh, yeah. I figure I have about two more minutes before I lose my position as the seductress and become the seduced."

"Damn right, if that means I'm going to fuck you." He walked her backward to the bed.

Gia bumped into the mattress, then scooted on her ass to the middle of the bed, unabashed and open to him. He grabbed a condom and kneed the bed, hovering over her. She laid her hand on his chest. His heart thumped hard against her palm and ricocheted back to him, and that power was nothing compared to the blood pulsing in his cock wanting inside of her.

He lowered his head and kissed her, dipping his tongue in her mouth and stroking. He never tired of her warmth, her taste, her eagerness.

Pulling back, he gazed down at her. She aimed her aroused look at him. He wanted to be the only person who ever got to see her with her emotions written all over her face and in her touch.

"Gia?" He closed his mouth, humbled over how close they'd grown and her level of trust.

She rubbed his sides. "What is it?"

"You're falling in love with me." He settled between her legs and lowered his upper body, bracing on his elbows. The words meant everything to him, and he had to keep repeating them in his head to believe she could see past all his mistakes.

"I am," she whispered. "Deeply."

He smoothed her hair off her forehead. Her devotion knocked him on his ass, and a possessive need to keep her in his life swept through him. "There's no way I'm letting you leave Haugan."

Her eyes softened. "Is that your way of telling me you feel the same way about me?"

He grunted in agreement.

She smiled in reply.

He reached back for the condom, went up on his knees, and rolled the protection on his hard cock. She understood him and accepted him.

His woman.

His girl.

His Gia.

Ownership felt good, and his body pulsed in pleasure. Gia had pushed her way into his life and ended up cooking for him. Hell, no. He wasn't letting her get away.

He pressed his cock against her pussy without going in, letting her heat wash over and caress him. Her hands trailed down his arms, and he linked his hands with hers, pinning her to the mattress.

Her breasts squished against his lower chest, and she trembled in anticipation. The ultimate thrill she got over being fucked by him always took him by surprise. He inhaled deeply to slow himself down. He could smell her arousal and feel the shudders rolling through her, and he wasn't even inside of her yet.

Skin to skin, he influenced every reaction, and in return, she had him bent in all different directions. He couldn't get close enough. The need to be inside her, be a part of her, was too much for him to go slow. He thrust into her with one plunge.

Gia arched her back at the sudden fullness. He held still and groaned as her pussy clenched around him, squeezing tight, stroking the length of him. And, damned if a chill hadn't swept over his skin and his balls warmed.

He tasted her, using his tongue, his lips, before pulling his mouth away and kissing her neck. "Hold on, sweet."

He pushed up using his hands. The pink marks along her neck pleased him. He wanted everyone to know, she belonged to him.

He withdrew, plunged, and stroked her with his cock. Slow and warm, until she closed her eyes and arched her neck to give him more room.

Wanting to touch more of her, he braced his weight on one arm and moved his hand down the side of her breast. His light touch hardened her nipple, and he licked his bottom lip. He could no longer tell who was turning who on more.

He cupped the back of her knee and brought it up to his shoulder, opening her wider and slipped his hand between their bodies without missing a stroke with his cock. He found her clit and circled the small nub with his finger.

She gasped and pulled her legs down closer to her chest, pressing her ass up against him.

He slid his cock in and out in determined and yet irregular sweeps. Any faster and he'd lose control.

Her breasts swayed with the movements.

Her wetness spread all over his fingers.

His dick powered by greed left him curling his toes as he dug his feet into the blanket at the end of the bed, aiding his need to be fully inside of her.

Gia reached for him, and he lowered his head and captured her mouth. His tongue mimicked the rhythm of his body as he fucked her.

Her hips came up, faster, urging and begging him for harder. He always believed he was in control, but damned if she wasn't a bossy woman in bed, demanding what she wanted and letting him know what to do. Her passion surpassed anything he'd ever experienced, and he'd become addicted to her. Morning, afternoon, night, it never mattered. His dick wasn't picky. His mind was obsessed.

She lowered her legs from his shoulders. He moved his arms wanting to feel her around him. She rubbed the inside of her thighs against his hips. Her urgency to orgasm grew and tightened around his body. He plunged harder, faster. In. Out. In. Out.

His jaw dropped open on a gasp of breath, and

he grunted with each stroke, pounding into her, moving her up on the bed with his demanding movements. His head roared. So close. So fucking close.

Her breasts squeezed together. Her nipples skimmed his chest, and his ass tightened.

"Come on, sweet," he said with a growl

"Yes. Yes." Her neck arched and her legs tightened around him, drawing him in more. He couldn't take anymore, and when her release hit her fast and hard, washing through her body, he exploded.

The pressure in his balls released, flooding his body with pleasure. His muscles seized. Unable to stop, his hips pumped fitfully as if his dick was happy to be home, buried forever in her.

He shuddered.

Jolt after jolt, proclaiming his territory. She was his.

The tension in Gia's muscles gave way to softness, and she let her legs widen and relax on the bed. He lowered his head and rested against her neck until he grew heavy on top of her and rolled to the side. He held her tight until he had to finally leave her body and rid himself of the condom.

Using one of his shirts to wipe himself clean, he then returned to bed and held her longer.

She snuggled onto his chest with a sleepy sigh. He cupped her hip possessively. With her problems with Sparrows settled and behind her now, he should be able to get some sleep.

But, he was wide awake.

For the first time in over twenty-two years, he

couldn't beat back his need to see his daughter. What made her send Gia to him? Was Heather okay?

Questions he once refused to ask because it hurt too fucking much to think about came flooding back and opened up old hurts.

Chapter Thirty Four

Monday morning, Swiss kissed Gia goodbye as he walked out the door headed to Watkin's Repo and Towing. She stood in the doorway and watched him start the Harley— no doubt waking everyone on the street— and ride away. It was the first time since she'd moved in with Swiss that she'd be spending the day alone.

After an emotional weekend, she needed the time to accept and understand the many changes that had come over her life, not only running to Haugan but to realize what she'd gone through at work and accepting she'd lost two people she thought of as friends and never had a chance to mourn them. She walked back into the duplex and locked the door. Even now, she had a hard time understanding how she had ever taken each day for granted.

It was normal for her to fall into her routine.

She woke up every morning at six o'clock.

She went to work from eight to five and had an hour for lunch when she liked to walk with her Fitbit on her wrist.

She spent eight hours with her coworkers and generally enjoyed their conversations when business slowed in the office.

Most evenings, she'd go home to do laundry, clean, watch her latest Netflix obsession. Occasionally, she dated on Friday and Saturday night. Her bills were paid once a month. She shopped on Sunday mornings when the store was less crowded. Life definitely had a good versus bad vibe, and she let a lot of things go, letting karma play the role of her best friend.

Before the murders in Seattle, her biggest worry had been if she'd ever find someone she could love for the rest of her life.

During that time, if someone had asked her if she believed her life was full, she would've agreed. She was content. Happy.

She sat down on the stool at the kitchen counter. Now, she had no idea what was happening in her life, and yet she was more excited over her feelings toward Swiss and having them returned the euphoria left her intoxicated. Then, the next minute, guilt grabbed hold of her. Why had she lived and Trinity and Sean had not? Were her co-workers' innocent or involved in the Ponzi scheme?

What would've happened if she never ran to the woman's shelter and met who she believed was Bianca? What if she had never came to Montana and found Swiss?

She swiveled on the seat. Swiss had taken care of her and in return probably killed the men who had murdered her coworkers and she couldn't bring up an ounce of fear or regret for the loss of their lives. The police had taken a passive-aggressive stance from the beginning.

Life went on, and she had no idea what was expected of her.

The phone Swiss gave her sat on the counter mocking her. Never letting her forget there was one important person in the middle of everything which had changed her life—saved her life. Had Heather used her in a game against Swiss or genuinely believed she'd be safe in Haugan?

She picked up the phone. Having already talked to Swiss about her calling his daughter, she'd respected his stance that it was up to her if she wanted to make contact and since Heather already knew she was with Swiss, there was no problem with letting Heather know that she was aware of her non-existent relationship with her dad.

Swiss claimed he wasn't ready for any type of conversation and needed more time to understand how Heather became the one to send Gia to him. Yet, he assured Gia that she was free to call and reach out to Heather if that was what she needed.

She suspected Swiss's reluctance came from wanting to dig into Heather's past and find out how his ex-wife played into the situation before making any contact with his daughter. In some ways, she understood his reasoning.

His ex-wife ruined Swiss's life, and almost got him killed.

Gia rested her head against her upturned hand. She feared losing Swiss to the unknown and the ghosts that plagued him from the past. Their relationship was new and so far, abnormal, she wondered how they'd both survive.

Swiss had lived most of his life, protecting himself and alone. She needed to be loved.

But she couldn't let her fears stop her. Swiss had shown her that.

She tapped out the phone number for Heather with her heart racing and her stomach protesting, urging her to wait, to hide, to ignore the truth.

The phone rang in her ear.

After the third ring, Heather answered, "Hello?"

"It's me, Gia." Her voice shook.

"I'm so glad you called. How are you? Are you safe?"

Gia inhaled deeply. "It's over."

"Over?"

"The men are gone." Gia looked around the room in the duplex. "I'm free to go wherever I want without any worries now."

"The killers are locked up?"

"I don't know the whole story, but Swiss has assured me that there is no more danger for me. I'm safe."

"Oh, Gia." Heather's exhale of relief came over the cell. "I knew sending you to Montana would be the best choice. You're safe, and Trinity's killers were brought to justice."

Gia rubbed her forehead. Heather took her explanation that it was over without questioning every single detail. A concerned friend would want to know exactly what happened and where the killers were and how long they'd be locked up in prison because that was how the world worked.

"Yeah, it's great news," Gia whispered.

"Are you coming back to Seattle?" Heather paused. "I'd like to see you and talk about what you've been going through and be here if you need support."

"I, um..." Gia grimaced.

She couldn't do it.

Protective of the man she loved, she swallowed hard. It wasn't her place to step in between

Swiss and his daughter. Whatever the reasons behind Heather sending her to Seattle would come out later if Swiss and Heather decided to reconnect.

"I'm not sure." Gia turned on the stool and gazed at the picture of Heather as a child with her dad. "I might see what kind of jobs are open around here and start over fresh. I don't think I could go back to my condominium and feel safe again."

"I understand."

"I better let you go, but I wanted to update you on everything and tell you how much I appreciate your help." Gia slid off the stood and stood. "All your support and understanding helped to keep me safe, and…thank you, Bianca."

She couldn't call her Heather. She loved Swiss and would step back from the situation. She couldn't pick sides.

"No thanks are needed. It's my job." Heather paused. "Please, keep in touch, Gia."

"I will," she whispered. "Bye."

Gia disconnected the call, walked over to the couch, and sat down. Pulling her legs up, she hugged her knees and stared across the room until everything blurred and the first tear rolled down her cheek unchecked.

Her stomach seized into a tight ball. She rocked, pushing away the hollowness building inside of her, telling her life with Swiss would be impossible.

The amount of stress she'd lived through, the loss of her friends, her heart overfull of love, she couldn't hold any of it in anymore. She cried out, swallowing down her sob at the knowledge of what

Swiss had struggled through on his own. His family ostracizing him and turning their backs to the situation when he needed them most. His wife tearing his family apart. His little girl waving goodbye, never knowing that would be the last time she experienced Swiss's large hand holding hers and she'd never have his big chest to soften all of the big and little hurts life would throw at her.

She curled into a ball and cried for herself because her future teetered off-balance, and she only wanted someone to hold her and tell her everything would be okay.

Chapter Thirty Five

Heavy Metal music blared inside the clubhouse. Swiss leaned against the wall and held Gia in front of him, his arm hooked around her waist while holding a whiskey bottle in his free hand. He'd only drank half the bottle but damn was it a long time coming.

Once he had Gia safe, he'd put in an uneventful five-day work week. He'd almost wished for something to happen and distract him from what he'd put off all week.

But, he'd survived.

It was Saturday night.

He had his buzz on, his woman in his arms, and his club around him.

He fucking deserved to drink.

Gia shifted and gazed over her shoulder at him, smiled, and said, "Thanks for paying for the moving company to box up my things and bring them to Haugan."

She'd already thanked him twice. He gave her no choice. Either she let him take her back to Seattle to gather her belongings, or he'd pay someone else to bring them to her. No fucking way was he letting her travel alone in her piece of shit car or leave his side.

He held the bottle up to her mouth. "Drink up."

She laughed and his balls tightened. In the last week, she'd loosened up. Smiled more. Laughed more. And, challenged him in ways he could appreciate.

Her eyes lit up in amusement. "Doesn't

Ronacks believe in mixing their drinks?"

"That's weak, sweet." He placed the mouth of the bottle against her lower lip, teasing her.

Instead of taking the bottle from him, she dipped her knees, opened her mouth, and let him pour a shot of whiskey over her tongue. Her eyes rounded as the liquid hit the back of her throat. His cock hardened. She swallowed, and damned if he wanted to toss the bottle and take Gia home.

He captured her mouth, dipping his tongue. Drunk on her, he walked her backward without stopping the kiss. His hard-on leading the way.

Gia wound her arms around his neck, bumping her breasts against him with each clumsy step. He pulled his mouth off her, took another drink, and walked her down the hallway.

She slipped her fingers under his belt and held on. "Where are you taking me?"

"The room in the back. Gonna fuck you hard. Then, you're gonna fuck me slow." He licked his lips and aimed for her mouth.

Her feet found ground, and she pushed against him. "No way."

He stopped. "Huh?"

"Swiss, honey. Baby." She shook her head. "Whew. You can't really expect me to go there."

"You want me." He cupped her ass, pulling her to the front of him and showing her proof he wanted her, too.

"I do." Her laughter fell away, and her eyes sobered up. "When I first came to the clubhouse, a woman mentioned the backroom. What *happens* in the backroom, and while I respect all the Ronacks members, I'm not going to lay on a bed that has seen more traffic than Main Street in Haugan."

"Picky?"

She laughed loudly. "Oh, yeah."

He chuckled. "I'll take you home."

"Good idea." She patted his chest. "Except, I'm driving."

He'd brought the Mercedes with that plan in mind. He lifted the bottle, guzzled, and looped his arm around his woman's shoulders. "Take me home, sweet."

He walked her into the main room of the clubhouse and Raelyn stopped their exit. Swiss thrust the bottle forward. "Drink up, Rae. Everyone's celebrating."

"Hey there, yourself." Raelyn took the bottle, smirked at Swiss, and then turned her attention on Gia. "I heard the awesome news. You're staying with Swiss."

"Thanks." Gia curled against Swiss's side and put her hand on his stomach. "I couldn't be happier."

"Well, bottle that joy, girlfriend, because I've got a proposition for you." Raelyn put her hands on her hips and grinned. "Come to work at Pine Bar and Grill. Swiss can explain the Ronacks roster to you and the wage tier they use. You'll be employed by the club, but working for me. The tips you earn will be yours to keep."

"Raelyn, that's awfully nice of you to offer, but I've never worked at a bar or around drinks and food." Gia lowered her voice. "I'd fail, big time. But, I appreciate you asking. That means so—"

"No, no, no..." Raelyn shook her head.

"Unless you're an idiot, you'll learn how to carry drinks and set a plate in front of a customer. You're gorgeous and a clean freak, and that's all you need to succeed at the bar. If you like it, stay on. If not, you can go get a different job. No worries."

During the conversation, Swiss remained quiet and yet he knew Gia worried about money and finding a job in Haugan. Though he hated the thought of other men appreciating what he had at home, Gia could do anything she put her heart into and then some.

"Try it out. I work in town and can take my lunch at the bar." Swiss kissed the top of Gia's head. "Now, tell Raelyn yes, and let's go home."

"So, is that a yes?" Raelyn tilted her head and grinned.

Gia reached out with one arm and hugged Raelyn. "When do you want me?"

"Monday. I'll start you off slowly." Raelyn bounced on her toes. "This will be great. We're losing a couple of girls next month who are going off to college. I needed you."

"Okay, the deal's done. Let's go home." Swiss pulled Gia to the side.

Raelyn slapped Swiss's arm. "What's your hurry?"

Swiss opened his mouth. "I want to F—"

Gia dragged him away from the conversation on a laugh and pulled him outside. She stopped him at the sight of Mel kneeled down beside his mangled motorcycle. He studied the kid, intent on straightening the forks.

"I feel so bad for him. If it weren't for me, he'd

still have a bike to ride," whispered Gia.

Swiss let go of Gia and walked over to Mel. Compared to last week, the bike looked better, but it was a long way from becoming rideable again.

Mel caught sight of him and lifted his chin. Swiss lit a cigarette and strolled around the Harley. An older model that the kid had taken care of before the hit and run.

"Where'd you get the bike?" asked Swiss.

"Uh…" Mel stood, wiped his hands on his jeans, and then hooked his thumbs in his pockets. "It was my dad's motorcycle."

"Is he around?"

Mel looked Swiss in the eyes. "He died when I was fourteen. My mom got remarried a couple of years later to an asshole who sold all my dad's stuff and moved my mom to California. I took the bike before he could get his hands on it and rode back to Haugan."

Fuck. Swiss whistled. Mel had been a sixteen-year-old kid bent on keeping his dad's memory alive and set out on his own. He'd paid his time prospecting for Ronacks, and ended up coming out half-way decent.

"Have LeWorth load the Harley up in the trailer and bring it to my place tomorrow night. And, make sure you bring that set of balls it took to keep your dad alive in here." He tapped his head with his finger. "You'd do him proud becoming a lifer."

Mel lifted his chin. "Yes, sir."

Swiss turned around and mumbled, "Knock that sir shit off, kid."

"I will." Mel's voice grew deeper behind him.

"Swiss."

Swiss joined Gia at the Mercedes and handed her the keys. She smiled crazily up at him without saying a word, and he hooked his finger at the top of her shirt and pulled her forward. "Why are you looking at me like that?"

"You're an amazing person." She kissed him, humming in anticipation, and then broke away from him. "Hurry and get in the car. We're going home."

Finally.

He rounded the car and slid into the passenger seat. He hoped like hell she could drive fast.

Chapter Thirty Six

Swiss's cock, hard and waiting, stood up for Gia. She trailed her finger over the warm, smooth length, wrapping her fingers around the thickness. Swiss sucked in his breath. She lifted her gaze at the sound without letting go of him.

"What you did back at the clubhouse for Mel was a good thing, honey," she whispered.

His intense gaze was his answer. "A condom is a good thing."

"I'm serious." She let go of him, retrieved protection off the top of the dresser, and handed it to him.

"I'm serious, too." He opened the foil package.

She took off her Tee. "I overheard Mel talking about what happened with his dad and taking off to come back to Haugan. He was so young, and he's grown up a lot since his dad died. I mean, he's what…twenty-four or twenty-five years old now. He practically raised himself during the years his dad would've taught him how to be a man if he was alive."

"Sweet, I'm not feeling like talking about Mel. You feel like talking, let's talk about fucking." He ogled her breasts overflowing her bra as she leaned forward to remove her jeans.

"Okay, okay," she said, removing her bra and panties. "But, one more thing. Mel looks up to you."

"He what?" he mumbled.

"He respects you and listens." She nodded. "I know I don't have a say in what Ronacks does as a club, and I'm an outsider, but I think you should seriously think about letting Mel wear a Ronacks patch."

"You do, huh?" he said, rolling on the condom.

She moved closer and placed her hands on his chest. "Yeah, I like him."

He lowered his head and kissed her lips softly. "You're right. You have no say in club business, but I hear you, and since I'm done listening to you, it's time to fuck."

Her stomach fluttered, and she walked with him to the bed.

He stretched out to his full height beside her and laid his hand on her bare hip. "Gia?"

"Yes?"

"Never stop talking to me," he said.

She gazed into his eyes, melting. Because Swiss, despite his gruff ways, his often one track mind, he actually listened to every word she said. He might not always agree but he took everything into consideration, and she trusted him to know what was best for both of them.

He lowered his mouth, wrapping his arms around her and rolling to his back. She straddled his hips while caressing his tongue with hers. His hardness settled between her legs. She couldn't move because he was giving her the control.

She pressed her hips toward him. His cock slid between her legs. Warmth flooded her sex. Pleasure came with each thrust of her pelvis, and she continued rocking.

Swiss held her hips, moving her against him.

She lowered her head. The closer she got to his body, the more she wanted.

"Damn sexy, sweet, sitting on me, looking at me, feeling me." He brushed his mouth below her ear.

Her spine tingled at the touch of his breath against her neck. Then his tongue was on her skin. She threw her head back giving him more access. He licked in languid swipes against the sensitive spot, sending wave after wave of pleasure to her core. Her legs and arms trembled. She pressed herself against his hardness.

He lifted her up. She arched, lining up his cock and plunged down on him at the same time he thrust his hips off the bed. A moan of happiness bubbled out of her. His vulnerable position allowed her to take every exciting inch of him, and she braced herself against his chest as she adjusted to having him inside of her.

"Tight, sweet," he whispered.

She sighed. "Mm-hm."

His hands spanned her hips, lifting her. She sprawled her fingers on his chest and rose, and then let herself ease down on him. Her eyelids fought to close and yet, she wanted to watch him. To see the moment he came.

"Lean down," he said.

She moved her hands to the bed, one on each side of his head. He lifted his mouth, his tongue swiping her hard nipple. Her hips rose and fell on their own, taking up a natural rhythm and going with what felt good for her. He sucked on her breast. Her sex spasmed, and her body tightened.

His ass came off the bed, meeting her moves.

She rocked back and forth. The wild sensations swirled in her body, and she moved, catering to the deep pulse inside of her screaming for more.

Swiss removed his mouth from her nipple and flipped her over onto her back. She stared up into his face, gasping in shock at finding herself underneath him.

His rough, possessive dominance of needing to be the one in control turned her on. He gave her permission to take. And, take.

In long, complete strokes, he let her feel his weight, his size, his love. She clutched his shoulders, meeting each of his plunges. His eyes took on the squint she'd come to love and his gaze burned into hers as his lips parted and he groaned going faster.

He pressed, circled, rubbed, and teased with his lower body between her legs. She reached out and held onto the blanket for stability to match him thrust for thrust. Her back arched with the ever tightening sensations in her body. God, he was unbelievable.

Spiraled tighter, hotter, and higher, she desperately reached for him. Her fingers dug into his biceps. The solidly muscled arms grounded her to the moment. She panted, unable to beg and plead for him to take her to climax.

"Yeah, Gia. Don't stop," he said.

She couldn't stop if she wanted. Linking her ankles together around him, she stayed with him as he rode her. Each brush of his body against the aroused flesh of her sex caressed her until she burned in the most mind-blowing way. "Swiss…?"

In a rush of pleasure, her body froze on a final high. Every muscle constricted, winding tight and suspending her. She held her breath, straining with a pent-up scream. Seconds ticked by, locked in ecstasy.

Swiss's harsh breath came heavier and more rapid as he sunk into her bowed body and held himself still. Only when he trembled inside of her had her body unwound in a propelling display of pleasurable jolts.

"That's what I'm talking about…," he mumbled as his climax rocked his body.

She held on, absorbing his reaction, savoring her pleasure, and stunned speechless.

Every single time with Swiss left her in awe. That one man, this man, could bring out such a perfect array of emotions spanning so many areas in her life.

It was incredible.
He was incredible.
They were incredible together.

Chapter Thirty Seven

Swiss stepped out of the bedroom in the middle of the night carrying his jeans and his phone. Gia slept in the bed, out cold after having sex. His earlier liquored buzz gone, he couldn't put off the phone call he wanted to make any longer.

Good or bad, he needed to hear Heather's voice. At the very least, if she refused to talk with him, he needed to thank her for sending Gia to him. He held out hope that she'd sent Gia to him, because somewhere in her heart, his daughter still believed in him.

He stepped into his jeans and sat on the couch. His body trembled from fear. He was scared shitless. It was irrational to believe Heather even remembered him.

At four years old, his daughter still forgot to put her shoes on and half-hour cartoons were a challenge for her to stay seated long enough to finish the show.

He'd let his daughter go without a fight, believing his hands were tied. The Army had mentally beat him, forcing him to sign away his responsibilities, and he'd said 'Yes, sir. I'll sign now, sir.' to ease the pain.

Pain that killed him.

He took the piece of paper he'd jotted Heather's phone number down on out of his pocket, spread it on the coffee table, and tapped out the numbers on the screen. He hovered his thumb over the *send* button.

His chest constricted, and he grimaced. He was going to have a fucking heart attack.

He pushed the button and put the phone to his ear before he changed his mind. His pulse roared in his head.

"Hello?" said a female in a groggy voice.

He stood up, sat down, and cleared his throat. "Heather?"

Her silence broke him out in a sweat.

"Who is this?" she asked quietly.

"It's...Swiss." His chest tightened more, realizing she would only know him by his real name. "Greg. Greg Jones. Your dad."

He held his breath. She never acknowledged whether she remembered or her mom mentioned his name. He exhaled knowing he put her in an impossible situation calling in the middle of the night, out of the blue, with no warning.

"I..." He clenched his teeth, fucking the whole conversation up. "I've made a lot of mistakes in my life. Shit happened, and I lost you."

She hadn't hung up, and he kept going.

"You probably don't believe this, but not an hour goes by that I don't miss you and wonder how you're doing and what kind of woman you turned out to be." He stood, unable to sit still. "I've got a, uh, picture of you here. You were four years old. It's hard to imagine what you look like now, all grown up. I remember how you used to run out the door when you knew I was coming home and you'd—" He sniffed, needing to validate his relationship to her. "You'd hold your hands up and beg me to carry you on my shoulders into the duplex. And, at night, you liked two stuffed animals tucked in beside you in bed. You called them Rufus and —"

"Ringles," she finished for him.

"Yeah." Hope surged through him. "Ringles."

He swallowed. "How are you doing? Are you happy?"

"I'm good. After mom died—"

"Anita's dead?" He looked at the floor, feeling nothing but surprise over the news.

"She remarried after Brad passed away to a man who treated her badly. He was physically abusive, and she hid it from me and everyone who knew her. I was away at college and had no idea what she was going through until I was notified by the hospital that she'd been beaten and died on the way to the hospital." Heather paused. "It was because of her that I'm working at the woman's shelter helping other women out of unsafe situations."

"Jesus Christ, baby. I had no idea." He cupped the back of his neck. "I'm sorry to hear that."

"There's more, but I'll save it for another time."

"You're okay with me calling you?" He walked over and picked up his pack of cigarettes off the kitchen counter. "Or, if you want, you can call me, anytime."

"I'd like that."

He put the smoke behind his ear with a trembling hand. "Me, too."

"You're not upset that I sent Gia to you, are you?" she asked. The hesitation in her voice gripped him.

"No. No, not at all." He wanted to reach

through the phone and assure her. "Gia told me how you sent her to me. Well, Bianca had, and when I was checking out her story, we got some information that gave us your real name. I don't know what you were thinking or why you'd believe that I could help Gia when you don't even know me anymore, but I wanted to thank you. Everything turned out well in the end."

"I've heard. Gia called me a few days ago," said Heather.

"She did?" He paced the living room, surprised over the information. Gia hadn't mentioned the phone call to him. "She's a good woman."

"I think so, too."

A million questions raced through his head, and he had no idea how to ask a single one. His legs trembled, and he sat down on the couch. There were years he missed. Heather's whole life. He had no idea what kind of woman Heather turned out to be, what she liked to eat, or if she had a boyfriend. Shit, she could be married.

"Heather, I need you to know that if I could go back and do things differently, I would. It's my fault that you never knew me growing up and I wasn't there for you." He inhaled in an attempt to stop his voice from breaking. "So many fucking times, I wanted to find you and I…"

Soft crying came over the phone. His spine straightened, knowing he'd do anything to make things better.

"Don't cry, baby. I'm sorry." He squeezed his eyes closed. "This sits on my back, Heather."

Heather sniffled. "It's not all your fault. After Mom had been killed, I found some papers and notes she'd had hidden in her house from back when she was married to you. And, the court papers. It wasn't until then that I knew what happened. Mom and Brad never wanted to answer my questions about you."

"Fuck," he mumbled.

"I think I've put the pieces together enough to understand why you stayed away initially." Heather breathed over the phone and continued. "I-I don't really want to talk about it on the phone."

"No, I understand," he said.

"I'd love to see you, though. If, you know, that's okay. Whenever you feel like it, I mean."

"Yeah?" His throat closed up, strangling the ball of emotion choking him.

"Yeah." Her voice came across the phone louder. "Maybe we can work something out later when I can think again. I don't know what to say right now. I was sleeping and..."

"I can come to Seattle, anytime. Just say the word."

"Maybe, but I think I'd like to come to Montana. I tracked you down a couple years ago and figured out you still live in the house I lived in with you and mom."

"The duplex." He wiped his arm across his face. "I never left. I couldn't. It's where you lived. I couldn't leave."

"Dad?"

"Yeah, baby?"

"I'm really glad you called." Her voice came out squeaky grabbing his heart and twisting. "I was scared to call you."

"Ah, Heather." He leaned over and braced his

elbows on his knees, weakened. "Never be scared. Head up."

She sniffed. "You used to tell me that when I cried. 'Head up, baby. Show everyone what you're made of.'"

"That's my girl," he whispered.

He remembered everything about her. Her tiny hand in his. Her thin arms around his neck. The sweet, sweet smell of her laughter as she buried her head in his neck when he tickled her.

His eyes burned and he closed them before he lifted his chin. "I'll make this right. I can't make up for the time we've lost, but I want you back in my life."

"Okay. I'll see what I can do about getting some time off work. It might not be soon, but we'll talk more, right?"

"Absolutely." He blew out his breath. "I guess I should let you go, and you can go back to sleep. You probably have to work in a few hours, huh?"

She laughed softly, sniffling. "Yeah."

"I'll let you get back to sleep," he whispered, weakened at what he'd done.

"Okay." She paused without disconnecting. "Dad?"

"Yeah?"

"Thank you for calling."

He nodded, unable to take credit for something that should've been done twenty-two years ago. "Talk to you soon, baby."

"Okay. Bye."

"Bye." He held on to the phone until she disconnected the call and then he just sat, motionless, overfilled with thanks, and still scared to death.

Heather listened, talked, and wanted to see him. His chin hit his chest, and he squeezed his eyes closed.

He had no idea how long he sat there, going over and over the conversation, memorizing her sweet voice, when arms circled his stomach and Gia pressed her body against his, kneeling between his knees. He held her to him as if everything good was going to get stolen from him and he was scared of letting go.

The experience of losing his family, fighting for a marriage he recognized as more an idea in his head than felt in his heart, had him desperate to hold on to Gia. Her love and dedication were real. He could feel it beating throughout him, making him stronger. While he'd live with regrets on how he'd lived his life, he had the maturity and mindset to recognize what Gia gave him and what he wanted to give her in return.

Or, maybe he could explain his connection to her more simply.

"Love you, sweet," he whispered.

She held him tighter. "I love you, too."

Picking her up, he set her on his lap and held her. And, he planned for their future.

Epilogue

Three months later ~

"Fuck." Swiss dropped the wrench and shook his hand in pain. "Jesus Christ. Who was the son of a bitch asshole who put this God damn nut on so cocksucking tight?"

Gia stood in the doorway of the duplex, bundled in her heaviest coat, and watched Swiss continue cussing to the air as he worked on his motorcycle at the curb. Nothing was wrong with his bike, and he most likely was the asshole who tightened the nut the last time. Gia's stomach fluttered in happiness knowing he'd get his biggest wish today. He'd soon forget about his impatience and his clumsiness working on his bike.

What bothered him was the fact that Heather should've arrived for her first visit with her dad a half hour ago, and she was late.

Gia had watched Swiss count down the days until the visit and become more nervous the closer Heather's arrival day came.

There was snow in the forecast, and Swiss worried about her driving over two mountain passes, even though they'd watched the road reports for the last three days. The interstate remained plowed, and Heather had promised to call if she wanted to stay at a hotel along the way and wait out the weather.

No phone call meant she was driving.

Poor Swiss had barely slept last night and to keep his mind occupied, he'd pulled out his tools and set to working on his motorcycle at four o'clock in the morning.

Gia sighed in contentment. He had nothing to worry about. Heather was excited to finally come see her dad after all these years. The reunion helped by the constant contact the two of them kept since Swiss made the initial phone call. Heather called twice a week like clockwork and Swiss had reclaimed his right as her dad.

He went right to work fixing what he'd put off for twenty-two years and bought the duplex from the owner and had Ronacks members renovate the other side in their free time.

He hadn't said anything to Heather or her about his reasons to set down roots, but she understood what he was doing. If there was any chance that Heather wanted to stay in Montana, she had a home and her private space to live.

A low rumble filled the air. Gia pushed away from the door and peered up the street. Then, she looked at Swiss who'd gone still. Pride filled her, and she walked to the curb.

"You couldn't wait, could you?" she asked, leaning in and kissing him.

Swiss put his hand on her hip and held her close. "Just making sure she got here safely."

She leaned her head against his chest. Having Ronacks Motorcycle Club escort Heather home would surely be a moment his daughter would never forget.

Swiss's body stiffened at the sight of the first riders rounding the corner and coming down the block. She peered up at him, her heart bursting with excitement, and hoped Heather would realize how much love Swiss had inside of him to give.

"You'll do fine," she said.

He kept his gaze on the street. "I keep thinking she's going to run to me and hold up her arms, but she's not a baby anymore."

Ah, Swiss had a lot to learn about girls and their fathers. Gia blinked to clear her vision. She missed her dad every single day and was grateful for the loving relationship she had with him, and her mom when they were alive. Hugs, no matter at what age, were always needed.

"There she is," he whispered, grabbing Gia's hand.

A tug came to her arm as Swiss stepped forward. She held her position, and he looked back at her, desperation in his gaze.

"Go to her. I'll be here waiting for you both," she said, swallowing the hard lump settling in her throat. Swiss needed the moment and to know he stepped forward alone, under his own power, to fight for his daughter in his life.

He hesitated, his squint became more pronounced until he looked at her with one eye. She raised her hand and caressed his scar. There was a load of questions in his look.

"She will love you. I promise." She kissed him lightly. "Go get your daughter."

She stepped back and lifted her chin, letting him go.

Swiss turned around and faced the caravan filling the street.

The car door opened, and Heather stepped out,

set her purse on the hood of the vehicle, and strode straight toward her dad, her steps getting bigger, faster, the closer she came, until Swiss opened up his arms, and then Heather lunged for the big, solid chest welcoming her home.

Gia swiped her hand across her cheek and smiled. She couldn't see either of their faces, only Swiss's body. His back sloped, vulnerable, protective.

Battery stepped up beside her. "This whole time, he never said one word."

"It was his scar to carry, and he was too strong." Gia lifted her chin and gazed out at the man she loved. "Now, he can heal."

Several minutes later, Swiss walked Heather toward her. Gia stepped forward and smiled. The last time she stood before Heather she'd been in tears, fearing for her life, and had reached out in desperation.

Gia grabbed Heather and hugged her tightly. This time in thanks.

"It's so good to see you again." Gia pulled back, looked at Heather, looked at Swiss, and laughed. "You both have the same smile, too."

"I was just telling him that I remember how big he always seemed to me." Heather sniffed through her laughter. "I thought it was because all children see adults as big, but he's huge. I had no idea."

Swiss leaned over and kissed Heather's forehead. "Everything go okay on your trip?"

"Pretty much." Heather glanced behind her and wrinkled her nose. "There was a little confusion at the pass in the Cascades when I came out of the restroom and found a bunch of bikers surrounding my car."

Gia snorted. "Get used to it. Your dad's not very subtle."

"You could say that again." Heather's smile fell. "I've apologized to the man…"

Heather half turned, searched the row of bikers sitting on their motorcycles, and turned back around to her dad. "Who is the man on the black bike? Third from the back. He has a black stocking cap on."

Swiss gazed down the line. "That's Rod."

"Well, he should never step between a woman and her car." Heather's mouth thinned. "Regardless, I did suck it up when I realized Dad had sent his club after me, and I apologized to him."

Swiss marched off, heading toward his MC brothers. Gia studied Heather. Swiss's daughter watched her father closely and bit her bottom lip.

"Why would you need to apologize?" asked Gia.

Heather shook her head, remaining quiet. Swiss strode back to them with Grady by his side and the other club members following.

"It'd probably be a good time to go inside," muttered Heather, stepping closer to Gia.

Gia couldn't question her because one look at Rod's face beside Swiss, she understood what had caused Heather to apologize. Gia covered her mouth to keep her smile of amusement from showing to the others.

The Vice President of Ronacks Motorcycle Club had a split lower lip that was swollen twice as big as normal and looked painful.

"Heather, this is Rod." Swiss lowered his voice. "The other men behind him are Grady, LeWorth, Mel, JayJay, Sander, Choke, Roller, Chuck. The one behind you sitting on his bike is Battery, the President of Ronacks.

"It's nice to meet you all." Heather stared at Rod's face.

Hands were shaken, hello's given, and finally, each Ronacks member rode off leaving the block a quieter place. Gia rubbed her hands together to take the chill out of her fingers.

"Swiss, why don't you get Heather's luggage and I'll take her inside, and we can all warm up." Gia kissed Swiss. "Lunch should be ready soon."

"Good. I'm starving." Swiss walked to his daughter's car.

Gia led Heather inside. Swiss's daughter only made it two feet inside the living room, and she looked at the picture frame on the television stand. Gia let Heather have time with her thoughts and went to the kitchen to check on the stew.

Swiss made two trips inside with Heather's belongings before he shut the door and came to Gia's side. His hand came to her hip, pulling her closer, and he gazed at his daughter in the living room looking at the picture.

"She's beautiful," he whispered.

"Yes, she is. Inside and outside." She set the lid on the pot and turned into Swiss's chest.

Swiss dropped his gaze to Gia. "She's home."

"Of course, she is." She kissed Swiss softly. "Everything will work out. You'll see."

"Hey, Dad?" said Heather.

He kissed Gia quickly and walked over to his daughter. Gia's heart burst with love. Bad circumstances brought her to Swiss, and bad circumstances had torn a young family apart. Because of Heather's extraordinary ability to care for others, they had all found each other. It was time for each one of them to experience the good. Together.

Dear readers —

Thank you so much for reading Don't Say It.

In a world where children are often raised in one parent homes, and there are more deadbeat fathers than anyone likes to hear about, I wanted to show you a man's side of the story. Through Swiss, we learn what made him lose his family, and why he chose to protect his love for his daughter by alienating himself from everyone else in his life. While we, as outsiders, might not agree on how he lived his life or approve of the choices he made, it's not up to us to judge. Instead, it's an opportunity for readers to see what Swiss did to reconnect with his adult daughter.

It's a reminder that in real life, we often are quick to judge. Because that's human nature.

As with all my books. I enjoy showing you a different side to characters than relying on stereotypes and assumptions. While maybe not conventional in the romance category, I'm a true believer in if a book can open your mind, the story is much more enjoyable to readers.

As series go, the more you read, the more you fall in love with secondary characters, too. I'm thrilled to tell you that there will be another Ronacks Motorcycle Club series book, starring another Ronacks member soon. As planned, each book is a complete standalone. You can read out of order or only the books that appeal to you. Or, you can start from the beginning and learn about each character as they show up in the stories.

I'd like to invite all of you to follow me on

Facebook and visit my website to keep up on my books and what I'm writing next.

    Love,
    Deb

Author Bio

Best Selling Romance Author, Debra Kayn lives with her family at the foot of the Bitterroot Mountains in beautiful Northern Idaho. She enjoys riding motorcycles, playing tennis, fishing, photography, and creating chaos for the men in the garage.

When Debra was nineteen years old, a man kissed her without introducing himself. When they finally came up for air, the first words out of his mouth were...will you have my babies? Considering Debra's weakness for a sexy, badass man, who is strong enough to survive her attitude, she said yes. A quick wedding at the House of Amour and four babies later, she's living her own unbelievable romance book.

Website: www.debrakayn.com
Twitter: www.twitter.com/DebraKayn
Facebook: www.facebook.com/DebraKaynFanPage

Debra Kayn's Backlist

…or something – Ronacks Motorcycle Club
Blow Softly – Red Light: Silver Girls series
Touch Slowly – Red Light: Silver Girls series
Fall Gently – Red Light: Silver Girls series
Wrapped Around Him – Moroad MC series
For Life – Moroad MC series,
His Crime – Moroad MC series
Time Owed – Moroad MC series
Falling For Crazy – Moroad MC series
Chasing Down Changes – Moroad MC series
Breathing His Air – Bantorus Motorcycle Club
Aching To Exhale – Lagsturns Motorcycle Club
Soothing His Madness – Bantorus Motorcycle Club
Grasping for Freedom – Bantorus Motorcycle Club
Fighting To Ride – Bantorus Motorcycle Club
Struggling For Justice – Bantorus Motorcycle Club
Starving For Vengeance – Bantorus Motorcycle Club
Living A Beautiful War – Bantorus Motorcycle Club
Laying Down His Colors – Bantorus Motorcycle Club, anthology titled Melt My Heart
Archer, A Hard Body Novel, book 1
Weston, A Hard Body Novel, book 2
Biker Babe in Black, The Chromes and Wheels Gang, book 1
Ride Free, The Chromes and Wheels Gang, book 2
Healing Trace
Wildly, Playing For Hearts, book 1
Seductively, Playing For Hearts, book 2
Conveniently, Playing For Hearts, book 3

Secretly, Playing For Hearts, book 4
Surprisingly, Playing For Hearts, book 5
Chantilly's Cowboy, The Sisters of McDougal Ranch, book 1
Val's Rancher, The Sisters of McDougal Ranch, book 2
Margot's Lawman, The Sisters of McDougal Ranch, book 3
Florentine's Hero, The Sisters of McDougal Ranch, book 4
Suite Cowboy
Hijinks
Resurrecting Charlie's Girl
Betraying the Prince
Love Rescued Me
Double Agent
Breaking Fire Code

~ Sneak Peek ~
Fall Gently — Red Light: Silver Girls series
By Debra Kayn

Chapter One

Roni turned the faucet on until her minty spit circled the drain and cleared the sink. She ran her tongue over her front teeth, assured the taste of latex was finally gone. The job to rid her mouth of any foreign taste had only taken her three brushings, two swishings, and—she popped a wintergreen Lifesaver in her mouth—one mint. At least until the next customer finished with her and the routine started all over again.

The crunch of breath freshener between her teeth gave her something to concentrate on while she ignored the crick in her neck. She put a new rubber-backed throw rug on the end of her bed. The rules at Red Light Bordello surprised her.

Yesterday when Tiff, the madam of the illegal establishment in Federal, Idaho, gave her and the other three ladies from the prostitution Network their orientation, she realized how nice it was to work in a clean, organized building where everyone associated with the bordello treated her with respect.

Everything had its place and clothes stayed on the visiting customers, no matter the sexual request. Roni swallowed the tiny bits of mint left in her mouth, sat down in the chair, and looked at the clock. She still had five minutes until Tiff escorted the final customer of the night through the yellow door to her room.

She raised her hands and rubbed the back of her neck. Colored doors were also a new thing to her. The other three bordellos she'd worked at since signing up with the Network used a sign on each door to keep track of what lady performed which sexual favor.

At Red Light, each color represented the prostitute's skill. Yellow—blowjobs only. Red— Anything goes, but hard limits per the prostitute's choosing. Green— straight sex and blowjobs from a dominating sex worker. Blue— power sex and blowjobs from a submission prostitute. Roni checked the clock again and stood. Sometimes she wondered if she changed her paperwork to regular sex on top of the blowjobs it would be easier and less nauseating. The taste of latex left her gagging and by the end of the evening, her neck and jaw killed.

But, she couldn't. She knew the rules. Not the rules at the current bordello or even past houses, but the rules put in place by Vince.

He never allowed another man to take her through normal sex. Her body was his and what he owned would not be shared with any other man, except her mouth.

Vince believed her mouth was free to use. He believed her mouth didn't matter. He believed having a dick shoved in her mouth shouldn't bother her.

She shuddered. Her rational fear had not lessened when she escaped the boss of the Yesler Street Gang that got ahold of her outside the homeless shelter three years ago. Vince made sure she ate fear for breakfast and kept her afraid.

Until the day she no longer feared death, and instead feared to live.

She'd reached her limit when Vince had backhanded her hard enough she lost consciousness, and she'd used his negligence to escape his house.

Over nine months of being on her own and protected by the Network, she still waited for the door to open and Vince to drag her back out on the street.

The door opened.

Her body tensed. She swallowed the shock of surprise and smiled.

Tiff raised her brows, holding a hand under her swollen belly as if comforting the child that wouldn't be born for three more months. The tautness in Roni's neck eased at the sight of her madam.

"You have twenty minutes." Tiff stepped back into the hallway letting the customer inside and shutting the door.

The man looked up, found Roni, and stepped closer.

The large man stood confidently in the room. His short brown hair and intensely dark eyes topped off his rough appearance in a worn flannel shirt, faded jeans, and black steel-toed boots. Roni's head pounded, and she broke eye contact with him. Looking down at his hands, she gasped. He had a tattoo of a bird's head on the back of his hand between his thumb and index finger.

Sparrows!

A sudden chill left her shaking, and she reached behind her for something to use to protect herself.

How many times had she stared at the same

tattoo marking on Vince and the Sparrows members and thought she'd die?

The man stepped forward. "It's okay. I'm not here to hurt you."

She finally found her feet and moved back, pressing against the top drawer, and blindly searched for the handle. With only the minimum of necessities to her name, she only had clothes inside the dresser. But, she needed something to use as a weapon. Even a shirt might help her stay alive.

"Please." The man's deep voice softened. "I'm only here to talk to you."

"W-who are you?" she said, hating how weak her voice came out.

"My name's Carver." He ran his hand over his whiskered jaw. "Dawson Carver."

She inched backward, sweeping her hand along the top of the dresser and found the topless female figurine that came with the room. She snatched the object in her hand. A surge of energy burst through her fear at the added protection.

She lifted her chin. "I'll scream."

The tight security in the building, guarded by bikers and an alarm system, would protect her. The legal adult entertainment business, Silver Girls, downstairs in the Sterling Building remained locked during Red Light's working hours. If she yelled for help, someone upstairs would hear her.

"Please, don't." Dawson held his hand out in front of him.

Her gaze flickered between his hands and his tattoo. She'd seen most of the men who worked for Vince. They all had a sparrow head on their hand.

Vince had flaunted his tattoo many times in her face and drilled the meaning into her head with his fist.

A sparrow represented fear, courage, loyalty, and strength.

"I only want to talk to you." Dawson pointed at the bed. "I'm not going to hurt you. I'm not going to touch you. I'm not going to make you leave the bordello."

She remained where she stood, not believing a word.

"It took me longer than I thought to find you." Dawson eyed her carefully. "I'm here to make sure you're okay. That you're safe."

"Please leave," she whispered.

"I will." His dark brows lowered. "When my time with you is up, I'll walk out of the room, and you'll stay here. You're not in trouble. What I have to tell you is only for your ears only."

Deep lines etched the corners of his eyes and mouth. Roni's fingers ached around the figurine at the death grip she maintained. She no longer believed the words of others.

A dark stubble of week-long whiskers shadowed Dawson's jawline. She lowered her gaze to his hand and stared at the black eye of the sparrow tattooed on his skin, glaring at her in contempt. The tattoo mocked her.

The organization Vince ran followed his orders without mishap. The dedication to one man, one boss, went beyond her understanding.

"What do you want from me?" she said, squelching the rise in her voice.

"Nothing." He exhaled slowly. "I've come

here to tell you that Vince is dead."

No way.

Impossible.

She shook her head and refused to believe him. Nobody messed with Vince. Even those not belonging to Sparrows stayed out of his way. Nobody else would dare step in Vince's territory between James and Yesler Street, the underbelly of Seattle.

"He's been…" Dawson's mouth tightened. "He's been dead since August. I've been trying to find you for the last nine months."

The way he talked, he seemed to want her to relax and let down her guard. She wasn't stupid.

She looked down at the figurine in her hand. At one time, Vince had pretended to care about her. He'd swept in and put a roof over her head and gave her a bedroom to herself. Until he moved her into his bedroom, into his bed, a week later and refused to let her leave. Then, he'd supplied her with a new outfit. When she'd expressed her thanks, he proudly informed her he'd taken the clothes off a dead girl, not even eighteen years old, who police found in the alley. Raped. Strangled. Naked.

"I only have five more minutes before the madam will escort me out of the building." Dawson reached behind him.

She sucked in her breath and pressed against the dresser.

"It's okay." He held up a cell phone. "I only wanted to give you this."

Dawson tossed the phone on the bed. "My number is programmed in there. If you have any questions after I leave, call or text. If you need any help…"

She raised her chin in refusal. Her plans changed the more he spoke. She planned to leave the Network the moment everyone turned a blind eye to her. Her safety at Red Light compromised, she needed to run far away.

"There's information on the phone to back up the news I gave you, so you can relax knowing I'm telling you the truth." Dawson stepped toward the door and lowered his voice. "House rules let customers come back every other day. I'll check in with you on Thursday. If you need anything before then, text me."

The madam's knock came and echoed in the room. Roni shoved the figurine she still clutched behind her back to hide it from Tiff.

Dawson removed cash from his pocket, dropped it on the shelf by the door, nodded at Roni, and followed Tiff out of the room.

The door closed.

Caught in her current troubles, she remained standing. Where would she go? How was she going to get somewhere far away?

Having never been in Federal, Idaho before, she had no idea how to seek transportation out of here. She'd arrived by plane and landed in Washington via California. A private car brought her and the other three ladies from the Network to Red Light. From her view out the window, she'd be surprised if the town offered any public transportation to the residents. Federal looked no bigger than three blocks wide and sat snug between mountain peaks covered in snow.

A knock startled her out of her plans. She set the figurine back on the dresser, tightened her robe, and hurried to the door. Her hand shook on the handle.

Tiff stood in the hallway. "I wanted to check in with you before you go have dinner. The last customer, Dawson, has prepaid for three visits this week. Considering he's a new customer, please keep me informed if you have trouble with him following rules. While our business thrives on regulars, we also want to make sure you're comfortable. We also try not to let the men get attached to you during your stay."

Perspiration broke out on Roni's forehead, and warmth flooded her face. She nodded.

"You're a shy one." Tiff laid her hand on Roni's arm. "Relax. We really are easy to work for once you learn the rules."

"O-okay." Roni smiled, the muscles in her cheeks ticked. "Thank you."

"Go ahead and get dressed for dinner. The other ladies are already at the table." Tiff stepped into the hallway. "It's fish and chips night."

"Sounds good." Roni waited until Tiff walked away before she shut the door.

Until she figured out how to get out of the Sterling Building and away from Federal, she'd need to go along with the schedule and act as if everything was fine. She hurried over to the bed and picked up the phone. It took her a few minutes to figure out how to turn it on. When the screen stopped flashing, she found her name underneath a yellow square and tapped the screen.

A picture of a newspaper article appeared. She scanned the headline.

Vincent Pladonta died from three gunshot wounds to the chest inside his house on Yesler Street. The leader of the Yesler Street Gang was found...

Her legs gave out, and she caught herself on the bed, speed reading the rest of the article.

Seven women in his employment were arrested.

One female, Jane Doe, white, approximating twenty-six years old, found dead in City Hall Park and believed to have ties to the Yesler Street Gang AKA Sparrows.

She raised her hand and cupped her throat.

One woman, name unknown, missing.

She turned the phone over, unable to read more. Vince kept nine women. Considering she wasn't arrested or dead, the missing woman was her. Were the police looking for her?

Which one of the girls was found dead? She'd only known one of Vince's girls personally.

Sadness clogged her throat, and she inhaled through her tight chest. Jackie nursed her back from every injury Vince laid on her, always telling her everything would be okay. She'd clung to the only friend she had and yet refused to acknowledge her friendship in front of Vince to protect Jackie.

Vince favored Roni and kept her in the house, while he sent out the other girls to work the street. She hoped Jackie was one of the women arrested, and maybe her dear friend would get to start over someday and not live in fear.

Not wanting anyone to find the phone, she

shoved the cell between the box springs and the top mattress of the bed. She got dressed and walked to the kitchen.

If the article was true, and Vince was dead, why would a member of Sparrows come looking for her? She sat down at the table, deaf to the conversation going on around her.

Unless, Dawson Carver planned to pick up Vince's business and take her back to Seattle.

"Roni?" Shana tapped on the table.

She lifted her gaze from her plate. "Yes?"

"We're all going into Ella's room to watch Netflix." Shana dipped her French fry into the pile of tartar sauce on her plate.

The youngest out of the group of prostitutes, Shana let nothing stop her. From day one, she stepped forward and took the position of leader amongst the ladies, despite her age and barely one-hundred-pound body. Shana stood a head shorter than Roni and blew her long caramel colored hair out on the sides and top, so the only thing you noticed was massive, beautiful hair.

"Not tonight. I need to catch up on my laundry." Roni moved the breaded fish around on her plate. If she found a chance to take off without anyone noticing, she wanted to be ready.

"You can still hang with us." Ella wiped her fingers on the napkin beside her plate, careful of the long nails that she bragged about having professionally painted with no chips, worn edges, or smudges. "I don't care if we pause the show. You can do laundry, and while you're busy folding clothes or whatever, we can pop popcorn or something while we wait for you."

Roni put her hands on her lap under the table, hiding the torn and chewed fingernails. A nervous habit that had only intensified under Vince's care until she made them bleed.

Lynn pushed her plate away from her. "I can't do it."

"Do what?" asked Marci, the madam's assistant who ruled the upstairs when Tiff wasn't around.

"Eat fish." Lynn leaned back in her chair. "It's not my favorite thing in the world. It's at the top of my list of things to avoid, like sushi."

"But when we went over the menu, you said you liked fish." Marci tilted her head and smiled. "Should I change the menu while you're here."

"No. No. You don't have to do that." Lynn's cheeks reddened, and she mumbled. "Sorry. I can eat it if I have to."

Marci's gaze softened. "Nonsense. We can order you chicken and fries next time."

Roni looked away, her appetite gone. Lynn's need to please everyone backfired on her. Somewhere in Lynn's past, someone pressured her to accept everything thrown at her without question. Roni picked up her plate and carried it to the sink. Not that she had room to talk. She understood the need to do whatever made someone else happy, even if it killed her.

She dumped her food in the garbage, rinsed her plate, and loaded the dish in the dishwasher. Shortly, the music would start downstairs for the Silver Girls dancers and the ladies in Red Light would be left to entertain themselves until two o'clock in the morning.

The free time upstairs came with a cost. Roni couldn't leave the building, except to go up on the roof where Tiff had set up an entertainment area where the women could get outside without being seen by the public or to step out on the small balcony outside her room.

Once Silver Girls closed, and there were fewer people around, Red Light's security alarm came on, and her chance to escape without everyone noticing would be impossible.

While the others talked, she slipped out of the kitchen and grabbed her dirty clothes out of her room. Carrying the basket to the end of the hallway, she pushed through the last door with her hip and entered the small laundry room. Inside, she dumped her dirty clothes in the washer. Nothing she owned needed separated into similar colors or washed on the delicate cycle. What little belongings she owned had come from the homeless shelter or one of Vince's girls. The colors no longer ran together, but muted into a bland, washed out blah of their original color.

The washer began to fill with water. She shut the lid and returned to her room. No longer able to ignore Dawson's visit, she removed the phone and reread the article on Vince.

Then she read it again.

Instead of relief that the man who'd held her prisoner, abused her, treated her like a whore, and gave her mouth away free to Sparrows members whenever he snapped his fingers was dead, she only dreaded what would come next.

Dawson would be back, and her safe haven with the Network was over.

Genesee District Libraries
Montrose-Jennings Library
241 Feher Dr.
Montrose, MI 48457 MAR 17 REC'D

CPSIA information can be obtained
at www.ICGtestin
Printed in the US.
LVOW13s14472
522286LV

F KAY
Kayn, Debra
Don't say it

526049